TO TAME A COWBOY

Books by Jody Hedlund

The Preacher's Bride
The Doctor's Lady
Unending Devotion
A Noble Groom
Rebellious Heart
Captured by Love

Orphan Train

An Awakened Heart: An
Orphan Train Novella
With You Always
Together Forever
Searching for You

Beacons of Hope

Out of the Storm: A Beacons
of Hope Novella
Love Unexpected
Hearts Made Whole
Undaunted Hope

The Bride Ships

A Reluctant Bride
The Runaway Bride
A Bride of Convenience

Colorado Cowboys

A Cowboy for Keeps
The Heart of a Cowboy
To Tame a Cowboy

COLORADO
COWBOYS
3

TO TAME A
COWBOY

JODY HEDLUND

BETHANYHOUSE

a division of Baker Publishing Group
Minneapolis, Minnesota

Published by Bethany House Publishers
11400 Hampshire Avenue South
Minneapolis, Minnesota 55438
www.bethanyhouse.com

Bethany House Publishers is a division of
Baker Publishing Group, Grand Rapids, Michigan

Printed in the United States of America

Library of Congress Cataloging-in-Publication Data
Names: Hedlund, Jody, author.
Title: To tame a cowboy / Jody Hedlund.
Description: Minneapolis, Minnesota : Bethany House Publishers, a division of
    Baker Publishing Group, [2022] | Series: Colorado cowboys ; [3]
Identifiers: LCCN 2021051764 | ISBN 9780764236419 (paper) | ISBN 9780764240102
    (casebound) | ISBN 9781493437269 (ebook)
Subjects: LCGFT: Novels.
Classification: LCC PS3608.E333 T6 2022 | DDC 813/.6—dc23/eng/20211021
LC record available at https://lccn.loc.gov/2021051764

Scripture quotations are from the King James Version of the Bible.

This is a work of fiction. Names, characters, incidents, and dialogues are products of the author's imagination and are not to be construed as real. Any resemblance to any person, living or dead, is purely coincidental.

Cover design by Kirk DouPonce, DogEared Design

Author is represented by Natasha Kern Literary Agency.

Baker Publishing Group publications use paper produced from sustainable forestry practices and post-consumer waste whenever possible.

22 23 24 25 26 27 28   7 6 5 4 3 2 1

The Lord is merciful and gracious, slow to anger,
and plenteous in mercy.

Psalm 103:8

CHAPTER

1

FRONT RANGE, COLORADO TERRITORY
MAY 1867

Savannah Marshall's heart pulled taut like a rope in a tug-of-war.

In the darkness of predawn, she paused inside the front door, glancing behind her at the winding grand staircase. She ought to march right up to her room, climb back under her covers, and stay.

But her feet seemed to tangle with the plush entryway rug, preventing her from spinning around. She couldn't go through with the weddin'. She had to slip out, saddle up, and ride away today.

But could she really do this? Leave without saying any good-byes?

She gripped the door handle. She had to. If she didn't,

everyone would convince her to marry Chandler Saxton—just like they'd been doing for weeks already.

Pressing a hand to her chest, she tried to ease the battle inside. . . . She wasn't saying no forever. Just not yet.

Hefting her bag over her shoulder, she took a steadying breath, opened the door, and stepped onto the wraparound veranda and into the frigid May air.

At her appearance, Mr. Pritchard rose from the rocking chair, taking a puff on his pipe. The amber glow illuminated the kindly veterinarian's weatherworn face underneath the brim of his hat. "All set?"

Was she ready?

Pulling the door shut, she steeled herself against the need to retreat.

"Yes, sir." A cold breeze blew across the Front Range from the northwest, from the Rockies still covered in snow at the highest elevations. Savannah tugged her canvas coat closer. Painted with linseed oil to make it wind and water resistant, the coat was lined with flannel for warmth. It wasn't as heavy as her overcoat, which she wore on the coldest days, but it would hold her in good stead during the ride up into the high country. She'd already put on her calf-skin gloves and tucked her flyaway fair hair up into her hat—one that had once belonged to Hartley.

"You're sure you want to tag along today?" Mr. Pritchard started down the veranda steps, his boots clomping. "I know you're busy. What with getting ready for that fancy wedding of yours and all."

The weddin' was only three days away, and Momma was making a fuss over last-minute preparations. Actually Momma had been making a fuss ever since returning from their winter home in St. Louis earlier in the month, bringing with her a weddin' gown, decorations, and a to-do list as long as a prairie fence.

Savannah hastened after Mr. Pritchard. "I could use a break from the planning." Yes, her going away was a break. That's what it was.

"Alright then." His feet crunched in the hoarfrost that coated the grass. "So long as you're sure."

Was she sure?

She glanced behind her at the dark windows of the mansion, where everyone was still asleep. Daddy had built the beautiful home for Momma in order to entice her to live on the Colorado ranch, which she still only did for half the year. With the long colonnade spanning the full length of the front façade, the Greek-Revival style was similar to the Georgia plantation home they'd lived in before the war. The inside was just as beautifully decorated as the outside. Momma had made sure of it.

Savannah's footsteps slowed. What would her parents do if she didn't marry Chandler and his money? They needed the wealth the marriage would bring, allowing Daddy to invest in railroads again. But what would she do with her life if she became Mrs. Chandler Saxton? Especially since Chandler had made it clear that he didn't want her doing menial labor as a southern gentleman's wife. He'd agreed with Momma that she'd need to focus on their home and children and that her days as a veterinarian would have to come to an end.

Would she have nothing better to do with her days than decorate her house?

She didn't want to end up unhappy, like Momma. Sure,

her elegant and sweet-natured mother tried to hide her discontentment. But it was easy to see and was one of the reasons why Daddy was so anxious to go east, to Atlanta and civilization, where Momma would have more friendships and socializing.

Savannah shifted her attention to the large horse barn and to Silas, who'd roused to saddle their mounts and now stood by the wide door, yawning noisily. He held a lone lantern that illuminated her black Morgan, Molasses, although she normally rode Sugar, her Appaloosa.

The problem with Sugar was that she was unique. With her silvery white coat and dark leopard-like spots, the horse was sure to stand out. When Daddy and Chandler started searching for her, one mention of the horse's description and they would be right on her trail.

Taking Molasses would give her more time. And she needed more time, didn't she? A few weeks or even a month to gain perspective. Maybe after that, she'd be able to make herself go through with the marriage.

"I'm sorry, Daddy," she whispered. "I know you'll be disappointed." Since coming west and helping manage the ranch, Chandler had become like a second son to him. After Daddy had experienced so much sadness with Hartley's death, she didn't want to cause him more grief in losing Chandler too.

Yet, *agreeing* to marry Chandler was different from actually *going through* with the deed. As the weddin' inched nearer, she'd felt more and more like a corralled wild mustang. She'd circled and circled, going first one way and then the other. . . . Now that she was facing a saddle and halter, she needed an escape. To be free so she could decide what she wanted for herself first.

"Thank you, Silas." Mr. Pritchard took his mount's reins from the middle-aged groomsman.

Savannah handed Silas a haversack, hoping he wouldn't question why she had the extra luggage. Of course, she always wore her leather satchel strapped diagonally over her shoulder whenever she went on calls with Mr. Pritchard. She was as prepared as the veterinarian for any animal ailment.

"Please tie the bag onto my saddle." She hitched her foot in the stirrup and hefted herself up.

The groomsman stared from her to the haversack and back.

She pretended to ignore him, making a show of situating herself in the saddle.

Silas lifted the bag hesitantly.

"Hurry on up, Silas. Mr. Pritchard and I need to be on our way." She arranged her split skirt on either side over the trousers she wore underneath and prayed Silas wouldn't voice the question that filled his warm brown face.

He set to work looping a rope around her bag and securing it to the saddle. After cinching the last knot, he stood aside and hooked his fingers through his suspenders. "Sure are takin' a lot with you, Miss Savannah."

In the process of releasing a pent-up breath, her lungs tightened again, especially when Mr. Pritchard looked at the haversack and raised a brow.

She waved a hand to brush off the concern. "It's just a few extra things. Nothing to worry about."

Silas pursed his lips, the sure sign he didn't believe her.

She nudged Molasses forward. Though the ranch hands would be awake and readying for the day in the predawn hour, their cabins and the livestock barns were located across

TO TAME A COWBOY

the east pasture, well away from the main house. That meant she wouldn't have to worry about running into Chandler or any of the other cowboys. But the house servants would be rousing soon enough, and she wanted to be on her way before anyone else saw her bag and wondered what she was up to.

"The master know where you going?" Silas called after her.

"Of course he does." She could only pray her letter of explanation was enough. She'd left it in an envelope on the chest of drawers in her room. The servants would see it today when they went in to tidy and clean, but they'd leave it alone. When she didn't come back, then Daddy would start investigating and find the note calling off the engagement.

After he read it, his shoulders would droop and the lines in his handsome face would deepen with more sadness.

Her throat tightened, and she blinked back tears. She had to stay strong. Surely after a few days he'd realize she'd been right to leave, that marriage was too big a commitment to enter into without making sure she was ready for it.

She hoped he'd come to that conclusion. If only he wasn't struggling to make up for all the wealth he'd lost in the war . . . If only his and Momma's future security didn't depend on the union to Chandler . . .

Her horse trotted ahead of Mr. Pritchard down the lane leading away from the house. Darkness shrouded the landscape, but the starlight illuminated enough to see the rocky plains of the east rolling outward for miles and miles, all the way to Kansas and the Missouri River. Though the land wasn't arable enough for farming, it was perfect for ranching, as Daddy had discovered shortly after the gold rush.

As one of the presidents of the Central of Georgia Railway, he'd sold off his stock in the company and invested in land out west before the start of the war. Savannah suspected he'd done so to avoid the growing conflict, especially to keep Hartley away from combat. Little good it had done. Hartley lived through the war years, but an accidental kick in the head from a horse had caused trauma to his brain and killed him just as surely as a battle wound.

As she unhitched the gate and guided Molasses under the metal sign that spelled out the name of their ranch, the Double L, she allowed herself a final look at the place that had been home for the past seven years, the mansion set against the backdrop of the red-rock sandstone formations and the mountains in the distance.

"Love you, Momma," she whispered. "Love you, Daddy. I promise I'll make this up to both of you." The trouble was, she didn't know how.

"First stop, Smith Fork Ranch." Mr. Pritchard took a puff on his pipe and moseyed up next to her, the horses' hooves loud against the hard earth. "They've got a couple of calves with scours."

"And what about the Middletons? Their foal is having a hard time latching on." The Middletons lived close to Fountain near Ute Pass, and she needed to reach the wagon road before the teamsters left so she could ride along with them for safety. The road leading up Ute Pass was one of the main transport routes through the Pike's Peak region, winding through South Park and going all the way to Leadville.

Just last week Mr. Pritchard had mentioned the growth of ranches in the South Park area and that ranchers there wanted to hire a vet. He said he'd go himself if he were a younger, sturdier man who could handle the harsher conditions of the high country.

Ever since Mr. Pritchard brought it up, Savannah had been able to think of little else. She might not have gone to college or earned a degree like Mr. Pritchard, but he claimed she was as good as any vet he'd ever known.

Of course, the news of the need for a veterinarian had come just when the weddin' pressures had been building to unbearable proportions. Then, yesterday, when she'd heard the teamsters were heading up into the mountains, she'd known this was her chance—maybe her last chance—to taste freedom before having to return to the paddock.

"If you want," she said, "I can ride over to the Middletons'. You know I'm good with foals. I'll have that sweet thing nursing before you get there."

"You have a gentle touch with all horses. Not just foals." Mr. Pritchard's voice contained a note of pride.

"I've learned everything I know from you."

"No, Savannah. The truth is, some men—and women— are born with a natural ability to relate to creatures. And you're one of them."

If only everyone felt the same way. Even though Daddy was more supportive of her tramping around with Mr. Pritchard than Momma had ever been, he still held to the traditional view that such work was best left to men. But he'd humored her and allowed her more freedom in that regard.

Savannah smiled. "So you'll let me ride ahead to the Middletons'?"

He chuckled at what he must have perceived as her eagerness. "I'll deliver you there and then head over to Smith Fork."

"Thank you, sir."

"Just don't let your father know I left you unattended. If he finds out, he'll never let you accompany me again."

"I promise I won't say anything if you don't." She swallowed the discomfort at knowing she was putting Mr. Pritchard into a difficult situation.

She had to push it aside. This once. And pray that eventually everyone would forgive her for what she had to do.

CHAPTER 2

"You kick that horse one more time, I'll be kicking you." Brody McQuaid spread his feet wide and crossed his arms.

Though Brody's voice was low and quiet, traffic on Fairplay's Main Street came to a halt around him quicker than if he'd shouted. The cowhand, in the middle of lifting his boot, paused.

The mustang lay on the ground right where it'd collapsed, a dun mare, her flanks heaving in and out, showing ribs and a whole passel of scars and open wounds. Worst of all, a gouge in the horse's forearm oozed blood. She was injured. Bad. And needed attention, not a savage beating.

With fingers spread clawlike over his six-shooter, the cowhand straightened and pivoted. The evening sun hit the man full in his face, revealing the broken teeth and bent nose of Lonnie Quick. Stirrup Ranch foreman. An ornery cuss of a man if there ever was one.

Brody shoulda known. Nearly every horse at Stirrup

Ranch wore marks. And nearly every horse there was scared of his shadow and jumped at the sight of a June bug.

"I don't think I heard you right, son." Lonnie Quick's bottom lip bulged, damp pieces of chewing tobacco speckling his beard. "You sure ain't telling me how to take care of my own horse, are you?"

"Yep. That's what I'm telling you." Brody's muscles tensed with the need to lash out, to punch someone or something. The anger inside raged like relentless artillery day and night. But at times like this, it took a battering ram to his chest and demanded to be let loose.

He fisted his fingers, half hoping Quick would kick the horse again. Give him a reason to teach the snake-blooded foreman a thing or two about how to treat a mustang.

Stirrup Ranch's buster—like too many others—was of the mind to rough break wild horses—roping, blindfolding, and then saddling the green broncs without so much as a howdy-do. That kind of buster preferred to dig in with spurs, slam with a quirt, and fight it out. The rough-breaking methods rarely produced a good horse.

Which was probably why Quick's mustang was giving him a heap of trouble.

Quick glanced at Brody's balled-up fists then to his busted lip and black eye. The evidence from the last brawl was fading, but his reputation for packing a wallop was only growing.

Trouble was, Flynn got his bristles up every time Brody was in a fight, telling him it was bad for ranch business. Flynn had bawled him out something fierce earlier in the week for his sour attitude. And when Brody yelled back that he would leave the ranch and take his attitude with him, Flynn's shoulders deflated.

"Don't want you leaving, Brody." Flynn's voice had been drenched with enough sadness to douse a fire. "I'm just worried about you. Worried you're going on the warpath for every blasted thing so you can punish yourself."

Brody could admit he'd wanted to die a hundred times over during those early months after Newt's passing. He'd taken the loss of his best friend hard, blamed himself, hadn't wanted to go on, hadn't cared about recuperating, even though Flynn and his wife, Linnea, had done everything they could to help bring him back to life.

He'd been a difficult patient for those long weeks they stayed in New York City with Linnea's family. He'd been belligerent and resistant, and tried to end it all. If not for sweet little Flora . . . he wasn't sure he would have made it.

But after living in South Park for the past year and a half, he was beyond all that now. Wasn't he? Or was Flynn right? Was he still trying to punish himself?

He cocked his head, his sights homing in on Quick's revolver. Did he actually hope to get shot?

Naw, he couldn't leave Flora. At three and a half, his niece needed him. He wasn't about to chance getting killed and leave her heartbroken.

Besides, he'd told Flynn after their last argument that he'd try harder to control himself. He didn't want to embarrass Flynn and Wyatt and cause trouble for their ranch after how hard they'd worked to build it up over the past five years. With their land combined, his older brothers had the largest spread in South Park and one of the biggest in all of Colorado.

Brody loosened his fists and took a steadying breath before he nodded at the wounded mustang. "I'll take your horse to Healing Springs and finish taming her for you."

Quick's lips turned up into a sneer. "This here sorry excuse for a horse ain't going nowhere but to the closest farm as pig feed."

"No!" A woman's cry rose into the deathly silence that had settled over the usually busy thoroughfare. "She just needs a bit of tender care, and she'll be fine."

Before Brody could figure out what was happening, a woman dismounted from a fine-boned, well-groomed Morgan and was on her knees in front of the mustang. She slipped a leather satchel off her shoulder, flipped it open, and removed clippers, a glass bottle, a metal tin, and gauze.

Quick took a step away as though he didn't know what to make of the newcomer any more than Brody did. "What do you think you're doing there, little lady?"

She expertly wielded the scissors near the wound site, cutting away hair with one hand and stroking the flank with the other.

The horse lifted her head and whinnied.

The woman leaned in and spoke quietly, holding out a hand toward the mustang's nostrils, giving the creature a chance to sniff her.

Quick cleared his throat. "Listen, miss. I don't know who you are—"

"I'm Savannah Marshall, South Park's new veterinarian." She brushed a hand over the horse's neck and shoulder, gliding her fingers with such gentleness, the mustang laid her head back down and released a soft snort, the kind that radiated trust.

How had this woman gained this half-wild horse's trust in a matter of seconds?

Fascination wound through Brody, and he stared at her—

Savannah Marshall—dumbstruck like all the other onlookers. She wore a man's felt hat, black with a wide brim. While it shielded her face from his view, it didn't conceal her long blond hair that hung down her back and was gathered by a thin leather strip at her neck.

Her clothing was dusty but of fine quality, and her open coat revealed the slender figure of a young woman.

A woman veterinarian? Who'd ever heard of such a thing? Where was she from? And was she qualified?

As a murmuring made its way around the crowd, Brody could hear some of the men voicing his questions aloud.

"Never heard of a woman horse doctor."

"Woman can't be a real veterinarian. Just ain't right."

"She's too young to know anything about anything."

Savannah Marshall kept working on the mustang, talking and stroking, and all the while she continued snipping away the hair near the wound. If she'd heard the comments, she was ignoring them, likely not the first time she'd faced that kind of reaction.

Finally, Quick released an exasperated breath. "Listen, miss. I ain't got the time for this."

"It won't take long. I promise." Her reply was just as gentle as her touch, likely more for the horse's sake than for the foreman's.

The horse snorted again.

She pressed her hand to the creature's cheek, as though reassuring the horse she meant no harm.

Quick bent and shoved his Colt into the horse's head. At the click of the hammer, Brody jolted forward and dropped his shoulder into Quick, knocking him aside.

Quick cursed and tried to gain his balance. But with Brody's thick frame plowing into his, he fell to the ground. Brody was on top of the wiry man in an instant, slugging one fist into Quick's jaw and using the other to slam the revolver loose.

The gun spun through the dirt until a familiar limping boot stepped on it and halted the momentum.

Flynn.

Brody glanced up in time to see the frustration on his brother's rugged face. Before he could explain the fight, Quick smashed a fist into his nose, knocking his head back.

Pain shot through his bones, but he settled more heavily upon Quick, throwing one hit into the man's gut and another into his face. He forced himself to stop and shove his hand into his pocket. With blood dribbling from his nose and over his lips onto Quick's shirt, Brody pulled out several silver dollars and dropped them onto the man's chest.

"There. That's more than any farmer'd give you for the mustang."

"What if I don't wanna sell her to you?" Quick tried to buck, but Brody sat down on him hard again, this time on his ribs.

Quick cussed.

"You can take it or leave it, but the horse is mine now." Brody held Quick's gaze for several heartbeats, long enough to let the foreman know he intended to get his way, and there wasn't nothing anyone could do about it.

Brody stood and looped his fingers in his gun belt. Quick climbed to his feet and scooped up the silver dollars that had fallen to the street. It was the last of the money Brody had made from the sale of two mustangs he'd tamed over the spring to freighters who'd come up from Denver. Meant he was broke.

Didn't matter. Wild horses ran all throughout the high country, and he'd catch and tame more soon enough.

Quick sauntered toward Flynn. His brother nodded at Stirrup Ranch's foreman and handed him his revolver. "Sorry about the tussle, Quick." Flynn lowered his voice, but the apology struck Brody hard and loud anyway. "You know Brody don't mean nothin' by it."

Brody turned his back on the two and the rest of the men still looking on, and he knelt beside the veterinarian. He'd embarrassed his brother again, but he sure didn't need Flynn apologizing for him.

"Keep your boy on a better leash, McQuaid," Quick said belligerently. "He's just stirrin' up trouble everywhere he goes, and you know it."

Another burst of anger swelled inside Brody's chest. He wanted to get up and pound Quick a few more times. But he crossed his hands over his bent knee and pretended to watch the vet as she dabbed what seemed to be saline into the horse's wound.

She set aside the bottle, rolled out a piece of gauze, and ripped it with her teeth. Without taking her attention from the mustang, she held the cloth out to him.

Hesitantly, he took it. What did she want him to do with it? He might be good with livestock, but he didn't like doctoring their wounds. Though the blood and open flesh didn't make his stomach squeamish the way it had before the war, he still wasn't real good at watching the suffering.

Savannah resumed her efforts at cleaning the forearm gash.

From the corner of his eye, Brody watched Quick holster his revolver and continue across the street toward the Senate

Saloon. Flynn didn't budge from where he stood, likely with those deep, frustrated creases lining his forehead.

Brody fingered the piece of linen, then he held it out to her.

"It's for your nose." For the first time since kneeling in front of the mustang, she shifted her attention, tilting her head enough that he found himself peering into a pair of blue eyes as soft and endless as a summer sky. The gentleness within their depths reached out to soothe him as swiftly as she'd soothed the horse.

He released a taut breath, but before it left his lungs completely, she shifted, giving him a better look at her face. Her very pretty face.

His heartbeat stalled.

Every line, from her high cheekbones to her elegantly rounded chin to her perfectly proportioned nose, was exquisite. Her lips were sweetly curved, and he found himself staring at them and at the pretty dip above her upper lip.

She tugged at the gauze dangling in his fingers, took it from him, then lifted it to his nose. He needed to stop her—would have stopped anyone else. But he couldn't move as she touched the linen to the spot underneath his nose. Gently she pressed it to the bridge.

He winced.

"Sorry." She loosened the hold, her eyes softening even more as her gaze strayed over his face. "Thank you for what you did to rescue this beautiful creature."

He wanted to say something, but his tongue felt roped and hog-tied.

She wiped at his nose again. "I didn't mean for you to get hurt on account of the horse."

He needed to let her know none of this was her fault. He

would've taken issue with Lonnie Quick even if she'd never shown up. But he kept staring at her like a blamed fool.

"And I certainly didn't mean for you to pay for the horse." She moved the gauze lower, grazing his upper lip.

She was touching his lip. Heaven help him. A rough string began to gallop through his chest.

"Soon as I can, I'll pay you back." She dabbed his lower lip before moving on to his chin.

The rough string picked up pace so that he was afraid his heart would burst clear out of his chest. When was the last time a woman had touched him? Other than the nurses after the war, he couldn't think of when he'd interacted with a woman who wasn't family.

It had been years. Clearly too long, considering his reaction.

She finished wiping the blood from his chin. "There." She offered him a smile, one that went down inside and warmed him. And as her eyes connected with his, the warmth spread to his limbs.

He had to get himself under control and stop acting like a dumb and mute dolt. He reached up and took hold of the gauze. In his bumbling, his fingers brushed hers. The contact sent a strange current through him, making him fumble the linen and almost drop it.

She didn't seem to notice, had turned her attention back to the mustang. "She's been roughed up. With a little doctoring and tenderness, she has the potential to make a good ranch horse."

"Reckon so." His voice sounded strangled, so he cleared his throat.

"I promise I'll take her off your hands once I'm settled."

He cleared his throat again. "No hurry."

She opened a tin and dug her fingers into an oily salve before gently slathering it on the horse's wound.

Was she here with a husband? She wasn't wearing a wedding band. But still, most women didn't come up into the high country without a man.

He glanced around, but he didn't spot any fellas out of the ordinary. "You settling here with—family?" He couldn't make himself say *husband*, but no doubt a woman like her already had a man.

Her fingers stilled.

His breath stuck in his lungs as he waited for her response.

She shook her head. "No. I came alone." From the note of sadness in her tone, she must've left a fella behind. Who was he? Someone special?

For the next few minutes, Brody silently watched as she finished rubbing in the salve and proceeded to bandage the spot.

After securing the gauze in place, she sat back on her heels and wiped her hands on a rag she'd pulled from her satchel. "I'll come by your place in the morning to clean the injury and change the dressing."

"Much obliged." He'd get to see her again. He didn't know why that thought should please him so much, but it did. A whole heap.

CHAPTER

3

She'd made it to Fairplay. But now what?

Savannah started to pack her supplies, but she moved slowly, hesitantly. The cowboy next to her—the one someone had called Brody—didn't seem in a big hurry either, although the lean man standing above them was fidgeting with his leather gloves, slapping them lightly against his palm.

The others who'd stopped to watch her interaction with the injured horse had moved on. Even so, she was still drawing plenty of stares from men passing by.

Yesterday after starting up the wagon road with the teamsters, she'd tried to devise a plan for what she'd do when she reached South Park. But the traveling had been rigorous, and even when she'd been resting, she had to stay alert and fend off undue attention. Last night when the freight wagons stopped at a cabin that hosted travelers, the woman of the house had given her a spot inside away from the teamsters who set up camp outside. After the strain of the day, Savannah had fallen asleep the moment she'd lain down.

Today, as she'd journeyed, she'd tried again to plot how to convince the area ranchers to use her as their veterinarian—at least temporarily.

But she'd been distracted, too riddled with guilt over running away from home to think ahead. She'd pictured Daddy finally reading her letter, collapsing into his chair in despair, and Momma pressing a hand over her mouth to hold back her distress.

But now, she had to put the self-reproach aside. She was here. She'd bought more time, and now she needed to use it wisely.

She glanced toward the businesses lining the wide, dusty street. From the signs painted in bold letters on the buildings or on false fronts, the mountain town had more to offer than she'd expected. Fine establishments were interspersed with the taverns—McLaughlin's Livery and Feed Stable, Hyndman Bro's General Merchandise, Simpkins General Store, Hotel Windsor, and Fairplay Hotel.

To the west of town, the sun started to drop behind the bold peaks still draped in winter snow. The shadows cast a purple hue and turned the sky lavender and the thick pines on the mountain slopes a dark blue. Night would settle soon, which didn't leave much time to figure out what to do.

Although she'd brought along the cash she'd earned in her animal doctoring, she had to use it sparingly. It would cover the hotel stay and food, but not much more. Hopefully, after she started working, she'd be able to find a way to pay Brody back for what he'd spent on the mustang. *If she started working . . .*

Maybe he could put in a good word for her. "I assume you live on a ranch in the area?"

"Yep." He sat back on his boot heels and crossed his arms. Just as quickly he uncrossed them and braced them on his knees for the span of two seconds before crossing them again.

For the first time since she'd slid off Molasses and intervened to help this man save the horse, she took a good look at him. He was handsome in a rugged sort of way. He wore the typical heavy-duty, dark-colored wool trousers tucked into his boots, a blue cotton shirt with an unbuttoned vest over it, and a blue neckerchief worn loosely and tied with a square knot.

With how thickly muscled and brawny he was, she could see why he'd easily managed his opponent. She guessed he was in his early to mid-twenties, although something in his expression aged him beyond his years. The layer of dark unshaven scruff covering his jawline and chin lent him a haunted fierceness.

But it was his eyes, the rich dark mahogany, that drew her in. They were windows to his soul—a badly damaged soul—crying out for help. She could see it in him the same way she'd sensed the hurt in the mustang.

"Do you mind my asking which ranch you call home?"

He started to uncross his arms again but then, as though using extreme willpower, dug his fingers in and held his hands in place. "Healing Springs Ranch. To the southwest about an hour's ride."

Healing Springs Ranch. She'd heard Daddy and Chandler talk about the booming South Park cattle ranch owned by the McQuaids and how it was becoming one of their biggest competitors for the cattle markets in the East. A ranch like that would surely be interested in having a veterinarian on location. Maybe instead of staying in a hotel, she could use the ranch as a base, just like Mr. Pritchard used the Double L as his main residence while branching out and attending to the needs of other ranches.

"Do you think there's a chance your boss might consider . . ." She hesitated. She'd always had everything she ever needed or wanted handed to her, and asking for help was new and uncomfortable. She took a deep breath, then forced the words. "Do you think your boss would hire me on as the ranch veterinarian? Not permanently, but for a short while?"

He glanced up at the lean man standing above them. Though his hair was a lighter brown than Brody's, the resemblance in the shape and cut of their handsome features was too strong for them to be anything but brothers. His attire was similar but slightly newer and better quality, like the clothing Chandler wore. Nothing pretentious but enough to set them apart.

She could see lines of protest creasing the brother's forehead. She had to finish making her case before he shot down the idea. "I heard the ranchers in South Park have a tremendous need for a veterinarian."

Brody nodded. "Yep."

At the same time, his brother shook his head. "Don't rightly know."

"Don't rightly know?" Brody shot to his feet, his arms stiff, his body rigid. "That ain't true. You were just jawing earlier today about the need for a vet to tend to the horse with colic."

"I can treat a horse with colic," Savannah said quickly. "I've done it a hundred times."

The brother slapped his gloves again. "We've already got word out in newspapers that we're looking for a vet up in these parts—"

"Blast it all, Flynn. Can't you give her a chance?" The anger rolled off Brody in waves, and she held in a breath, praying he wouldn't haul off and hit his brother—Flynn—over her. The last thing she wanted was to cause more strife.

Flynn held his ground, but his brows rose, revealing surprise at the passion in Brody's request.

"Thought of everyone you'd understand." Brody spat out the words. "With how hard it is for Linnea to be taken seriously with her botany and all."

"That's not it." Flynn studied Brody's face before glancing to Savannah and then back, as though attempting to figure out a riddle. "I was just thinking we needed to run it past Wyatt first."

"Why? Ain't you half owner? Reckon you can decide."

Ah, so Flynn and Brody were McQuaids.

At the commotion of the two men, the mustang began to thrash. Savannah rubbed the mare's ribs and flank, reassuring the creature that all would be well. At least she hoped so.

When Savannah glanced up again, both men were watching her. "It was just a suggestion. I understand if it won't work." She offered them both a smile to let them know she wouldn't hold a refusal against them.

"It'll work." Brody stared at her smile as though it were a lifeline that he needed more than anything else.

Flynn's mouth stalled around a response. He watched Brody, and from the concern radiating from Flynn's face, she guessed this older brother was more like a parent than sibling. What was their story? Whatever had happened to Brody, it appeared Flynn was trying to fix it by any means possible, including giving in to his whims.

Flynn shifted his attention back to her. "You said your name is . . . ?"

"Savannah Marshall." Would Flynn figure out who she was now too? After all, most people in Colorado knew Sawyer Marshall and the Double L Ranch. She'd contemplated providing a false name. But she wasn't in the practice of lying and hoped instead that up here no one would connect her to her family. She wanted to remain in obscurity for a couple of weeks without Daddy or Chandler getting word of her whereabouts.

As Flynn gave her a nod, recognition didn't register on his face. "Mrs. Marshall—"

"Miss Marshall. But call me Savannah. Please." She laid on the southern accent and charm, just the way she'd learned from Momma.

"I'm Flynn McQuaid, and this here is my brother Brody." He cocked his head toward Brody. "So you're a veterinarian?"

Was he interviewing her for the job? Right here? Right now?

She sat up straighter. "I won't lie to you, Mr. McQuaid. I haven't been to college. But I've been training with a veterinarian for many years, and I know everything he does and then some."

Flynn hesitated. "We've got a lot at stake. Can't afford to make any mistakes—"

"She done proved herself right here with this mustang," Brody interrupted. "What more do you need to know?"

Flynn glanced at the bandage on the mare's leg. "What are your fees?"

For the first time since she left home, a tiny whisper of excitement shimmied through her. Maybe she'd be able to get more work than she'd thought. "I only require room and board from my host family. I'll collect payments from my visits to other ranches."

"Seems fair enough," Flynn responded.

"I hope so." It worked for Mr. Pritchard. Surely it would for her too.

Flynn and Brody locked gazes before Flynn gave a curt nod. "Alright."

Brody nodded back.

Flynn started to tug on his gloves. "You're responsible for overseeing her duties."

"Yep."

"That means everything."

Had Flynn hired her? The excitement inside clamored louder. "Don't worry. I won't require much overseeing, except perhaps a little direction when I need to make calls."

"Brody'll need to go with you." Flynn was focused on his gloves. "Everywhere."

Savannah balked. Daddy had laid down the same rule with Mr. Pritchard accompanying her. The difference was that the vet was already going on visits.

She waited for Brody to protest, but he remained silent.

She tightened the lid on the saline and stuck it back into her satchel. "I don't want to impose and make more work for Brody."

Flynn lifted his shoulder in a slight shrug. "Brody?"

Brody gave a shrug too. "You won't be imposing none."

She paused in repacking her supplies. "Are you sure?"

"I'm sure." He gave her a quick, almost shy glance. And though his skin was tanned, she could see a slight shade of red working its way into his cheeks.

She was used to men finding her attractive. It was part of being a woman living in the West among so many single cowboys. The sideways looks, the admiration, the good-natured teasing, even the outright declaration of love from time to time. She'd heard and seen it all over recent years. The men were usually respectful, especially the cowhands at the Double L under Daddy's and Chandler's watchful eyes.

Even if she wasn't within the safe confines of the Double L, she'd learned how to rebuff interest when it came on too earnestly. She was a full-grown woman of nineteen and no longer a naïve southern belle.

Besides, she doubted a little attention from a handsome cowboy like Brody would amount to anything. She'd come to the high country to untwist the knots she'd made of her life, not ravel them tighter with more complications.

She gave the mustang a final pat before she pushed to her feet. Brody was at her side in an instant, wrapping his hand around her arm and helping her up. His touch was firm and polite, and he released her as soon as she was standing.

"Thank you kindly, Brody." She smiled at him as she slung her satchel over her shoulder so that it hung diagonally.

Brody nodded and then rubbed a hand down his scruffy jaw.

"And thank you, too, Flynn." As she turned to speak to him, she caught him watching Brody's interaction with undisguised interest. As he appraised her again, she understood that Flynn McQuaid wasn't convinced of her veterinary skills. He'd hired her because of Brody.

She admired Flynn for caring so deeply about his brother. But she wasn't getting caught up in a matchmaking scheme if that's what he had in mind. She'd have to make that clear to him as soon as possible.

CHAPTER
4

"You're good with horses." Savannah glanced behind Brody to the wounded mustang trailing after his chestnut horse. At seventeen hands high, Brody's gelding rippled with muscle and power—like its master.

Brody gave a curt nod in response, a move that was apparently his normal mode of communication. He hadn't strung more than a couple of sentences together the entire ride to the ranch. She guessed his temperament tended toward silence and solitude but that whatever had hurt him made him even more reserved.

She hadn't minded the quietness. She'd learned over the years that wounded creatures often required more time and patience before being willing to trust. And she sensed Brody needed an extra dose of time and patience.

Besides, she was enjoying the stillness of the night, with only the occasional call of a fox in the distance. The silence was a reminder of the higher altitude of South Park, where some animals had yet to come out of hibernation since the temperature dropped below freezing after sunset.

She was cold and her fingers stiff, but she wasn't ready for the ride to end, even though the outline of buildings ahead told her they'd reached their destination.

A half-moon pushed out from behind clouds to reveal a simple two-story house made of clapboards. A large barn and several other outbuildings a short distance from the house attested to the prosperity and magnitude of the cattle operation of Healing Springs Ranch.

Of course, her daddy's ranch was bigger and finer than any other ranch in all the West, and Daddy was known as the Cattle King of the territory. But it was clear the McQuaids were doing a fine job. No doubt with the abundance of wild grasses to fatten their cattle, they didn't have to resort to hand-feeding or sheltering their livestock except during the severest parts of winter.

She guessed operations here were similar to those at the Double L, where they could let their cattle roam at will on the prairies, only mustering, counting, and branding a time or two a year. In the autumn, they separated out the three- and four-year-old cattle to sell to dealers who transported them to Chicago for slaughter and tinning.

The ranchers up in South Park had an additional market among the mining districts, turning a profit from the miners who were willing to pay a pretty penny for beef.

As she and Brody rode into the ranch yard, the lights glowing in the windows of the house beckoned with warmth. But Brody rode directly toward the barn with adjacent well-built paddocks.

Savannah stifled a yawn, the past two days of traveling

taking their toll. Although she wanted to remain strong and introduce herself to the ranch hands as the new veterinarian, she barely had the energy to stay on her mount, much less start working.

Outside the barn, Brody reined to a stop, and she followed his lead. He dismounted, and before she could swing her leg around, he was beside Molasses, reaching up to aid her down. He assisted her just like Chandler always did, and even though she was perfectly capable of taking care of herself, she allowed it, knowing he was doing his best to respect her.

He released her right away, as he'd done in town. But this time, she swayed, exhaustion and hunger making her weak. She groped for Molasses, but Brody was there first, taking hold of her arm and bracing her.

"Thank you, Brody." She closed her eyes and fought back a dizzying wave. "I'll be alright in a second."

He held her steady, and everything about his touch radiated patience and gentleness.

As she opened her eyes, she caught him studying her face, his brows drawn together. She offered him a smile. "There. Better." She stretched after Molasses's lead line. From the soft snort and bent head, her Morgan was as tired and hungry as she was, if not more so.

Brody swiped up the rope, adding it to the two he already held. "I'll take care of her tonight."

She tugged it. "No, I don't want to make more work for you. I can do it."

"Reckon you can." He moved the rope out of her reach. "But I want to."

From the stubborn edge to his voice, she knew there was no point in arguing with him.

She side-stepped to untie her haversack from the saddle, but Brody beat her to that too. In no time, he hefted it down and over his shoulder as though he had every intention of carrying it to the house for her.

Flynn's words from earlier in Fairplay rang in her ears. *"Brody'll need to go with you. Everywhere."*

Apparently Brody was taking his brother's instructions literally.

She skimmed her fingers up Brody's arm until she reached the strap. He reacted to her bold touch just the way she'd hoped. His eyes rounded, and he didn't resist as she tugged the bag loose.

Her move hadn't been fair, and as he stood motionless, not even breathing, she silently promised herself she wouldn't use womanly wiles on Brody again. For now, though, she had to make sure both he and Flynn knew she didn't need someone to shadow every step she took.

She hefted her haversack up higher on her arm. "Are you sure you don't want me to help with the horses?"

"Naw." He shook his head. "Go on to the house and get something to eat."

"Thank you again, Brody." She started across the stubby patches of grass, and with every step, she could feel him watching her intently. Halfway across the yard, she stopped and turned, expecting him to hurriedly pretend to busy himself with the horses.

But he remained in place, his attention boldly upon her, unperturbed to have been caught staring. His face was shadowed by the night, but there was no hiding how darkly handsome he was. And how appealing.

She could admit she had a soft spot for dark-haired

and dark-eyed cowboys. But she'd long past decided feelings for a man didn't matter. Or at least they didn't matter with Chandler. With his auburn hair and hazel eyes he was good-looking in his own way, but she wasn't attracted to him physically. Sometimes when choosing a spouse, other factors had to take precedence. And in Chandler's case, his desire to help her family out of their financial troubles was more important.

Brody spread his feet and folded his arms as though he planned to stand there all night and stare at her if she but dared him to.

At the feathery flutter in her belly, she ducked her head and continued toward the house. She wasn't planning to foster any attraction to Brody McQuaid no matter how eye-catching he might be.

Even so, as she strode forward, she was entirely too conscious of his attention to every swish and sway she took. When she reached the door, she was tempted to glance over her shoulder at him and was relieved when the door opened wide before she could manage a knock.

A plump middle-aged servant with a bright blue turban tied around her head filled the doorway. She fisted her hands on her hips and narrowed her eyes at Savannah. "You must be the veterinarian."

"Yes." Savannah glanced into the hallway, the open doors on either side revealing a parlor and a dining room. She guessed the kitchen and perhaps a bedroom occupied the rear of the house. Although not as luxurious as Momma's, the home was tastefully furnished with elegant items that had likely been imported from the East.

"Guess you better come in." The servant's expression was

as welcoming as if Savannah had announced she was a dance girl from the nearest tavern.

Savannah entered and shrugged out of her coat. As she handed it off to the woman, she heard voices, one of which belonged to Flynn, coming from the parlor. He'd ridden home ahead, able to go faster without the injured mustang slowing him down.

He appeared to be in the middle of an explanation. "Brody yammered on more in a few minutes around her than he has in an entire year."

A woman responded, but Savannah couldn't hear over the servant's rustling and huffing as she hung the coat.

"Couldn't say no to him." Flynn spoke again. "Not with the way she brought him to life."

Savannah rubbed her arms and looked around, pretending that she couldn't hear the conversation, which was clearly about Brody and her, confirming her suspicions about why Flynn had hired her.

A long silence ensued, followed by soft gasps and then womanly laughter.

The servant rolled her eyes, but a slight smile tugged at her lips. "Those two. Always acting like newlyweds . . ."

Newlyweds?

If she'd stayed at the Double L, tomorrow would have been her weddin' day. She couldn't imagine gasping and laughing with Chandler, not as a newlywed and not even when she was old and gray. He was a proper southern gentleman. He didn't give way to displays of emotion. Even in the few private interactions they'd had, he maintained a measure of reserve. And he'd expect her to behave like a lady, just like Momma did.

"Guess you'll be wanting something to eat." The servant started down the hallway.

Savannah hesitated. She didn't want to disturb Flynn and his wife and their newlywed activities.

"Come on with you," the servant called. "You here now, you may as well eat."

"Who's here, Vesta?" came the feminine voice from the parlor.

"The lady you all going on about. That who."

An instant later, a woman stepped into the hallway. She was straightening her short-waisted bodice and matching walking skirt, the fashionable style showing her to be a woman of some means. With long red curls hanging in disarray, the woman had a wild, almost exotic beauty to her. A smile curved her lips, making her breathtaking.

Flynn stepped out of the parlor behind her, and his attention lingered over his wife, his eyes brimming with adoration.

"Savannah?" The red-haired woman studied her. "I can see why Brody is taken with you. You're so lovely."

Savannah shook her head, needing to explain herself before everything spiraled out of control. But before she could say anything, the woman approached and held out a hand. "I'm Linnea. Flynn's wife and Brody's sister-in-law. I'm so pleased to meet you."

"Pleased to meet you too, Mrs. McQuaid, ma'am."

"Just call me Linnea." The beautiful woman shook Savannah's hand. "What brings a single woman like you up to Fairplay all by herself?"

It wasn't the first time Savannah had been asked the question, and it wouldn't be the last. While she hated misleading people, for now she had to remain as vague as possible. "I needed work and heard the ranchers up here were searching for a vet."

"You're from Denver?"

"South of there."

Linnea opened her mouth to ask another question—like exactly where Savannah was from, if she had family, or how she'd gained her experience.

Savannah stiffened her shoulders in preparation for the interrogation.

As if noticing the unease, Linnea closed her lips and curved them into another warm smile. Then she slipped her arm through Savannah's and drew her down the hallway while Flynn headed out the front door. In moments, Savannah found herself seated at a large table in the brightly lit kitchen with Vesta dishing up more food on a plate in front of her than she could possibly eat—beef with onions and potatoes along with greens Linnea said she'd discovered and picked herself just that afternoon. With Linnea's cheerful and sweet disposition, Savannah felt at home in no time.

She learned that Wyatt, the oldest McQuaid, lived on the southern half of the ranch. He had claimed his original 160 acres under the Homestead Act back in '62 and had been buying up land around his property ever since. Originally he'd purchased cattle from miners and settlers coming west but had expanded so that now he had close to two thousand head of cattle. His wife, Greta, had a thriving jam business and was pregnant with their third child.

Linnea also shared how she and Flynn had ridden west together in 1863. Flynn had been driving a herd of Shorthorns while she'd been a part of her grandfather's botany expedition. During the months of traveling, they'd fallen in love. Shortly after arriving, they'd gotten married, and now they lived on the northern half of Healing Springs Ranch on land Flynn had claimed under the Homestead Act. Like Wyatt, Flynn had also purchased most of the land surrounding his ranch from other homesteaders. And now he owned close to a thousand acres.

They had one daughter, named Flora, who was three and a half and was already in bed and asleep for the night.

"So Brody came with Flynn to the West?" After finishing the meal, Savannah sipped from a mug of coffee, letting the warm brew seep down and chase away the chill of the cold night. Her thoughts skipped back to Brody and the bold way he'd watched her walk away. She tried not to let the image stir flutters inside, but it did anyway.

Linnea sat across the table and plucked at the roots of what appeared to be a handful of weeds. Savannah had been surprised earlier when Linnea had explained it was just one specimen of many she was studying as part of her ongoing classification of plants in the Rocky Mountains.

Her love of botany was evident everywhere from the dried herbs hanging in bunches from the rafters, the jars on the windowsills filled with soil and live plants, and even framed sketches of flowers on the walls.

"Ivy and Dylan came with Flynn that year. But unfortunately, Brody did not." Linnea was using a tiny pair of tweezers to examine the roots. "He enlisted in the Union army instead, much to Flynn's dismay."

"But he survived and is here now. Flynn must be happy about that." Savannah was fishing for information. Her curiosity about Brody McQuaid kept growing with every passing moment, and she didn't care anymore if she was being nosy.

"I wish my dear husband was happy." Linnea set down the tweezers, and her pretty brown eyes filled with sadness. "Brody might have survived the war physically, but it damaged a part of his soul."

Savannah nodded in understanding. In a small way, that's what had happened to Daddy. He was living on the outside, but something inside died the day he laid his son in the grave.

"Brody spent six months in Andersonville." Linnea whispered the words as if the name of the notorious Confederate prison was a curse. "When we tracked him down, he was barely alive, not more than skin and bones."

Savannah hated to think of anybody having to suffer in such a place. After the war, the news reports had described the horrors of life in Andersonville, especially during the publicized trial of the camp commander, Captain Henry Wirz, who was executed for war crimes.

The prison had only been big enough to hold, at most, ten thousand prisoners, but three times that many Union soldiers had ended up there. The overcrowding had led to food and water shortages. And of course, it also caused unsanitary conditions so that diseases ran rampant, killing thousands of prisoners.

"With as sensitive as Brody is, Flynn thinks the war sucked the life out of his brother long before he landed in Andersonville."

"Poor Brody." Savannah wrapped her hands around her mug to ward off a shiver. "I'm so sorry."

"I'm sorry too." Linnea sat quietly for a moment. "Flynn worries about Brody all the time."

Savannah was beginning to understand why. "Because of the fights he gets into?" She'd witnessed how easily Brody jumped into the one today. The bruises on his face were evidence of more.

"He's had a hard time adjusting to life. And at times he doesn't know how to handle his confusion and anger except by using his fists."

"Sounds like he still needs time to heal."

Linnea nodded. "He loves our daughter, Flora. He loves training wild horses. I want to believe he's on the road to healing. But Flynn isn't so sure."

Savannah stared at the redheaded beauty, trying to comprehend everything. Flynn hadn't just given in to Brody's whim to hire her as the ranch veterinarian. Nor had he brought her to the ranch to play matchmaker between Brody and her.

Rather, he was seeking anyone and anything that might possibly bring Brody out of despair and breathe new life into him. If she had the ability to do that earlier in town, could she do it again? "I had the feeling Flynn was hiring me for Brody's sake. Now I understand why. I hope I truly can help."

Linnea reached across the table and took hold of Savannah's hand. "Flynn didn't bring you here expecting you to work a miracle in Brody's life. Only God can do that."

Savannah released a taut breath and prayed Flynn agreed with his wife.

"But while you're here, it might do Brody some good, draw him out of his shell, show him that he has something more to look forward to."

"You should know, I'm not interested in getting involved with a man right now."

"I understand. Even so, Flynn saw a side of Brody today he hasn't seen in a long time. And he'll take whatever help he can get for his brother, no matter where it comes from or how long it lasts."

Savannah squeezed Linnea's hand, knowing she would like this kindhearted, wise woman. In fact, from the sounds of things, she would have no trouble liking all the McQuaids, including Brody. After Linnea's story about his hardships, she ached for him more than she already had.

She would just have to pray that she didn't give too much of her heart to Brody and hurt them both in the process.

CHAPTER
5

He didn't need someone watching over him every blamed minute of every blamed day.

With a half growl of frustration, Brody scraped the last bite of grub from his plate, thrust it away, and rose.

At the table's end, Elmer took a long swig of coffee, shut his Bible, then pushed up from his chair. The house was quiet, everyone already getting shut-eye.

Elmer should be asleep now too, should have gone with Vesta hours ago. Instead, he lingered, like he did every night. Only after Brody snuffed out his light and climbed into bed did Elmer close and lock the kitchen door and start across the yard to his own place, which sat beyond the garden.

As Elmer bent to bank the fire in the stove, Brody paused and watched the faithful ranch hand. Elmer's legs bowed out from so many years riding a saddle, and his shoulders contained a permanent hunch. He'd moved up from Texas with his wife, Vesta, to search for gold like thousands of other prospectors. It hadn't taken him long to get tired of the mining life and realize he wasn't gonna get rich quick. Even though he hadn't taken a liking to mining, he'd taken a liking to the mountains and hadn't wanted to leave.

Elmer had made it clear he didn't want to ride with the herd anymore and had accepted Flynn's offer to manage the day-to-day operations in and around the homestead while Vesta cooked, cleaned, and helped care for Flora.

Brody guessed Elmer never expected that part of his duties would include watching over a grown man. The time or two Brody had brought up the issue, Flynn had waved him off, making the excuse that Elmer liked to go to bed late. But Brody knew Flynn was paying the older man to play nursemaid.

His muscles tightening, Brody shifted his feet awkwardly, an apology pressing to be said. At the very least, he oughta tell Elmer he didn't have to sit up with him anymore. But saying so would end like it had every other time he'd told Elmer to go home. The man would shrug, keep on sitting in his chair, drinking his coffee, and reading his Bible.

At least Elmer was content with silence. Even so, Brody chafed under Flynn's overprotectiveness. Maybe it was time to build a place of his own.

Elmer closed the stove door, then stood and arched his back all in one motion. "'Night, son."

"'Night." Brody hesitated but made himself turn and go. About the only thing he could do was hop in bed. Then once Elmer left, he could do what he wanted like he usually did.

The moment Brody shuffled up the steps, his thoughts turned to Savannah. His pulse surged, as it had every time he pictured her. All the while he'd groomed the horses and calmed the new mustang, he relived the way she'd glided her fingers over his arm when she'd taken her bag from him. He doubted she meant anything by the touch. Probably hadn't known she'd done it. But just thinking about the caress made the hair on his arm tingle again.

He'd never seen a woman as pretty. Or as kind. She'd fussed over the mustang off and on during the ride back to the ranch and had taken better care of her own horse than she had of herself. Weariness had marked her features long before she'd started yawning.

He didn't know her history, and it wasn't his place to probe. But if he had to guess, he'd say she was running from someone or something. No other reason a respectable woman like her would be wandering around South Park by herself without any traveling companions.

She'd needed a place to stay in a bad way. And he figured Healing Springs Ranch was safe. Besides, they had the room. . . .

A room . . . across the hallway from his.

He halted abruptly.

Ivy stayed in that room once in a while when she came over from Wyatt's, and Linnea's grandfather had used it when he visited for a few months last summer.

Brody stared through the darkness and swallowed hard. It wasn't a good idea for Savannah to be upstairs near him. It was gonna be hard enough during the day to keep his thoughts in line around her. And her sleeping nothing but a hop away was only gonna make his thoughts wander all the more.

Naw. He shook his head. He was getting worked up for nothing. Even if they shared the upstairs, they wouldn't be alone. Not with Flora sleeping in the room right at the end of the hallway.

At a whimper and then a cry, his senses heightened. Flora. He listened for a moment, waiting to see if the little girl was waking up.

When her cry came again, this time louder, he took the remaining steps two at a time and crossed to her room. Faint moonlight streamed past the flowy white curtains and outlined her delicate shape sitting in bed amidst the tangle of her covers.

She held up her arms toward him, crying softly.

He wasted no time in lifting and cradling her against his chest like he always did. She wrapped her arms around his neck and laid her head on his shoulder . . . like she always did. Her tiny body was warm, and her curly red hair tickled his face. As he breathed in her soft scent of sunshine and prairie grass and rosewater, peace flooded his soul.

"You're gonna be fine," he whispered. "Ain't gonna let nothin' happen to you, darlin'."

She nodded, and her crying tapered to sniffles.

He didn't bounce her like he used to do when she was younger and woke at night crying. Last time he'd tried, she giggled and told him she wasn't a baby anymore. Instead, now he just held her and swayed. That seemed to comfort her.

The earaches didn't bother her as much anymore. And he had to admit, he was gonna miss these days once she did grow up. He'd already overheard Linnea telling Flynn that a girl of three and a half shouldn't still be waking up almost every night. For once, Flynn hadn't been the one worrying and had said that Flora was probably awakening out of habit more than anything, and if that didn't bother Brody, then it didn't bother him.

Didn't bother Brody one lick. Never had, not from the day he'd arrived when he offered to do it since he was awake anyway.

He rocked back and forth, caressing her hair. When her breathing evened and she relaxed her hold, he knew she was asleep again.

Carefully, so he wouldn't rouse her, he tiptoed to her bed, lowered her as gently as possible, and situated her stuffed rag doll back in her arms. As he lifted the covers over her and tucked them around her snugly, she opened her eyes. "I love you, Uncle Brody."

With her big brown eyes peering up at him, his heart melted like always. "Love you too, darlin'." He bent and placed a kiss upon her forehead. As he straightened, her eyes closed, and she snuggled her doll, falling asleep again in an instant.

He gazed at her, love filling all the broken places inside him. Though he wasn't on speaking terms with the Almighty and hadn't been for a long time, he could admit the Almighty had given him a lifeline in this child. She'd been the one thing that had kept him going during those times when all he'd wanted to do was fall into the abyss and drown.

With a last tuck of her blanket at her shoulders, he turned. Then froze.

Savannah was leaning against the doorframe, watching him.

For an instant, neither of them spoke or moved.

"I heard crying," she finally whispered. "And I wanted to make sure everything was okay."

"It's okay."

She nodded but made no move to leave. Her fair hair was loose from the leather tie and flowed in long waves over her shoulders. Her nightdress flowed around her too, so that she was almost angelic. Her attention shifted to Flora. "She's the sweetest and prettiest thing I ever saw."

Standing there in the soft moonlight and in the quiet of the night, Savannah was the sweetest and prettiest thing he'd ever seen.

"You're really good with her." After another moment, she looked at him again.

He still couldn't tear his sights from her, almost like in front of the barn after they'd arrived. A part of him had known he oughta be polite and drop his gaze. He hadn't wanted to make her uncomfortable. But another part of him hadn't cared, the part of him that had seen and experienced too much to be embarrassed by anything anymore.

"I can tell she adores you." Savannah's whisper was filled with admiration.

"Don't know why." He honestly didn't understand what the little girl saw in him. But Savannah was right. Flora had adored him almost from the moment they'd met in the hospital in Virginia after the war. Not more than a year and a half old at the time, she'd held out a hand to him, and he'd clung to it ever since.

"I can see why." Savannah's low voice made his insides flip.

He couldn't think of a response and so watched her mutely.

"You'll make a very good father someday, Brody."

He shrugged. Never thought about becoming a father. Never imagined himself living long enough to get married or have children.

"I think you should have at least a dozen babies."

"A dozen?" His question came out with a note of surprise and a twinge of flirting. Trouble was, he was mighty rusty at flirting. Never had been all that good with it to begin with.

"Yes, maybe two dozen."

"Don't get much sleep with one babe. Wouldn't get any with a dozen."

Her laughter, soft and lilting, wafted across the dark room, and the tension eased from his shoulders.

"Linnea and Flynn are really lucky to have you doing night duty."

"That's why they keep me on."

She laughed again. And the sound was sweeter than anything he'd heard in a very long time, if ever.

As the silence settled around them once more, Savannah hugged her arms over her chest, but she couldn't hide a shiver.

He'd installed a stove in Flora's room the winter she moved upstairs out of her cradle into a bed. But now that it was May, he didn't light it anymore. Maybe he should . . . for Savannah's sake.

"You're cold." He started toward it in the corner. "I'll get a fire going."

"I'll be alright once I'm back under the covers. . . ."

He was already at the little cast-iron stove before the words left her mouth. He opened the door, then dug into the tin pail beside it for shavings.

"Brody. You don't need to."

"I want to." He laid in the shavings and began layering the twigs.

"Really. I'll be fine."

A moment later, he had a small blaze lit. He watched it

crackle and pop before standing. When he turned, she was still in the same spot.

"You'll make some lucky lady a very fine husband."

The very prospect of marriage shot heat into his neck. "Guess I oughta get me a wife before having those two dozen babes."

Her laughter rang out louder. She cupped a hand over her mouth and glanced at Flora. The little girl didn't move, oblivious to their presence. Thankfully. Flora was smart and would pick up on his attraction toward Savannah. No doubt she'd blurt something indecent.

Warmth seeped from the stove, and it wouldn't be long before it wound through the hallway and into the other two bedrooms—as long as Savannah kept her door open.

His mouth suddenly turned dry. What in the blazes was he doing? He had a hard enough time sleeping, and seeing Savannah from where he lay in bed wasn't going to make matters easier. Even so, he didn't want her to be cold.

"You'll need to keep your door open—at least partway—if you want some heat." He didn't dare meet her gaze. "Promise you ain't got nothin' to worry about on account of me."

She was silent, and when he chanced a glance her way, she was studying him. "I know that, Brody. In my prayers tonight, I kept thanking the Lord for letting us meet. I don't know where I'd be if not for your helping me."

"Ain't nothin'."

"It's everything." Her voice rang with sincerity. "Thank you."

He nodded. Then before he could think of a flirtatious comeback, she tiptoed to her room. He didn't want their conversation to end. But it was for the best if they didn't make a regular habit of being together late at night alone in a dark bedroom.

As he exited Flora's room, a small thrum of anticipation flowed through his blood.

When he reached his bedroom, he forced himself not to look across the hallway to her bed. Instead, in the darkness he shed his garments, letting them fall to a heap on the floor. Then he climbed into bed and stared at the low ceiling.

Savannah's room was a mirror image of his, with only enough space to hold a bed and a chest of drawers. Each bed was placed lengthwise against the wall opposite of the doorway. The position allowed him to sleep on his side and see into the hallway . . . and into the other room.

He tilted his head to the side. The moon and starlight poured through Savannah's windowpane and seemed to fall right upon her.

She faced his direction, watching him.

A strange burst of heat surged through his blood.

"Good night, Brody," she said softly, as if there wasn't anything unusual about the two of them bedding down a dozen paces away from each other.

"'Night."

She gazed at him a moment longer before her lashes fluttered closed and sleep claimed her.

He shifted to his side and curled an arm under his head. She was so beautiful with her hair tousled around her and her lashes resting on her cheeks.

But more than her beauty, she radiated peace. A peace he wanted to watch all night long. Maybe if he did, he'd soak in some of it and stave off the nightmares that tortured his soul every time he shut his eyes.

CHAPTER

6

"They're making target practice of the wild mustangs again!" A young woman's shout reached Savannah where she knelt in the barn beside a yearling with a fractured leg.

Brody, crouching beside her, stood and went to the wide-open door. Savannah glanced past him to find a woman riding bareback and careening to a halt in the ranch yard a dozen paces away.

Savannah finished tying off the splint, then stroked the calf's muzzle, earning a soft snort. "You'll be just fine now." Now that the leg was set properly.

Apparently during a recent stampede, the yearling had stepped into a gopher hole. The impact from the other cattle had only wedged and twisted the leg deeper.

Flynn had brought the yearling to the barn, and Elmer had tried to doctor the poor thing. But it hadn't stopped bawling from pain.

Elmer had suggested putting the creature out of its misery, but Savannah had asked for a chance to reset the bone. After administering a painkiller, she'd done the deed quickly. Now it was resting more peacefully.

"Brody! You've got to help me!" As the young woman slid down from her mount, Savannah could tell from her features she was a McQuaid, likely the lone sister, Ivy, that Linnea had mentioned. At nearly seventeen, she shared Brody's dark brown hair and eyes but had a vivaciousness and beauty uniquely her own.

"They won't stop." Her voice rang with distress. "Even after I warned 'em that I'd come get you."

Brody glanced at Savannah as though gauging how much work she had left on the yearling.

"You go on, Brody. I can finish up here by myself." She began to repack the supplies into her satchel.

Ivy stepped into the door. "Who's the lady?"

Savannah started to stand, and as usual, Brody was quick to come to her assistance. At his touch against her elbow, her thoughts flew back to the night hours, to seeing his exquisite tenderness with his niece, to exchanging banter with him, and to feeling cherished when she climbed back into bed. Though she'd only just met him, she'd fallen asleep knowing she had nothing to fear. In fact, she almost felt that he was watching over her like a guardian angel.

When she'd awoken at first light, he'd been gone. She'd found him in the barn, gently grooming the injured mustang. He hadn't spoken to her, but his eyes had welcomed her. Wordlessly, she joined him in grooming all the horses, sensing he needed the peaceful silence of the barn to start his day. He'd helped her tend the horse suffering from colic. And he'd stayed by her side when she changed the bandage on the mustang's leg, watching and assisting her.

Vesta had clanged a ladle against a pan when breakfast was ready, and Savannah and Brody strode quietly to the house together, her heart filling with wonder at the beauty of the sun rising above the eastern peaks. She'd felt at that moment she was exactly where she needed to be. The regrets of leaving Daddy and Momma and her weddin' had faded—at least for a little while.

Of course, it was hard not to think that today would have been her weddin' day, that if she'd stayed, Momma would have been overseeing the preparations for the feast they'd planned to have for the Double L cowboys as well as neighbors. Momma also would have made sure the servants groomed Savannah to perfection, turning her into the refined southern lady she'd been born and bred to be.

Now with breakfast over and her duties keeping her busy, she prayed Daddy and Momma weren't too sad.

"This here's the new veterinarian." Brody steadied her before taking a polite step back. "Savannah Marshall."

"Veterinarian?" Ivy's eyes widened. "Well, howdy-dowdy. Ain't that somethin'?"

"You must be Ivy." Savannah offered the young woman a smile.

"Pleased to meet you, ma'am." Ivy touched the brim of her hat. "We sure could use a vet up in these parts."

"That's what I heard. I sincerely hope I can be of some assistance."

Ivy stared back and forth between Brody and her the same way Flynn had yesterday. "I reckon you already have been."

Brody crossed his arms, his bulk imposing, as though warning Ivy not to say any more.

Ivy's eyes danced with amusement. "She's mighty pretty, ain't she, Brody. You sweet on her?"

Brody's brow furrowed. "Hush up, Ivy."

Ivy's smile broke free as quick as a ray of sunshine emerging from behind the clouds. "Guess you are."

Brody didn't bother with an answer, and instead he spun away and stalked toward the horse stalls.

"'Bout time you got yourself a woman," Ivy called after him. "Even if I can't see what a pretty lady like her sees in a big ol' grump like you."

Brody swung open a stall door and disappeared inside.

Savannah was tempted to race after him and reassure him Ivy was just teasing, that he had nothing to worry about from her. But she held herself back, guessing Ivy was the only one in the family who didn't treat Brody like he was a fragile piece of cracked clay. And maybe being treated like he was normal was just as important to his healing process as the tender loving care the rest of the family lavished on him.

"Glad to see you could fix up the little fella there." Ivy took in the injured yearling lying on the bed of fresh hay.

"A few days of resting, and he should be well on his way to walking again."

Elmer shuffled into the barn on his bowlegs, bumping up the brim of his hat. He cocked his head toward the yearling. "I can keep my eye on 'im if you got a mind to ride along."

Savannah had heard about the wild horses that made the Rockies their home. Old tales pointed to the Utes acquiring the horses from the Spanish centuries ago, but because the natives hadn't corralled their horses, so many had escaped into the wilderness that now undomesticated herds roamed much of the Rocky Mountains.

While horse hunters could obtain wild stock anywhere in the mountains and attempt to break them, the mustangs weren't easy to tame. The bronc busters weren't always successful—as evidenced by the battered and bloody mustang Brody had rescued yesterday in Fairplay. Even though the mare's owners had attempted to beat her into submission, she bucked easily and wasn't the kind of horse anyone wanted to be riding on a mountain trail near the edge of a cliff.

"Brody won't mind if I tag along?" she asked.

Ivy sized her up. "Reckon Brody'll wanna drive some of the mustangs into his corral. We could use the help if you're up for it."

Savannah's blood thrummed at the prospect of getting a closer look at the mustangs in the wild. "I'm up for it."

In no time, they were on their way, galloping east into the foothills. Savannah marveled at the beauty of the high country as she had yesterday when the caravan had ridden down out of the snow-covered Ute Pass into South Park. Surrounded by mountains on both the east and west, the rolling prairie stretched out for seventy-five miles from north to south. And though the grassland was flat, the elevation was close to ten thousand feet, a good five thousand higher than the Front Range.

She'd had some shortness of breath while making the gradual climb up. But since arriving, she hadn't experienced any of the usual mountain-sickness symptoms other than her lips and mouth being dry.

Though Brody was mostly silent, Ivy chattered nonstop about the mustangs, filling Savannah in on the ranchers' growing frustration with the wild herds eating up the grass meant to fatten the cattle, especially in the winter and spring when the naturally cured hay was less plentiful.

Ivy's eyes flashed with indignation. "Some ranchers have taken to corralling the weak and injured mustangs, selling them for a few cents a head to area farmers to turn into dog and pig feed."

That was exactly what the fellow had been planning to do yesterday to the mustang. Savannah could only shake her head in dismay.

"Then we've got some good-for-nothin's who've been shooting the mustangs and leaving their carcasses to rot in the sun." Ivy fingered the revolver holstered at her hip, as if she'd like nothing better than to shoot at those good-for-nothin's.

From the firm press of Brody's lips, he seemed inclined to join Ivy.

Savannah lifted her face, letting the bright sunshine warm her skin. "I understand the need to keep both the cattle and horses from overgrazing and starving to death, but surely the area ranchers can come up with a better solution than killing the horses."

"Most don't care," Ivy said, her tone laced with disgust.

"It's all about profit." Brody's few words were clipped but packed with meaning. The ranchers could make money from the cattle. Lots of it. But the mustangs were nothing but a liability.

"I'm sure the wild horses must be a threat to Healing Springs' cattle and grassland too." Savannah was glad the Double L didn't have to face this problem on the Front Range.

"We grow our own alfalfa." Ivy spoke with a knowledge that likely came from listening to the menfolk discuss the matter. "Wyatt started off doing it, and now Flynn's taken over."

"Seems like a wise plan." Too bad more ranchers in the high country didn't do the same thing. But why should they make the time and effort when they had free-range grass? Daddy and Chandler wouldn't do it.

As they began the climb into the hills, Ivy took the lead. The pine trees thickened, and so did the patches of slushy snow full of pine needles, making the ascent more difficult. As they neared the crest of the first ridge, the echo of gunshots reverberated in the distance. The trees thinned enough to give a view of a valley with a wide creek running through it.

Savannah guessed such an area was a natural place for horses to congregate. If anyone was interested in killing them, the fortress of the surrounding rocks provided plenty of overlooks.

"There." Ivy pointed to a cove upriver. In the shelter of trees and boulders, Savannah could make out a dozen or so mustangs. Several were a golden-tan dun and stood out among the pine, as did the roans and sabinos. The bays and blacks blended in better within the thick branches and shadows.

Compared to other breeds, the mustangs tended to have wide foreheads that tapered to small muzzles, giving their faces a V shape. Their eyes were large and expressive, but their ears were smaller and pointed slightly inward.

Even now as Savannah glimpsed one of the faces peering from behind the branches, she was struck by the potential of such horses. They could be friendly and trusting companions if trained properly and given the right care.

As another shot rang out and pinged against a rock near

one of the horses, the herd shifted, clearly agitated enough to remain under cover. She could almost sense their fear as if it were a real, living creature hovering around them.

"We have to do something." Desperation drenched Savannah's whisper.

Ivy nodded solemnly downriver. Several horses lay unmoving along the creek bank, blood running in rivulets from their bodies, turning the water a reddish tint.

Savannah gasped and almost cried out. But at Brody's warning glare, she caught herself and bit back her dismay.

"If Dylan were along, he'd be able to pick off each one of those pesky cowhands." Ivy's dark eyes flashed. "He's the best sharpshooter this side of the Mississippi."

Savannah had heard Flynn mention something about Dylan over breakfast and how he was drinking too much and getting himself in more gambling debt. From what she'd gathered, Dylan was the youngest brother and had developed a wild streak, which had given both Wyatt and Flynn trouble.

As Brody regarded the dead mustangs, he didn't speak, but the muscles in his jaw flexed and his nostrils flared. The anger flowed off him like a thundershower. He pulled out his revolver, flipped open the cylinder, and checked the chambers. Then he closed and shoved it back into the holster on his belt. He lifted the coil of rope from the saddle and looped it around his shoulder.

"Once I'm downriver, I want you to hightail it to the fork and wait there for me." He slid his rifle out of the scabbard and tucked it under his arm before his gaze locked on the opposite side of the ravine, where the shot had come from.

Ivy nodded.

When he turned to Savannah, the brown of his eyes was as rich and luxurious as the thickest and brownest of mink fur. "Promise to stay by Ivy?"

At the concern in his expression and voice, she could do nothing but acquiesce. "Of course."

Brody surveyed the landscape again. Like Ivy, she had to trust Brody, that he'd do the right thing to keep the horses and himself out of danger.

But as he nudged his mount over the crest and guided it down the rocky descent toward the creek, Linnea's warning from the previous evening wafted back: *At times he doesn't know how to handle his confusion and anger.*

Was Brody throwing himself into the fray, knowing he was putting his life in peril but not caring? Maybe she and Ivy should go with him. At least with three of them, they'd provide a united front.

She pressed a trembling hand to her chest. "Ivy, he's out in the open. What if they shoot him?"

"These here fellas won't harm Brody." Ivy narrowed her eyes upon an outcropping almost directly across from where they waited. "They might be bullies pawing for trouble, but they're all horns and rattles."

Savannah peered through the brush, trying to find the culprits, hoping Ivy was right.

"Ain't that right, Jericho?" Ivy shouted, sitting up straighter on her horse. "You're a big bully is all."

"Thought I told you to go home, Ivy." The reply echoed in the ravine. "A little girl like you shouldn't be riding around out here by herself."

"I ain't a little girl no more. And I can go wherever I blamed want to."

Silence filled the air, except for the calls of a broad-winged hawk flying overhead.

"You need to stop following me around" came the young man's voice.

"I ain't following you around, you arrogant cuss." A flush moved into Ivy's cheeks.

Savannah located a young man sighting down his rifle barrel at the mustangs. From what she could tell, he was a good-looking fellow a few years older than Ivy with a strong, lean body and brown hair showing underneath his hat.

"Brody's goin' down there and rounding up that herd," Ivy shouted again. "You let him be, do y'hear?"

At that moment, Brody came into view, riding down an invisible trail into the ravine. His horse slid, causing a shower of gravel to cascade toward the creek.

Savannah sucked in a breath and whispered a prayer.

Another shot rang out, this one from a different area farther up. The bullet hit the creek, but the horses whinnied in fright nonetheless.

"Jericho, you tell those boys of yours to stop their shootin'." This time Ivy's voice rang out with anger. "Brody's coming to get the mustangs, and you better let him."

"You know you can't save all the horses."

"Won't keep me from trying."

"Blast it all, Ivy!" Jericho sat up and lowered his rifle. He glowered at her for long seconds before he rose, calling to two other cowhands hiding in the brush and boulders not far from his position.

Ivy released a whoosh of air, and Savannah hoped that meant the shooting was over, at least while Brody was out there.

As Brody's horse reached level ground, he nudged it faster, uncoiling the rope as he went and twirling it.

Jericho tipped up his hat and leveled another glare at Ivy. "You'll be the death of me, you know that?"

"Good." She glared back.

He shook his head, frustration etched into his forehead and mouth. "Now go on home and stay there."

A flash of hurt crossed Ivy's face, but it happened so quickly that Savannah wouldn't have noticed it if she hadn't been watching Ivy.

Without giving Ivy a chance to reply, Jericho and his men scrambled upward and away. Meanwhile, Brody edged closer to the herd, circling around to one side. He remained calm and slow and steady. Rather than shouting or shooting and using fear to provoke the horses from the cove, he was clearly attempting to win their favor and trust.

For long minutes, Brody rode back and forth, flicking the rope and making eye contact as if speaking another language altogether. At first, the horses shied away, but eventually they stilled, watching him with more curiosity than fear.

Though Savannah couldn't see Brody's face since his back was mostly toward her, she could see the life and energy emanating from him. With the horses, he was fully alive just as he'd been last night with Flora. This glimpse of him again, at the man he was capable of becoming, gave her a fresh burst of hope. She never believed any creature too scarred or hurt to find healing, even if just a little.

With more time and patience, he somehow nudged the dominant stallion from its hiding place. Once the stallion broke into the open, the rest of the herd—made up of his mares and their offspring—rushed out to follow him.

As the wild horses raced through the water, sending up a spray of dazzling droplets, the sunlight shimmered over their rich coats. Their manes and tails flowed with abandon. And the power of their muscles and bodies rippled with each thundering gallop.

Savannah's lungs stopped working at the beauty of the sight. Only Ivy's urgent tug and command to follow prevented her from marveling over the mustangs until they disappeared. As it was, she tried to keep pace with Ivy's descent, knowing Brody was counting on them to meet him at the fork, where they'd turn the herd and direct them to his corral.

Savannah considered herself to be an expert horsewoman, having spent many hours in the saddle over the years. But Ivy's skill and natural ease with riding made Savannah look like an amateur.

Thankfully, they reached the fork ahead of Brody. Only minutes later, the majestic creatures came racing toward them, Brody to their left flank. Somehow the stallion recognized Brody's assertive but respectful leadership, for though the horse's nostrils still flared and his eyes radiated fear, he wasn't panicked.

Ivy seemed to know just what to do to help Brody, spurring her mount to the opposite side of the herd. Savannah joined her, galloping alongside the horses, admiring their rough and rugged beauty.

They were doing something so right, protecting the mustangs. As wild as they were, they had incredible potential if tamed by the right hands.

Wasn't that how it was with God? When others gave up, He kept going, kept pursuing, always seeing the potential of a person tamed by His hands.

Her sights strayed to Brody, to the confident way he held himself, the determination in the bend of his body, and the strength of his arms and legs in tandem with his horse. This sensitive man had been broken—was still broken—but he was giving of himself anyway, even when he didn't have much left to give.

With the grit of the dust on her tongue and the wind sweeping against her face, joy welled up within her. For a few moments she could forget about the confusion and frustration that had fenced her in over recent weeks. For today, she was riding free.

As they drove the horses across the open prairie, two riders came from the southwest. At first, Savannah couldn't distinguish who they were, assumed maybe they were ranch hands riding out to help. But as the pair drew nearer, she saw that the long black braids, dark skin, and buckskin shirts and breechcloths belonged to natives.

At the realization, an icy chill brushed across her skin. The warring with the Plains Indians had been ongoing for the past several years in eastern Colorado. While the Double L hadn't been close to the conflict, everyone had heard the tales of the violence perpetrated by natives as well as the military. In fact, for a while travel to the West had been dangerous. Roads were closed. And Denver and other Front Range towns had been isolated with delays of supplies and mail.

Even though news was circulating that the military was attempting to gather with the Plains Indians near Fort Larned for peace talks in an effort to end the hostilities, everyone was afraid and alert.

What did these two natives want? Were they upset Brody

was taking the mustangs to the ranch? And would they try to stop him?

She expected Brody to slow down, to at least acknowledge the natives drawing near, but other than a nod in their direction, he kept his focus on the herd.

The men didn't speak either, and their faces didn't contain any animosity. Instead of a confrontation, they veered alongside the wild horses, riding low and hard, as though they intended to help.

As the ranch came into sight, Brody guided the herd into a narrower formation. He'd camouflaged the corral entrance with sage and brushwood, and the mustangs didn't know they were entering until they were forced to slow up and turn.

When the last of the dozen or so galloped inside, Brody swung the gate closed. Then Savannah—along with the other riders—sidled up to the fence and watched the horses race in a circle around the corral, frightened and trapped.

The fear in their beautiful eyes tugged at Savannah, making her wish she could set them free to roam at will. But all she had to do was picture the slaughtered horses in the ravine to know they were safer in the corral. And hopefully, Brody would be able to calm them.

She didn't realize Brody had positioned his horse next to hers until one of the natives spoke, a shorter, stouter man with dark, keen eyes. "You have a wife?" He nodded curtly at Savannah.

"Not yet." Brody didn't take his gaze from the mustangs.

"Soon?"

Brody shrugged.

The other native, a younger man with a leaner face, made a comment in his language.

The stout one grinned. "Yes, soon."

Savannah got the impression they were talking about her. She'd never interacted with a native this closely before and didn't know what to say.

Ivy had already hopped down from her mount and climbed onto the fence. She grinned at Brody from her perch. "Sitting Bear is never wrong about anything. Right, Brody? Guess that means you're gonna marry Savannah."

Brody didn't respond.

The natives again spoke in their language, then laughed. Clearly these men were well known to Brody and Ivy, and Savannah could feel the tension easing from her shoulders.

The one Ivy had called Sitting Bear nodded now at the mustangs. "You need help with taming, send me word."

"Will do." Brody touched the brim of his hat.

"Before we are forced to leave."

The statement brought Brody around, and he gave the natives his full attention, his expression growing serious. "I didn't think the Ute representatives would agree to a meeting."

"We might not have choice."

Sitting Bear's English, while stilted, was clear enough. And Savannah guessed he was referring to the push from the U.S. government for a treaty with the Utes, one that would move them to a reservation in the western part of the state.

"There's plenty of land here for everyone." Brody scanned the surrounding open acreage as if to make a point.

Savannah didn't know enough about the situation to join in the conversation—only the grumbling from ranchers on the Front Range who believed the Utes were a nuisance to progress. Brody's friendliness with these men was flipping her perceptions upside down.

The two spoke only a few minutes longer to Brody and Ivy before riding out. As Savannah watched them fade into the distance, she felt Brody studying her.

She wanted to turn and catch him in the act. But she guessed she'd have the same results as last night in the barnyard when he'd stared at her—he'd keep on doing what he wanted. Brody was a man who didn't care what anyone else thought.

Was he wondering what her real story was? Where she was from? And why she was here?

He hadn't pressured her into saying anything. And even though she'd divulged only a little to Linnea last night, it had apparently been enough for the McQuaids. They didn't need to know much to open their hearts and home to her.

Savannah was grateful for their easy acceptance. This place, the people, the work—everything was much more than she'd expected, and it would be all too easy to let herself get attached. That would make the leaving harder. Because she would have to leave eventually, wouldn't she?

CHAPTER

7

Brody straddled the paddock fence, trying to keep his focus on the wild stallion but failing. His attention kept shifting to Savannah outside the barn, where she was tending a lame chestnut gelding.

She'd scraped away dirt caked in the hoof, tapped to find the painful area, and then cut right in with a knife blade. She'd drained a steady trickle of pus before disinfecting the cavity. Every move had contained a proficiency and steadiness that had added to his growing admiration.

"You losing your touch?" Ivy sat on the beam a few feet away, her bare feet hooked into the middle rail.

He raised his brow.

"Last couple of roundups, you were already on the ground by now, approaching the stallion with your stick."

Since returning with the herd, he'd been determining the pecking order of each of the mares, colts, and fillies in one paddock. And he'd been studying the stallion as it ran the circle of the fence in the other paddock, searching for a way out. Once he gained the cooperation and trust of the lead male, the others would be more willing to fall into line. But stallions tended to be aggressive, stubborn, and spirited, some more than others.

"Still watching him."

"Sure you are." Ivy was too perceptive for her own good. Any minute she was gonna start bellowing about how much he liked Savannah.

Even if it was the truth—and he felt a surge of life whenever he was by her side—he didn't need Ivy making a big deal about it.

"You wanna let me try some taming this time?" Ivy chewed on a long piece of grass, twisting it around between her lips. Even though his brothers' wives had both been good influences on Ivy, she was still a tomboy and maybe always would be.

"I reckon I'm getting as good as you." Ivy tossed the piece of grass behind her and started to unhook her feet from the post.

He hopped down before she could and slipped the stick from his belt. When Ivy made a motion to follow him, he held out a hand and growled at her. "Stay put." It was too dangerous for her to be inside either paddock until he'd had time to work with the mustangs and calm them some.

"Fine." She tucked her feet back into the fence post. "But I know exactly why you're losing your touch. 'Cause you can't keep your eyes off Savannah."

He'd never admit it to Ivy, but when his mind wasn't bounding straight over to Savannah, it raced back to thoughts of her from earlier in the day when she'd come out to the barn and helped him with the morning chores, how beautiful she'd been with sleepy eyes.

Brody blew out a tense breath. "Don't you need to be heading home?"

Ivy smiled. "Nope. I'm staying for supper. Linnea already told me to." Early on, Ivy and Dylan had lived with Flynn on his claim. But when Flynn and Linnea had gone east to care for him, Ivy and Dylan had moved to Wyatt's ranch and resided there permanently.

Brody couldn't blame Ivy for hanging out at Flynn's ranch now and again. After all, Flynn had stepped in and raised her after Pa and Ma had passed away—raised them all, truth be told. And steady, responsible Flynn was still the one everyone leaned on.

Brody held out the stick, a four-foot rod he'd fashioned from pine. It functioned as an extension of his arm, teaching the horses at first that they had nothing to fear from him, proving he wasn't a predator or a threat.

Later, he used the stick to train the horses to yield forward, backward, right, left, and eventually up and down. He never hit them with it. But he sometimes used the pressure to firmly direct, getting the horses to be perceptive to his cues and communication.

As he started to approach the stallion, he squared on to him and maintained eye contact. He advanced a few steps, then retreated, working his way closer and holding out the stick. By nature, horses were flight animals, and his first job during the training was to give the stallion time to figure out who he was and what his intentions were. Mainly his goal was to build trust.

He kept his eyes locked on the stallion's, moving his gaze farther back to the shoulders, then hip. When the horse slowed and angled off the wall, Brody finally looked away and broke the silent interaction, allowing the stallion to trot around the fence.

Brody counted twelve revolutions before attempting to communicate again. He held the stallion's gaze, using his stick to guide the creature. The horse slowed until his ears opened, and he made a licking and chewing motion—the sign he was beginning to communicate back, deciding whether to trust Brody.

The stallion continued to trot, though less nervous now. And Brody waited patiently for the final signal. When the horse dropped his head, Brody knew the strong and proud creature no longer saw him as a predator.

For the next hour, Brody worked steadily, repeating the process until the horse approached and allowed him to stroke him between the eyes. As the stallion nickered softly, almost contentedly, Brody felt the immense satisfaction that came every time he succeeded in gentling a horse.

Gradually his thoughts shifted from the horse back to reality. What was Savannah doing? Was she still tending to the lame horse? He glanced to the place she'd been before he started his training.

"You looking for Savannah?" came Ivy's humor-laden voice from where she sat on the fence.

He leveled a glare at her that could have skinned enough cowhide to make a saddle cover.

"She's right there." Ivy nodded across the paddock.

He didn't want to prove Ivy right, but his gaze slid to Savannah regardless. She'd tilted up her battered black hat, and her gentle blue eyes met his. They were filled with wonder. "I've never watched anyone as good with horses as you are."

"Learned most of what I know from Sitting Bear."

"He taught you well." Her expression contained a sincerity that told him she meant every word. "You'll have that stallion bridled and saddled in no time."

"Maybe." He wanted to converse more, but the words got stuck inside. What could he talk about with this pretty woman? He didn't have much in him worth saying.

He lifted his hat and wiped at the perspiration with his sleeve, then settled the hat back in place. He couldn't keep from taking her in again, this time more fully. Her long hair was tied loosely back, but wisps had come free and dangled around her face. She wore the same garments that she had yesterday, except with the way she sat, her split skirt revealed her trousers and the outline of thin, lovely legs.

She was a fine, fine woman. What was she doing here in South Park? The question taunted him as it had last night. With the scarcity of women in the West, she was probably fighting the men away. And if not, she'd have a wagonload of proposals by week's end.

Brody gave the stallion a final pat before he released it. Thankfully, he didn't have to try to come up with anything to say because Savannah struck up a conversation with Ivy about the wild herds. Her tone, her mannerisms, and even her very presence were calming, so that within minutes, he felt his muscles relaxing as he moved on to the lead mare and began the process all over again with her.

Eventually Ivy went off with Flora. At some point Flynn rode in from the south pasture and stopped to watch him with the mustangs for a short time. And Elmer was in and out of the barn, pausing every now and then to take stock of the progress.

Savannah, though, she stayed. She switched posts, sometimes standing and other times sitting. But she remained throughout the afternoon, asking him questions once in a while about his methods, but mostly just offering encouragement.

When Vesta banged the pot for supper, Savannah hopped down.

"You have a gift, Brody." She helped unlatch and swing open the gate. "An incredible, God-given talent. It's beautiful to watch. I could do it all day."

He wanted to tease her that she *had* watched him all day, but before he could formulate the words, a shout from the west drew his attention. Someone was riding across the open prairie as fast as a red ant rushing out of a burning log.

By the time he and Savannah reached the ranch yard, everyone had poured out of the house to greet the newcomer, the mayor's son, Logan Steele. Brody didn't know his age but guessed he was a year or two younger than Ivy, a gangly boy in that awkward halfway point where he wasn't a boy anymore but not quite a man.

Though Logan had lived in Fairplay for several years, he hadn't shed his rich, eastern city-boy look with dark, neatly trimmed hair, hat without a perspiration ring, and tailored trousers, vest, and coat.

"Logan Steele." Ivy stepped forward to pat the boy's heaving horse. "Your pa know you're running around the range like a madman?"

Logan lifted his chin and straightened his thin shoulders. "He's the one who sent me."

"What for?" Ivy narrowed her gaze upon him as if she didn't trust him.

Linnea stepped forward and offered Logan a smile. "You're

just in time for supper, if you think your parents would allow you to stay."

Logan ignored Ivy and instead gave his full attention to Linnea. "Thank you, Mrs. McQuaid. I do appreciate the offer. But I came after the new veterinarian."

All eyes swung to Savannah. "I'm the new vet," she said kindly. "What's the trouble?"

Logan's expression held a wildness that only came from desperation, a desperation Brody knew all too well. "Our mare's been in labor for hours and isn't progressing. Mr. McLaughlin's been there the whole time, and now he's saying he'll have to cut up the foal to deliver it if he's to have any chance of saving the mare."

Savannah nodded solemnly. "I'll leave right now and see what I can do."

"Thank you, ma'am." Logan brushed a hand over his horse, trying to calm it.

"You'll need to water and rest your mount first." She looked pointedly at the horse's foaming muzzle.

"We can't waste another minute." The young man rubbed his mount, as though that could make it magically ready to ride again.

"I'll go on ahead." Savannah began to jog toward the barn.

"You won't know where I live," Logan called, unable to keep the waver from his voice.

"You tell me," she tossed over her shoulder, "and I'll find it."

Logan hesitated.

"I'll take her." The words were out before Brody could stop them. That's what Flynn expected of him. His brother had made it mighty clear yesterday that he didn't want a woman riding around South Park unattended.

While the population was growing and the towns becoming more civilized, the area was still full of too many rough characters and criminals to be entirely safe, especially since they didn't have a regular lawman in these parts. But more than that, Brody wanted to go with Savannah and help her. From the sounds of things, the situation was gonna be difficult, and she might need an extra hand.

❦

Except for the thundering of their horses' hooves, the ride into Fairplay was silent. Brody could sense Savannah's urgency. It pulsed from her as she pushed her Morgan hard. When they galloped up to the fancy house the mayor had recently built on the outskirts of town, Brody guided her toward the barn at the rear.

As they slipped from their mounts, Brody handed off their care to one of the mayor's servants before directing Savannah through the crowd that had gathered outside the barn. He elbowed people aside and forced himself not to take a swing or two at the underhanded slurs about having a woman coming to do a man's job.

Savannah didn't seem to pay the comments any heed. Instead, she rushed to the brightly lit stall where another crowd had gathered, including Mr. Steele, a couple of cowhands who'd likely been passing through town and offered to assist, and Mr. McLaughlin, who ran the livery.

The barn was large and clean and well maintained, with at least a dozen horse stalls. The scent of fresh hay wafted in the air, with hardly a trace of the usual manure scent.

Rolling up her sleeves, Savannah dropped to her knees beside a beautiful black Arabian. The mare was worth her weight in gold, likely purchased from breeders out east. She was whinnying and snorting, her eyes wide with terror.

"How long has she been this way?" Savannah grazed the distended abdomen.

"All day." McLaughlin's arms were coated in slime, and straw stuck to his face.

Landry Steele's expression was grim, and he stepped aside to allow Savannah the room she needed to work. She was already peppering McLaughlin with a dozen questions even as she dunked her arms into a bucket of water and lathered up with soap.

"Logan?" Steele pinned Brody with his question.

"On his way."

Steele scrubbed a hand across his face. "When the boy begged me to let him go after the new vet, I couldn't say no. But McLaughlin says that now we're putting the mare into more danger by prolonging the delivery."

"Won't hurt none to let Savannah have a look."

"Hope you're right, son."

Brody'd done his fair share of birthing calves, not only growing up but also since living on the ranch. Foals weren't much different.

The mare groaned and strained, but nothing happened.

Savannah lay down on the floor and slipped her arm into the womb. She probed for a moment, then pushed in farther. "Both feet are back."

McLaughlin sat on his heels. "Poor thing's gotten up and then lain back down, rolling around and trying real hard to change that foal's position."

Savannah stretched again, her arm inside the horse nearly to her shoulder. "And you tried manually maneuvering the foal?"

"There isn't enough room inside to shift it."

The mare whinnied and tried to move. Brody stepped around Savannah and knelt by the mare's head. He stroked her cheek back into her crest. His touch might not be as calming as Savannah's was yesterday to the injured mustang, but he could do his share of soothing.

Savannah cast him a grateful glance before biting her lip and focusing on what she was feeling inside. "It's a big baby, and she's a small momma, but with my slender hand and arm, I think I can make the adjustment without tearing her uterus and causing internal hemorrhaging."

Brody rubbed the mare as Savannah worked to turn the foal. She had to stop and wait during the contractions, no doubt pained by the constriction around her arm. But she kept at it quietly and calmly, until at last she smiled.

"There we go." She continued to maneuver, her movements now quick and sure. "The amniotic sac. Now I can feel the front hooves and nose."

As Savannah pulled her arm out, the mare stopped her whinnying and began to labor in earnest, likely sensing the difference in her baby's position and finding revived strength.

"The foal is coming!" McLaughlin called out in excitement and relief. "I can see the head!"

The chattering all around them rose. But Savannah concentrated entirely on easing the foal out, giving the mare a little assistance.

"It's out!" McLaughlin again shouted, adding his muscle to Savannah's in pulling the newborn the rest of the way.

As the slick black bundle lay in the hay with a membrane still covering it, Savannah clamped the umbilicus. But instead of moving and showing signs of life, the foal was deathly still.

A new sense of urgency seemed to take over Savannah, and she began clearing out its mouth and nostrils and rubbing its belly in an attempt to stimulate it.

When the foal didn't respond, she laid the creature out, then gave it two big breaths in its upper nostril while blocking the lower one. She rubbed the body again and repeated the breathing. McLaughlin offered to help, and after several minutes, she let him take over while she massaged the foal's body.

Silence had once again descended. As more time ticked past, Steele's shoulders drooped. He glanced frequently toward the barn door, as though dreading Logan's appearance. A sense of discouragement settled over Brody as well.

When McLaughlin finally pushed away from the foal, his breathing was labored and his face perspiring. Savannah resumed the respirations in his stead. Brody suspected it was time to let go, that the newborn was beyond help. But as long as she wanted to keep trying, he was gonna help her.

He positioned himself beside her and let her work a little longer before gently touching her arm. "Need a break?"

She sat back and stroked the foal's muzzle. "I think it's starting to breathe on its own."

He bent in and felt the slight whoosh come from the foal's nostrils.

She smoothed a hand over the ribs while pressing fingers against the artery above the fetlock, silently counting the heartbeats.

When she glanced up, everyone stared at her expectantly.

Logan charged through the silent crowd congregated near the barn door and stumbled to a halt at the sight of the foal lying motionless on the ground.

It chose that moment to give a weak nicker. At the sound, the mare raised her head and nickered in response.

Logan collapsed to his knees, the relief on his face tightening Brody's chest.

Savannah rubbed the foal vigorously. "The heartbeat is steady. This baby will be just fine."

McLaughlin gave a whoop, and everyone outside the barn erupted into cheers.

Savannah continued to massage the newborn but glanced up to meet Brody's gaze with a happy smile. The sight of it went straight to his heart. If a fella could fall in love right on the spot—then it happened to him at that exact moment.

CHAPTER

8

"You're fallin' asleep again," Brody said.

In the growing dawn, he sidled his horse next to Savannah's and braced her as she tilted in her saddle—thankfully toward him and not the opposite way.

He propped her up and waited for her to stir like she had the last few times she'd nodded off. But instead of straightening, she only leaned against him more, her eyes closed, her grip on the reins slipping away.

A glance ahead to familiar landmarks told him they still had a good thirty minutes of riding before reaching the ranch. She wouldn't make it, was too tuckered out after staying up all night with the foal. She'd wanted to make sure it was well on its way to recovery before leaving, and that had included ensuring its ability to nurse. Since it was weak, she'd assisted the wobbly-kneed creature for the first couple of feedings.

Logan had stayed in the barn with them long after darkness had fallen and everyone else had gone to bed. Savannah had spent hours with the boy, patiently showing him how to make sure the foal was getting enough to eat.

Brody'd heard the tales about Logan Steele and his difficulty adjusting to Fairplay. He'd made no secret of how much he disliked the town and wanted to return to the East. His horses were the only things he liked. Little did Savannah understand how important saving the Arabian and her foal was to the kid.

Finally, when Savannah was certain the mare and her newborn were well on their way to survival, she allowed Brody to help her up onto her Morgan, and they started home.

Through her yawns she'd apologized several times for making him stay up all night. He'd tried to assure her he didn't mind. But she'd shaken her head and blown out a breath, clearly frustrated at herself for imposing on him.

As the reins fell from her fingers completely, Brody snagged them and brought both of their horses to a halt.

Her body sagged against him. After how hard she'd worked, she deserved to rest.

He slid his arms around her.

As gentle as he tried to be, the movement jarred her, and she roused. "Brody? Are we back at the ranch?"

"Not yet." He hefted her from her horse and set her sideways across his lap.

"What are you doing?" Her voice was sleepy and filled with another yawn.

"Trying to keep you from falling off Molasses." He situated her against his chest. "Gonna have to ride with me the rest of the way."

He half expected her to protest and wasn't prepared when

she coiled an arm around his waist and leaned her head against his shoulder. "I'm sorry, Brody."

"Don't mind none." He could feel her breath upon his neck and the tickle of her hair against his chin. And suddenly his body was in tune with every inch of her.

"I'm sure you're tired too." When she snuggled in closer, he could hardly make his lungs work past the surge of wanting that rocked through him.

It'd been a real long time since he'd held a woman. Last time was the day before enlisting when he'd hugged Mary Carroll good-bye. He'd kissed her good and hard, and she promised to wait for him. He thought she would, until Newt's mother wrote that Mary had gotten engaged to a right smart Union officer she'd met at a benefit social.

Of course, by that point in the war, Brody hadn't cared. Never thought he'd make it out alive.

He leaned in, let his nose brush Savannah's hair, breathed her in. The same rush of emotion he'd experienced earlier in the night came back. He couldn't possibly be falling in love with this woman, could he? He'd just met her, hardly knew a thing about her.

"I'm so selfish."

He snorted. "You? Selfish?"

"Yes. Me. I kept you out all night."

"Wasn't nothin' selfish about what you did in saving that mare and her foal."

"But now you'll be too tired to do your horse training." She yawned again, and her long lashes fell to her cheeks.

"I don't need much sleep."

"You're too nice to me, Brody."

"You callin' a grump like me nice? *You're* the nice one."

"You're not a grump." Her tone contained mirth.

"If I ain't a grump, then what am I?" His flirting was getting easier, less rusty.

"Hmmm . . . you're many things. . . ." She shifted slightly, and her fingers skimmed his lower back, sending shivers of pleasure skittering across his skin.

Heaven help him. How could so slight a touch affect him?

"But if I had to pick one thing . . ." Her tone was contemplative. "I'd say you're a gifted man who has to learn to see the beauty of life through the ashes."

He couldn't think of a witty response, not even if his life depended on it. All he could think about was the ashes that covered him. Layers upon layers had piled up as the smoldering ruins of his life had fallen down upon him.

She lapsed into silence, and from the soft exhalations and steady rise and fall of her chest, she'd obviously fallen back asleep.

He nudged his horse forward and led her Morgan, going slow. Just so he didn't wake her up.

But as he ambled along, deep inside he knew he was taking his sweet old time because he didn't want the moment to end. He wanted to cherish every second with this gentle woman as long as it would last.

When he ambled into the ranch yard, the sun was above the eastern range and spilling its golden light across the frost-covered grass. From the scent of bacon and coffee in the air, Vesta must have already banged the pot, signaling the start of breakfast. Though his stomach rumbled, he had one mission—getting Savannah to her bed without disturbing her.

As he dismounted with her in his arms, she mumbled against his neck but remained asleep. He carried her up the front steps, managed to open the door, and treaded lightly through the hallway toward the stairway.

Flynn appeared in the dining room entryway holding a mug of coffee, his brow furrowed and his eyes dark with frustration.

"Where you been?" His question was loaded with all the clucking of a mother hen.

Brody cocked his head down at Savannah.

"I was about to set off in search of you."

"No need," Brody whispered, starting up the steps.

"Hi, Uncle Brody." Flora slipped out of the dining room, half-eaten toast in one hand and crispy bacon in the other. Her red curls cascaded in disarray, not yet having been tamed by Vesta into the usual braids. "Papa's been real worried 'bout you."

Brody continued up the stairs carrying Savannah, hoping all the commotion wouldn't wake her. As he reached the top, he glanced down to find her still asleep. And more beautiful than ever. The lines of her face were graceful and slender, and he had the sudden desire to trace each curve with his finger.

With Flora's short, choppy footsteps behind him, he reined in his runaway thoughts and forced his feet to move toward Savannah's bedroom. As he lowered her to the bed, she didn't let go. In fact, her hand around him tightened as though she wanted to drag him down beside her.

At the merest thought of lying next to her, heat surged into his blood. He'd denied his needs for so long, he hadn't thought they existed anymore, had figured they'd died just like the rest of him. But he was learning mighty fast that his manly desires were alive and well—especially around this woman.

Flora's footsteps halted in the doorway behind him. "You tucking in Miss Marshall same way you tuck me in?"

Not exactly. He slipped his arms away from Savannah, and she released her hold. Her eyes opened and latched on to his, the blue as wide and deep as a mountain sky. "Oh, Brody. You're a godsend." Then she rolled to her side and was back asleep in an instant.

As much as he liked—maybe even loved—her, he didn't deserve a woman, not after everything he'd done in the war to survive. The fact was, he was too damaged to be of any good to a woman or family. He'd long ago resigned himself to living as a bachelor and doting on his niece. That had to be enough. Couldn't start getting ideas about the first pretty young lady to light a fire inside him.

He tugged up the blanket on the end of her bed. Even if her clothes were dirty from the birthing, he didn't have the heart to wake her to change. He folded the blanket over her shoulders, then backed out of the room until he stood in the doorway and scooped up Flora.

"She napping, Uncle Brody?" Flora wound her arms around his neck.

"Yep." He pressed a kiss to her cheek, tasting the toast crumbs that lingered there. "Now, let's be real quiet-like for a bit and let her rest. Can you do that?"

"Yep." Her whisper was loud.

"Good."

"Do you need a nap too?"

"Maybe a little one." His eyelids felt heavy, but somehow the thought of sleeping didn't frighten him the way it usually did.

She pressed a hand against his cheek. "Kin I tuck you in?"

He never could say no to her. "Okay. You get my bed ready while I go talk to your papa."

She broke into an excited smile and squirmed to be let down. And though he wasn't keen on a lecture from Flynn, his brother deserved an explanation for why he hadn't come home. After he finished the brief conversation with Flynn, Brody climbed back upstairs to find Flora waiting next to his turned-down bedcovers, with a storybook and a cup of water.

She patted the mattress, mimicking what he did for her every night. And once he was stretched out, she pulled the covers up and made a production of tucking every hem of the blanket around him snugly. Then she sat on the edge and proceeded to tell him the story in a singsong voice that imitated the way he read to her.

He had to smother his humor at her antics and pretend to be serious. But by the time she offered him a sip of water, he nearly choked on it in an attempt not to laugh.

"Let me pat your back, Uncle Brody. It'll help get rid of the stuck water." She set the tin cup on the floor and then tapped his back with about as much force as a dandelion petal tapping against a fence post.

When she finished kneeling next to his bed and saying prayers, she stood and blew kisses on his cheeks before leaving him with the solemnity of a widow at the graveside. The minute she turned the corner, he couldn't contain his smile, only to have her peek around the doorframe two seconds later.

"'Night, Uncle Brody. Now, don't you go getting out of bed."

He brushed a hand over his chin, trying to wipe away his mirth.

"And make sure you call me if you need anything."

"I'll do that, darlin'."

"Come on down now and leave Brody alone." Flynn's gentle rebuke drew Flora away from the bedroom. The mirth in his voice told Brody he'd probably been sneaking looks at the bedtime ritual and had enjoyed it just as much as Brody, if not more.

Brody crossed his arms behind his head and listened to Flora's chatter on the way down the steps, telling Flynn everything she'd done. Brody couldn't understand why Flynn didn't want to have any more children. Faced with a choice, Brody'd have a whole bunch of kids like Flora. But Flynn and Linnea had both agreed one child was enough for them.

"She's so sweet, Brody." The soft comment came from across the hallway. Savannah was awake and watching him. Had she seen the whole thing?

Her broad smile and the twinkle in her eyes gave him the answer.

"Tried not to wake you."

She shrugged. "I'm glad it did. I've never seen anything so cute in my life."

He smiled again. Smiling twice in the span of a few minutes was out of the ordinary. But that's what Flora always did—she brought him joy in the most unexpected ways.

He realized then that he was sharing a smile with Savannah, the same way Flynn and Linnea often did over Flora. The connection with her was tender and stirred up a longing to have more such moments.

"You're cute too, Brody." Her lashes lowered, and she fought a yawn.

"That supposed to be a compliment?"

"Yes."

"Just so you know, kittens and babies are cute. Not full-grown men."

"Then how should I describe full-grown men?"

"I dunno. You tell me." He was surprised when his voice came out low and full of invitation.

She laughed lightly, and a flush moved into her cheeks.

He shifted and laid his head on his bicep, giving him a direct view of her. "Well?"

"Do you want to know my thoughts on men in general or you specifically?"

"You choose."

She was silent for a moment before lifting her lashes almost shyly. "You're a handsome man, Brody. Especially when you smile."

Her words sifted through him, awakening him, filling him so that his response got lost somewhere inside.

She didn't seem to mind his silence, held his gaze another second, then closed her eyes. "Good night, Brody."

He still couldn't speak. All he could do was watch her. And the longer he watched, the more his fingers itched to pick up his pencil and sketch her. He hadn't drawn anything or anyone since before his first battle of the war, when death and destruction had taken up residence within him and killed every ounce of creativity.

He pushed up, reached under his bed for his haversack, then dug inside until his fingers connected with the small sketch pad he'd taken with him to war. In those early days, he'd passed the time by drawing, as he'd taken to doing ever since he'd been old enough to hold a pencil.

Gingerly, he removed the pad. The pencil formed a lump

between the pages where he'd left it when he last closed the pad. He pried it open but then hesitated. Was he ready to see the pictures he'd drawn the day before heading into battle?

His blood chilled. No, he didn't want any reminders. He had enough nightmares that wouldn't leave him alone. Averting his eyes, he began to rip out the pages. He didn't have to look to remember the images of new recruits drilling in a dew-drenched field, drying socks with a stick over an open fire, playing cards on an overturned crate. As he reached the last one, he folded the stack and stuffed it into his haversack.

With a fresh page open before him, he picked up the pencil. His fingers trembled, and he twisted the stub around. It fell onto the page, rolled off, and dropped onto the mattress.

He wasn't ready to draw, couldn't do it, wasn't sure he'd ever want to again.

His attention strayed to Savannah. Bright sunlight fell across her, giving him full view of the gentle curves of her chin, the smoothness of her cheeks, that dip in her upper lip. She'd shed her hat, and tendrils of fair hair framed her face. The shadows under her eyes. The smattering of freckles on her nose. The elegant arch of her eyebrows.

He swiped up the pencil, and before he could talk himself out of it again, he stroked the lead against the paper, making the first line, then the second, until his fingers stopped trembling and took on a life of their own. Within minutes, a black-and-white drawing filled the page. It didn't do her justice, but it was good. Better than he'd expected after so many years of not sketching a single thing.

With a final shading at one edge, he tucked the pencil inside, closed the pad, and slipped it under his pillow. Then he laid his head down and closed his eyes, a strange sense of calm falling over him, a calm he hardly recognized, one he hadn't felt in forever.

Somehow he sensed he'd made progress in moving on from his past. He still had a long way to go, but at least he'd begun the journey.

CHAPTER

9

Savannah wasn't sure which was more captivating—the man or the stallion.

She leaned against the split-rail fence, her chin propped on her hands, unable to tear her attention from Brody leading the wild stallion with a rope halter.

In the late morning sunshine, Brody and the mustang radiated with power, their muscles corded and well defined with each move they made. Both held their heads stiffly, proudly, as if to warn away predators. If only Brody could see that no one meant him any harm, especially Flynn.

From the past few days of watching the two brothers interact, she could tell that as much as Flynn wanted to help Brody and tried to love him, Brody kept Flynn at arm's length. In fact, he kept everyone at arm's length except Flora.

The little girl brought him joy like nothing else.

Just thinking about the way the child and Brody interacted made Savannah smile.

Brody's gaze flitted to her before returning to the stallion, but it was long enough to feel his interest and to know he saw her smile.

After only three days, his progress with the wild mustangs was admirable, especially because he'd had to stop training on several occasions to accompany her on calls. After she delivered the mayor's Arabian filly, word about her skill had spread fast. She'd been called to take a look at a sick mule at one of the mines, relieved a cow of a milkstone, and performed an emergency rumenotomy on a severely bloated steer.

Now that her name was getting out, how long would it take for locals to identify her as Sawyer Marshall's daughter? How soon before someone questioned her? Or sent word to the Double L? Although she hadn't heard any gossip yet about the Cattle King's daughter gone missing, that didn't mean it wasn't happening.

"You ready to go?" Brody rolled his shoulder like he did once in a while, as if the pain from a war wound bothered him still.

"Whenever you are. I'm not in a hurry." She needed to return to the homestead to the north and check on the steer today, but she didn't like that she had to keep tearing Brody away from the training. She wanted to insist she could go alone, but she wasn't familiar yet with the area the same way she was with the Front Range for miles around the Double L Ranch.

Once Daddy and Chandler learned her whereabouts and came for her, would she be ready? And if she wasn't, could she gather the courage to tell them she needed more time?

Her stomach cinched like it did whenever she thought about her predicament. In fact, she'd been hesitant ever since her daddy hinted at a match with Chandler before Hartley died.

Chandler came from a good southern family, the son of a former business partner of Daddy's. He'd journeyed to the West and worked on the ranch almost from the start. He'd developed a passion for it and had learned the operations even better than Hartley. It hadn't taken Daddy long to hand over the management to Chandler. It was because of the young man's savvy leadership that the ranch had become as successful as it was.

When she was younger, Chandler had treated her like a sister. But over recent years as she'd matured, he paid her more and more attention, until at last it had become all too clear he loved her almost as much as he loved the ranch. And since she didn't want to leave and go east with her parents, their marriage made sense.

Perhaps if she'd fallen in love with him, too, she wouldn't be struggling with having to give up her vet work after their wedding. Maybe she would have been more willing to be the kind of wife he wanted.

She expelled a sigh, which earned her another glance from Brody.

He quickly wrapped things up. A short while later as they rode out of the ranch yard, she tugged her flannel-lined coat closer to ward off the cold breeze blowing at them from the north. The mountains sat in the distance, attired in regal pine and rising tall into pinnacles of frigid white. The bright-blue sky also had a coldness to it, as if to remind them that spring was something that could come and go at a whim.

He held his reins loosely. He rarely used them. Somehow, he directed his horse by simple body movement, as though one unit with his horse.

She tried to read him, but he'd pulled the lapels of his coat up and tugged the brim of his hat down, hiding his eyes. Was he irritated he had to accompany her again? "Maybe next time Elmer can come with me instead."

"He's not a slave and ain't at your beck and call."

"I realize that. I wasn't intending to make him come. I'll ask."

"He's got other work. Best leave him be."

Where was Brody going with the conversation? Maybe his scars reminded him of the battles he'd fought to free the blacks. And maybe he was more sensitive to the issue as a result.

What would he think if he learned she was from the South? That her family had once owned slaves?

He was beginning to trust her and allow her into his world. Telling the truth could create a painful wedge between them. But most likely he'd find out soon enough. She may as well confess it now. "I grew up in the South in Georgia."

At her revelation, he didn't flinch, and his expression remained unchanged.

"My family owned a plantation, and we had slaves. Do you hate me now that you know?"

"Already guessed it."

"How?"

"Hard not to."

It had been so many years since she'd left Georgia, she thought her southern accent and mannerisms didn't stand out quite as much anymore. "When Daddy moved to Colorado Territory, he freed all his slaves and gave them the opportunity to come west with us if they wanted to."

"Sounds like your father's a decent fella."

"He's wonderful. I love him dearly."

This time when Brody looked at her, his gaze stayed upon her longer, his brows raised, as though he was waiting for her to say more.

"He's had a difficult time since my brother's death, that's all."

"Your brother died in the war?"

"No. While roping a steer, he got tangled up and was pulled down and kicked in the head by his horse." She swallowed the sudden lump in her throat. "Hartley lived for several days, but the injuries were too severe."

Brody slowed his horse. "I'm sorry, Savannah."

The soft compassion in his voice brought the sting of tears to her eyes. She had no doubt he understood the pain of losing people, had likely witnessed much more loss than she had.

"Is that why you ran away?"

"What?" She blinked back the tears. "Who said I ran away?"

The breeze picked up, and he tugged at his coat collar. "Ain't hard to tell."

How much should she disclose? It wouldn't hurt if she told him the truth about why she'd come to the high country, would it? She bit her bottom lip and attempted to think of all the reasons why she should hide from Brody. But she couldn't think of a single one. "I ran away from my weddin'."

They were cresting a rise, and at her admission Brody halted abruptly. "Your wedding?"

She tugged on Molasses's reins. "Yes, Daddy wanted me to marry our ranch manager, but I broke the engagement."

He tipped up his hat and stared at her, his rich dark eyes full of questions. "The manager? Something wrong with him?"

"Chandler's a fine man—"

"Chandler, as in Chandler Saxton?"

She drew in a breath. "Do you know him?"

"Not personally, but he bought a dozen tamed mustangs from me."

"Of course those were yours. They were the gentlest wild horses I've ever seen." Savannah had been on hand when a couple of cowhands had arrived at the ranch with the new horses. They'd all remarked on the fine training.

Brody narrowed his gaze and studied her more closely. "That means you're Savannah Marshall, the daughter of Sawyer Marshall, 'the Cattle King.'"

"Yes. He's my daddy."

Brody muttered under his breath.

"What's wrong?"

"He ain't gonna take kindly to anyone helping his daughter hide. And Chandler's gonna shoot-to-kill any fella who comes within a dozen yards of you."

"They'll be grateful you offered me a place to stay."

Brody muttered again and shook his head. "Gonna have to send them word you're here."

"Please, Brody." She edged up and grabbed his arm. "Please give me a little longer. I need more time to think, to decide, to figure out what to do."

"Figure out if you're gonna marry Chandler?" Brody's voice turned hard.

She hunched deeper into her coat, the cold breeze sliding underneath and sending a chill over her skin. "It would make Daddy happy."

Brody's gaze dropped to her hand on his arm, and the muscles in his jaw twitched.

She released him and instead clutched the reins.

"And what about you?" he asked. "Would marrying Chandler Saxton make you happy?"

The last night she'd been with Chandler, she'd turned down his request to kiss her good-night. The request hadn't been inappropriate. Not with their weddin' only a few days away. But the thought of kissing him had sent a burst of panic through her. Maybe the request had even been part of the reason she'd felt the urge to leave.

At the time, she hadn't stopped to analyze why she wasn't ready to kiss Chandler, had just resolved to endure some aspects of the marriage—like the intimacy. But what if she wanted more than enduring? What if she longed to have something deeper?

Of course, some marriages that started as friendships turned into loving unions eventually. But she didn't feel that way about Chandler yet, and she'd tried to convince herself that mutual respect, kindness, and being together on the ranch would be enough. But would it be?

"He's a good man—"

"You think every man is good."

Did she? Her thoughts flashed over the various men in her life, and Brody was right. She couldn't think of anyone she didn't like. "Maybe I just try to see the good in everyone I meet instead of focusing on the bad."

Brody stared straight ahead. "Maybe if you took a better look at Chandler, you'd have an easier time making up your mind."

"And I suppose you're planning to tell me everything about Chandler I'm not seeing."

Brody was quiet for several long heartbeats.

She stared ahead too but didn't see anything. No, Chandler wasn't perfect. He was arrogant at times and liked to be in control. But he would treat her well, just like Daddy treated Momma.

Finally Brody released a taut breath. "If you need time, I won't send word to your father."

"Thank you." She expelled a breath too. "I promise you've got nothing to worry about. Daddy will be grateful you helped me."

Brody didn't respond, which told her he didn't believe her. But Daddy was a generous man, and he'd probably reward Brody for the time and effort he'd put into taking care of her.

As the silence stretched, she was keenly aware of how much talking they'd done. Even if it had been a difficult conversation for her, at least it had drawn Brody out of his shell.

"Do you love him?" His question was blunt and almost demanding.

A part of her was ashamed to admit she didn't love Chandler. What would Brody think of her for being willing to marry a man she didn't love? But the other part of her needed him to know the truth . . . because maybe he'd be able to help her sort out what to do.

She twisted her reins around her gloves. "I was hoping eventually I'd grow to love him. But . . ."

Brody rested both hands casually across his leg, and yet his shoulders and arms were rigid.

"But I can't make it happen, and the Lord knows I've tried very hard."

"Then there's your decision."

As always, the decision came back to the mutually beneficial arrangement. Chandler would gain the ranch, and in return he'd offered Daddy money to invest in railroads again. "My marrying Chandler would make things a whole lot easier for Daddy."

"That's his problem, not yours."

"You make everything sound so simple."

"Maybe you're making it too complicated."

"But that's because it is." Much more than she wanted to explain. The crushing weight of Hartley's death had simply been too much for both her parents to bear. Her marriage to Chandler would give them everything they needed to leave the West and start over in the East.

Brody's expression turned pensive. She waited for him to expound, to offer more of his simple wisdom, but his attention riveted on something in the distance. "There." He leaned toward her and pointed.

She followed his finger to the north. Aspens with new leaves covered the hillsides along with a few withered pines. To the forefront, a cluster of horses grazed on the patches of grass growing in tufts amidst the sage and stone.

"Another herd of mustangs?"

"Not just any herd." His voice contained a note of awe. "It's Hades's band."

"Hades?"

He nodded toward the lead pinto with a bay-and-white-spotted pattern and a two-toned mane of blond and bay. "Everyone 'round here calls him Hades for stirring up so much trouble."

Brody slid from his mount and offered her his hand, assisting her off. As her feet touched the ground, he didn't let go. Instead, he drew her toward a level spot, tugged her down, then released her hand.

When they were both stretched out flat on their bellies and peering over the crest, he pulled a spyglass from his inner coat pocket and squinted through it. He focused the instrument before he carefully handed it to her.

She peered through the lens. The horses appeared as though they were only a dozen paces away instead of a hundred. She shifted the spyglass until she had it pointed on the pinto. While he wasn't an especially large stallion—maybe fifteen hands—he was mantled with muscle and sheathed in scars. His presence exuded a power and purpose unlike any horse she'd ever seen.

"See the way their ears are flicking?" Brody whispered. "They sense our presence."

"This far away?"

"Yep. And the way Hades is circling and lifting his tail, he's letting us know he sees us and doesn't like it."

"Tell me more about Hades," she whispered reverently.

"From what I can tell, he's the strongest mustang out here. Has at least six mares and sired dozens of offspring."

Hades tossed his head, the uniquely colored mane blowing in the wind. Several jagged scars marred his nose and cheeks. His neck and ribs had splotches that had once been torn up and healed too. "Why does he have so many scars?"

"From all the fights he's been in."

"Fights from what?"

"Other stallions competing for his mares."

She knew enough about the mustangs to understand their lives were challenging, that they faced risks in the wilderness from predators, harsh weather, extreme winters, and the constant search for grass. She hadn't realized the threats they experienced from one another. And now the danger from area ranchers.

She surveyed Hades a moment longer, then handed the spyglass to Brody. "How is he stirring up trouble for the ranchers?"

Brody positioned the lens over his eye. "He has a knack for luring away tamed mares and making it real hard to get them back."

She could understand why that would be frustrating. A cowhand needed a trustworthy horse, often several.

"Hades's band made trouble over the winter too," Brody continued, "breaking fences and foraging grass meant for winter cattle feed. Riled up the ranchers something fierce, and now they're gunnin' for him."

Hades was magnificent, even with all his wildness and blemishes. Her heart ached just looking at him. "He was here first, before all the ranchers, and doesn't deserve to die."

"None of them deserve to die." Brody's voice was low, and his eyes distant. Was he talking about the horses or thinking back on the war?

She had the urge to lay a hand on his arm and comfort him, but he hadn't liked her touching him earlier, and she didn't want to push him. "Isn't there anything we can do?"

"Wish there was."

Hades bent his head and grazed, so scarred and yet so powerful. That was just like Brody. Broken but still beautiful. "Can you drive him and his herd to the ranch and tame him?"

Brody folded his spyglass. "Even if I could catch him, I wouldn't. He needs to be free."

"But with the ranchers trying to reduce the wild horse population, wouldn't you like him to be safe more than free?"

He stuffed away the spyglass and then pushed up. "Taming would kill him. I'd rather let him take his chances out here."

She started to rise, and he helped her to her feet. Once standing, she held herself motionless, not ready for the moment to end. The ruggedness of the hills and the mountains spread out in a breathtaking view with the mustangs poised in alertness.

As the herd began to move on, she and Brody watched until the last mustang disappeared from sight. Then wordlessly they mounted. As they started riding again, she knew that once she left the high country, this moment with Brody, watching Hades, was one she'd never forget.

CHAPTER

10

"She's a beautiful filly." Savannah glided her fingers over the soft mane as the creature stood wobbly kneed next to her mother in the corral, the evening sunshine turning their coats to ebony. "Looks like she'll make it just fine."

Logan stroked the mare, now completely revived from the birthing. With his dark hair and lean features, the young man was on track to be as handsome and distinguished as his father. "I can't thank you enough, Miss Marshall."

"I'm happy I was here to help."

Brody relaxed against the fence, both arms braced casually against the top rail, as if he had all the time in the world to wait on her as she made her visits. After stopping to watch Hades and then riding out to check on the bloated steer, she'd been surprised when Brody suggested swinging by Fairplay on their way back to the ranch.

She hadn't objected. In fact, she'd been grateful for his offer and was learning he was more perceptive than he let on. He'd noticed her dwindling supplies and had helped her find some of what she needed at several different stores. Then he'd directed her to the Steeles', somehow guessing she'd relish an opportunity to check on the mare and foal.

She appreciated Brody's patience. More times than not, he was right there beside her during her work, assisting her in whatever way he could. Even so, she'd taken up enough of his time.

With a final rub to the foal's flank, Savannah slung her satchel across her shoulder. "We should get going if we have any hope of making it back before Vesta bangs the pot."

She gave a few last instructions to Logan before following Brody to their waiting mounts. As they made their way down Main Street at the busy hour, her gaze strayed to his thickly muscled arms, his broad chest, and his strong hands resting upon his thigh.

As if sensing her looking at him, he slid a glance her way, and his brow quirked as though to ask her what she needed.

What did she need? Something strange and warm swirled within her, something she couldn't define but that was connected to him.

Before she could lose herself in the dark, rich depths of his eyes, his attention darted to a group of cowboys standing outside Cabinet Billiard Hall. One of them was hammering up a notice on the wall beside the door.

Brody studied the sheet, a frown creasing his brow.

She tried to read it, but more men crowded around, blocking her view.

In the next moment Brody hopped from his horse and started toward the billiard hall.

The man nailing up the notice was the same handsome fellow who'd been shooting at the mustangs earlier in the week. Ivy had addressed him as Jericho and had later informed Savannah that Jericho Bliss and his older brother, Nash, had been the cowhands who had accompanied them on their journey across the Santa Fe Trail back in '63.

Apparently after arriving, Jericho and Nash had gone up to Leadville and spent a year there mining for gold before calling it quits and returning to ranching. The two had helped Flynn for over a year, managing his ranch while he and Linnea went back east. But then Nash had suffered a deadly accident in the mountains when his horse was spooked and slipped over the edge of a cliff.

Jericho blamed the death on the presence of the wild mustangs, claiming they'd riled up Nash's horse. He'd wanted to take a posse out and eliminate the mustangs right then and there. When Flynn refused, Jericho quit and went to work for a rancher who hated the wild horses as much as he did.

Brody strode up to the notice, shoved Jericho aside, and yanked it from the wall.

Jericho grabbed Brody's arm and lunged for the sheet. "I have permission to post it, so give it back."

Brody threw off Jericho's hand and stared at the cowhand, his expression dark and dangerous. The crowd around the two tapered to silence.

Unease skittered through Savannah.

"Want it back?" Without taking his gaze from Jericho, Brody crumpled the paper into a ball and tossed it at Jericho's feet. "There."

Jericho tensed, his fingers tightening into fists. "You can take down the notice, but you can't stop us from doing what should've been done long ago."

Brody formed fists too. "Hades ain't to blame for your brother's accident."

"That devil-horse was there in the canyon the day Nash died, and everyone knows it."

"Ain't no proof."

"It doesn't matter." Jericho lifted his chin. "Three more of our mares ran off with Hades last night. The boss said that was enough. Had a meeting with a few other ranchers, and they decided to offer a reward to anyone who can bring them Hades's head."

Savannah drew in a sharp breath. So that's what the notice was about—a death warrant for Hades. She could understand the frustration the ranchers were feeling at losing mares to his band, but after watching the stallion today, she hated for him to come to harm.

Brody glared at the gathering crowd. "Nobody better go after Hades, y'hear?"

"Then what are you aiming to do with the devil-horse, McQuaid?" said another onlooker.

"Ain't taking him down, that's for blamed sure."

"Who put you in charge of the mustangs?" Jericho pushed forward, shoving Brody.

Brody jabbed him in return. "Stay away from Hades."

"Try and stop me."

In the next second Brody's fist plowed into Jericho's gut. Jericho swung back with a strength and determination that was almost frightening.

Her pulse pounding, Savannah slid from her mount. She'd seen enough cowhand brawls over recent years to know the onlookers wouldn't interfere. They'd let the pair fight until they tuckered out or were knocked out. If she wanted the altercation to stop, she would have to end it herself.

She glanced around for something—anything—she could use to get the men's attention. Her sights landed upon a bucket near a livestock watering trough. She rushed over to it, filled it, then crossed back to the men and tossed the water, making sure to aim directly into Brody's face.

As the murky liquid hit him, he stumbled backward. Thankfully, Jericho took several steps back too. She used the opportunity to plant herself between the two, eyeing first Brody as he spluttered and wiped his face, then Jericho, who dropped his fists, his eyes wide upon her, blood streaming from his nose.

"I'm so sorry, gentlemen." She schooled her voice into her most charming southern accent. "I was intending to water my horse. Guess I missed."

The other men standing around guffawed.

Brody removed his hat, shook the water off, and slapped it back on his head. Each movement was forceful, as though he hadn't released the pent-up anger inside him yet. But instead of resuming the fight, he stalked toward his horse, grabbed its line, and began to lead it away from the crowd.

She passed the bucket to the nearest bystander, swiped up Molasses's lead line, and followed Brody. His stride was long and swift, and she couldn't keep up. But she didn't mind. She guessed he was in no mood for her company, not after what she'd done.

When he reached the edge of town, he stopped, his back as rigid as a buckboard. Although he didn't turn around, she suspected he was waiting for her. Even if he was mad at her, he was too honorable to set off to the ranch and leave her behind.

Her steps slowed until she halted beside him. Maybe she shouldn't have intervened. She wanted to help him, but had she gone too far?

He stared straight ahead. Blood trickled from his nose. And a split in his lip had started to swell.

The more she got to know him, the more she wanted to ease his pain, had hoped he'd sense her concern, feel her kindness, and know he could be vulnerable with her. But so far, she wasn't making much progress, if any. Now she'd probably caused him to dislike her.

Her mind scrambled for a way to make peace with him. What could she say or do?

"Thank you." His voice was soft.

"What?" She surely hadn't heard him correctly.

"I'm obliged you put an end to the fight."

He *was* thanking her. What should she say in response? She couldn't think, could only stare at his rugged profile.

He slid a glance at her, his eyes brimming with sorrow. "Don't know why I'm so quick to fight. Ain't something I wanna be doing."

"You're fighting demons with your fists, but from what I've seen, no one ever wins a battle with fists or strong drink or even ignoring the hurts."

His jaw flexed.

By being honest, she was stepping into dangerous territory. But he'd cracked the door just a little, and she had to take advantage of it. "Demons have to be fought inside."

"Inside?" His brows rose.

"Here." She touched her head. "And here." Then she touched her heart.

He opened his mouth as though to protest.

But she spoke again before he could say anything. "When you're taming a horse, you don't overcome his fear by beating him or bribing him. You do it by getting inside his head and heart and working to overcome his fears and gain his trust and respect."

As he took in her words, he clamped his lips together.

"We're the same," she continued. "We can't beat or bribe our fears away. We've got to go inside and replace the fear."

"How?" The word came out raspy.

She paused and stared off over the dry grassland, the wind kicking up swirls of dust. "When you're training your horses, you know it's different for each one, and you use time and patience until you figure it out, right?"

"Yep."

"Then be patient with yourself. If you're on the lookout, you'll find ways."

He nodded.

Although she'd been able to easily tell the McQuaids were God-fearing people who took their faith seriously, she had the feeling Brody's demons had been driving him away from God. She didn't want to preach at him, but if he wanted to truly defeat the enemy, he would have to make his peace with the One who could help him fight.

"Try prayer, Brody. It's the best way to start."

He watched the horizon. "I ain't been on speaking terms with the Almighty for a long while."

"I guessed that was the case."

"I reckon He ain't holding His breath waiting to hear from me, not after everything I've done."

What could she say to that? She was just a simple woman with a simple faith. She didn't claim to have all the answers, especially for everything Brody had experienced in his short life. But surely God still loved this broken man and wanted to hear from him. "This week, watching you tame that stallion, I couldn't help but notice that you have the most patience for the wildest of creatures. Maybe God has the most patience with the wildest of us too."

"Maybe."

The breeze flapped against their coats, bringing a sharp chill. The sky was turning violet since the sun had already disappeared behind the peaks to the west.

"You're a good man, Brody."

"That's what you say about every man." He gave her a ghost of a smile and stared off into the distance again.

Yes, they'd had this conversation earlier. But it bore repeating. "Maybe I do see the good in people more than the bad. And maybe you should try it, too, especially with yourself."

He was quiet, and she hoped that meant he was taking to heart everything she'd said.

Finally, he tugged at his lead line. "Best get started home."

"Whenever you're ready."

He helped her up into her saddle. And as they directed their horses toward the ranch, she could only pray he was one step closer to being ready to start on his way back to the Lord.

CHAPTER

11

Brody's breathing was labored, smoke choking him. The bullet in his shoulder sent pain shooting through his arm.

Down! Get down! The shouts from his comrades and best friend clamored above the pounding artillery.

Brody hunkered behind the boulder on the ridge and wanted to plug his ears to drown the cries of hundreds of wounded and dying men in the blazing sun with no one to comfort them or come to their aid.

Gun smoke clouded the air, hazy in the thick July heat. Bloody limbs, mangled flesh, bloated bodies littered the ground around him. The stench of fear was as strong as the rancidness of decay. Was he in the pit of hell again? Every battle was exactly what he'd imagined hell to be like, only worse.

Brody shifted, needing to find an escape, but flames leapt up all around, blocking him in, pinning him in place. The heat seared his skin, and he cried out at the pain.

He had to get out, but he couldn't leave anyone behind.

"Brody?" someone called to him. A woman. Savannah.

His heart thudded even harder. Why was she standing in the middle of the fray?

Panic seized him. He reached for her and drew her down beside him where she'd be safe. Dragging her close, he sheltered her within the confines of his body.

He could feel her hesitation, but after a moment she seemed to relax and then wrapped her arms around him in return. Somehow her touch, her presence, her gentleness made the din of the combat fade.

"It's okay." Her whisper was soothing.

His throat was still too full of smoke to say anything. But the heat against his flesh disappeared and left him terribly cold, so cold he started to shake.

Her arms tightened, and she pressed closer, as though to give him her warmth. "You're fine, Brody. Just fine."

He had to get her out of here. Had to save her.

"Take a deep breath." Her soft voice beckoned to him.

He sucked in air and then released it.

"Good. Now take another."

He clung to her command, her voice, her touch, and he released a second deep breath. The smoke cleared, and he found himself staring at pitch-darkness.

He was in his room having another nightmare. The same nightmare that had haunted him for years. Except this time, Savannah had been in it.

"There you go," she whispered. "You're dreaming, that's all."

Had she heard him thrashing in his sleep? Embarrassment hit him hard. He rarely allowed himself to fall into a deep sleep to avoid this very thing—bothering people with his nightmares.

"Savannah." He shifted, trying to make his tremors go away. But then he froze. She lay in his bed beside him, in his arms.

The smoky world of the battlefield fell away altogether, and he was suddenly conscious of the length of her and all her womanliness crushed against him. Her fingers caressed his back, rubbing in circles.

Oh, heaven help him.

He had no doubt he'd been the one to pull her down into so compromising a situation. He hadn't meant to.

He had to release her. Fast. And put distance between them. He rolled, but she clung to him, whispering words of comfort again, likely not realizing he was fully alert.

Her soft exhalations against his neck tantalized him. The silk of her hair brushed his chin. And the warmth of her body soaked into him, setting him ablaze, but this time in a completely different way than he'd experienced in his nightmare.

Suddenly, he didn't want to let her go. His desire for this beautiful, intelligent, and compassionate woman swelled within his chest, and he had an overwhelming urge to let his hands and mouth explore where they wanted to go.

Her fingers rubbing his back came to a halt. Did she sense the changing nature of his wakefulness? It was probably hard not to, since his breathing and trembling had both ceased.

Her body grew rigid.

Yep, she knew he wasn't dreaming anymore. Expelling a terse breath, he loosened his hold. "Sorry . . ."

She unwound her arms from around him. "No, I'm sorry, Brody. I heard you crying out—"

"It's my fault." He shifted back, feeling cold and barren without her embrace.

"It's not your fault. You were having a bad dream." In the blackness of the room, she scrambled to sit up, her whisper filled with mortification. "I was just trying to comfort you, but I know you don't like being touched."

He captured her hand before she got too far. "Wait."

Thankfully she halted, didn't try to pull away.

Her fingers were long. And tender. He'd watched those fingers work their magic all week with every creature she doctored. "What makes you think I don't like being touched?"

"You pull away from me."

With only faint starlight coming through the window, he could see that she was sitting next to him on her knees. Her unbound fair hair spilled over her shoulders and around her, reaching nearly to her waist.

His fingers itched to comb through those strands, but instead of giving way to the urge, he brushed his thumb across her knuckles.

She sucked in a sharp breath.

The soft sound sent warmth spiraling through him again. "That's why I pull away."

"Why?" Her voice was breathless.

"Your touch is like a branding iron to my skin, like mine is to yours."

She ducked her head and tugged her hand loose. "That's not true. You shouldn't be saying such things—"

"Ain't gonna deny it, darlin'."

"Brody." Her chastisement was weak.

He reached for her hand again, slipping his fingers around hers. She stiffened. For just a heartbeat. Then she molded her fingers with his.

Immediately he wanted to jerk away—just as she'd accused him of doing. This connection with her was dangerous and made him feel things he wasn't sure he was ready to feel.

He let his body sink into the mattress, still keenly attuned to the way she'd felt in his arms. Even if she hadn't meant anything besides offering him comfort, she was a desirable woman, and a man'd have to be a saint not to want to hold her.

Had Chandler Saxton held Savannah? Brody hadn't been able to stop thinking about the manager of the Double L ever since Savannah had told him she'd run away from her wedding. From everything he'd heard about Chandler, the gentleman had been born and bred in wealthy, elite circles of the South.

He expected Chandler behaved perfectly in every way toward Savannah, keeping his hands to himself. Even so, the very idea of another man getting to spend time with her and maybe even kiss her sent a sourness worse than vinegar sloshing in his gut.

"Chandler's touch like a branding iron on your skin?" His whispered question was out before he could stop it or the jealous edge that hung in the air.

"I'd rather not say."

"Reckon if you were feeling this with him, you wouldn't be here."

She started to pull away. But he let his fingers glide against hers, the warmth of their palms brushing together and stirring his insides.

Her breath hitched, and her fingers pressed into his with almost a tremble.

At her reaction, a small measure of satisfaction curled through him. Chandler might have longed for more but hadn't been able to win Savannah over.

Brody wanted nothing more than to be the one to win her body, soul, and spirit. But old ghosts rose swiftly, taunting and telling him he wasn't worthy of a wife, a family, or a future. Was it time to battle those ghosts—demons, as she'd called them?

Her words from the evening had lingered with him all the while he'd eaten supper, done chores, and tucked Flora into bed. Savannah was right. He'd been fighting his demons with his fists, letting his anger get the best of him. And after every fight, he walked away feeling worse inside, knowing a better man wouldn't jump into a brawl and hurt people every chance he got.

She grazed her fingers against his, almost as if she'd never touched a man before. He stretched out his palm and fingers, giving her silent permission to explore. She traced first one finger and then the next before she moved to the grooves in his palm.

With each stroke, the heat inside spread deeper and fanned hotter. She was clearly an innocent to sit on his bed in the dark and caress him this way. She didn't realize how her touch was affecting him, or she would've hopped up and moved away.

As she reached his last finger, she drew a line up to his wrist. Could she feel the throbbing in his pulse?

"Brody? Can I ask you something?"

"Yep." Didn't she know at that moment, she could have asked him to do anything, even climb the highest peak in Colorado, and he would have done it for her?

She hesitated. "What are your nightmares about?"

He froze.

Her fingers returned in full force to tangle with his, telling him without words that she asked because she cared. Yet, just thinking back on the nightmare made the smoke rise to choke him again.

"You don't have to tell me." She spoke in a rush. "I thought maybe if you talked about it, you might loosen the chains just a little."

Would it loosen the chains or only rustle up the memories he wished he could forget? Except he wasn't forgetting them. The war had been over for two years, and he hadn't forgotten one gruesome detail.

"I'm sorry, Brody." She squeezed his hand in a sisterly way, the intimacy of moments ago gone. "You don't have to tell me anything—"

"It's Gettysburg." The whisper came out harsh and angry, but not because of her. Because of what a coward he'd been.

Images of the battle lingered from the nightmare—glints of hazy sunshine, bursts of bright blood, and flashes of cannon blasts. He wasn't sure he'd ever be able to talk about everything he'd experienced during the long hours he'd lain injured on the battlefield among the dead and dying. But he wanted—needed—to say something more to Savannah.

"I was shot in the shoulder. Tried to move, tried to get off the field, but I couldn't make it."

"Brody . . ." Her whisper was laced with such sorrow it brought an ache to his chest.

The cries and groans of the wounded had mingled with the deep sobs of other men who knew they weren't going to make it. "Was with two men in my regiment, injured worse than me. . . ."

His throat seized up. And he fought back the sights and sounds and scents embedded in the very fibers of his body.

She sat quietly, patiently, holding his hand.

He wanted to tell her more, but a tremble worked its way from his insides down his limbs.

"Shh. It's okay." Her fingers lifted to his face, to his hair, to his cheeks, and back into his hair.

Her touch, her words, her presence were like the salve she used so freely to ease the pain of the wounded creatures she doctored. He closed his eyes and focused on the softness and tenderness of her caress. After several moments, his chest loosened and peace settled over him.

His world, his life, had been upside-down for so long. Somehow with Savannah, it was tipping upright.

❧

Savannah grew more conscious with each passing minute of how intimate their situation had become. She'd only meant to soothe Brody for a few seconds. But she hadn't been able to pull away, especially as his tremors ceased and his body began to relax. She'd told herself she was the one who had caused additional agony by prying into his past and that she needed to make sure he was calm before leaving.

Even so, she couldn't deny how much she savored the scruffy feel of his stubble, the strength in his jaw, and the thickness of his hair. Though darkness shadowed his face, her fingers had memorized each line of his chin and cheek and temple.

From the evenness of his breathing and the way he'd slowly relaxed against the mattress, she could tell he'd fallen back asleep. It was past time to return to her own bed. But she wasn't quite ready to part ways with him.

Her stomach was aflutter with emotions Brody brought

to life inside her without even trying. Of course, he hadn't known he pulled her down onto the bed, hadn't realized he tugged her tightly against his body. But she'd been entirely too conscious of their proximity, of the long length of him, of his bulky arms surrounding her.

Even now just thinking about it, exquisite desire tensed her muscles. It was a shimmer of wanting she'd never experienced before, and she was embarrassed to admit how much more she wanted.

Brody had been right. Chandler's few touches hadn't scorched her skin. While he'd held her hand their last night together, all she'd been able to think about was how long she had to wait before she could slip away. She hadn't wanted to offend or hurt Chandler, and so had endured as long as possible.

If only she'd been a little attracted to him. Attracted like she was to Brody . . .

She brushed his hair back one last time, then forced herself to stand. She couldn't deny the obvious—she was drawn to Brody for more than his brokenness. His dark good looks held a sway over her that only seemed to get stronger with each passing day. Add to that his tender spirit, kindness, and sensitivity, and the combination was weakening her. She felt almost helpless to fight against the magnetism. Did she really need to? Couldn't she see where this attraction might lead? After all, he'd hinted at feeling the attraction, too, had admitted he felt powerful heat whenever they touched.

At a soft squeak on a floorboard in the hallway, she stiffened. Had Brody's thrashing awoken Flora? Had the little girl witnessed their touching? Savannah flushed at the prospect of being so poor a role model.

She exited the room and paused. Though darkness shrouded the narrow passageway, Flynn's lean, muscular outline was unmistakable from where he sat on the top step. He'd buried his face in his hands but, at her approach, lifted his head.

Did Flynn come up every time Brody had a nightmare? She didn't imagine Flynn went into Brody's room the way she had. Doing so would mortify Brody. But from the familiar way Flynn perched on the step, she guessed he'd sat there many nights over the past year, making sure Brody didn't do anything to hurt himself.

How much had Flynn overheard of her interaction with Brody? Did he know Brody had pulled her onto the bed next to him?

"I was just comforting him," she whispered. "That's all."

"I know." He stood and stuffed his hands into his trouser pockets. He didn't turn to descend, and from the rigidness in his shoulders, she sensed he had more to say.

She wasn't sure she wanted to hear it, but she waited, nonetheless.

"He shared more with you tonight than he has with another living soul in two years." Flynn's whisper contained appreciation but something else she couldn't define.

"Maybe he's reaching a point where he's ready to talk about it."

He plunged his hands deeper. "Or maybe he's finally met someone he feels safe enough to talk to."

"I'm sure he feels safe with you, too, Flynn."

"But he's taken to you in a way he hasn't with anyone else, except for Flora."

After how much time and effort Flynn had put into loving Brody so unconditionally, she could only imagine how difficult it was to keep on facing the same rejection from his brother day after day. "It's not you, Flynn. He's probably taken to me because I'm new and have a fresh perspective."

Flynn was silent for a heartbeat. "Don't get me wrong. I surefire ain't complaining. All I care about is Brody getting better."

"And because of that, he's very lucky to have you for a brother."

"Because of that, I've tried about everything on God's green earth I could to help him . . . including hiring you."

"I figured as much."

"Then you can understand why I wanna make sure whatever's going on between the two of you helps him and doesn't leave him in worse shape."

"Worse shape?"

He shifted and the floorboard squeaked again. "He's getting mighty fond of you mighty fast."

She wanted to deny it, but how could she? Not after the interaction she'd just had with Brody on his bed, not after how they'd both reacted to each other.

"Trouble is, Chandler Saxton doesn't strike me as the kind of man who's gonna share his woman."

Savannah clutched her robe tighter. How did Flynn know about Chandler? Had Brody told him? Or maybe he'd heard Brody bring up Chandler's name during their conversation. "I'm not Chandler's woman anymore."

"Reckon he ain't gonna see it that way. Might even decide to make Brody pay for being sweet on you."

"Chandler isn't like that."

Flynn shrugged. "As I said, I'm just aiming to help Brody."

"Me too."

"Good. Then we agree he's been hurt enough and doesn't need more pain?"

What was Flynn insinuating? That she ought to set better limits with Brody so that she wasn't leading him on only to break his heart when she left? If so, he was right. She needed to keep her relationship with Brody platonic.

"Thank you, Flynn. I appreciate the warning. I don't want to hurt Brody in any way, and I promise I'll be careful."

He hesitated, nodded, and then started down the stairs so soundlessly, she knew indeed he'd had many nights of practice going up and down them in his efforts to watch over his brother. She could only pray Flynn's concerns about her and Brody were exaggerated and that they had nothing to worry about.

CHAPTER
12

Savannah rubbed the calf's head captured between her legs. She pressed the bottle tip into its mouth, forcing it to ingest the brine. "Remember to dilute the solution with enough water and to wait at least two hours before feeding the colostrum."

"Then you think you'll save them?" Ivy sat on the stall's top railing. The sunshine coming in from the open window nearby swathed the area in a peaceful glow, soothing the half-dozen calves with scours Savannah had sectioned off in the barn.

"Oh, we'll save them." Savannah pinned the calf tight. "Just make sure the place stays clean and keep them hydrated with the salt solution, and then in a few days I'll come back and show you how to make an easily digestible food from steaming flax."

Nearing two weeks old, the calf's spotted cream-and-burgundy coat had begun to lose its curls and straighten. It broke from the nipple and chased after the container, licking it with natural curiosity.

"I think this little fellow will be just fine." Savannah gave the calf a final pat, then released it.

"Wyatt's gonna be real happy you could save all these calves." Ivy swung her long legs, her bare feet as black as the freshly plowed dirt in the enormous vegetable garden behind Wyatt and Greta's house.

Though Savannah had been in the high country for a week and a half, this was her first visit to Wyatt's homestead and her first introduction to the rest of the McQuaid family. She'd missed seeing them at church since she'd been tending to an emergency birthing of another foal. And today, she'd been hesitant to meet everyone else, didn't want anyone to get the wrong idea about Brody and her.

After her talk with Flynn several nights ago, she'd done her best to keep her interactions with Brody friendly and nothing more. He hadn't woken up again with nightmares, and she'd been able to avoid another middle-of-the-night encounter.

The past couple of days had been quieter, with fewer emergency calls. She'd doctored a cow with an eversion of the uterus after calving, and she'd treated a steer with a mild impaction of the rumen. She'd also doted on the mustang Brody had rescued her first day in Fairplay. It was healing nicely and flourishing under the tender care it was getting.

However, mostly she'd spent her time with Brody as he tamed the mustangs. She finally persuaded him to allow her to join him in the paddock and try gentling a few of the mares, following his lead and using his methods.

When Flynn had come in for supper the previous evening and lamented the scours passing through the newborn calves, Savannah suggested she take a look at them. He was surprised by her offer. Almost as if he'd forgotten he hired her to be the ranch's veterinarian and not just to help Brody.

She glanced through the open double gates to the corral where Brody worked with one of Wyatt's stallions. The ranch foreman, a short, white-haired and bushy-bearded man called Judd, watched Brody with keen eyes but said little. She could tell Brody liked Judd, that somehow the two shared an affinity that didn't need words.

"Brody kissed you yet?" Ivy was peering outside at Brody now too.

"Oh my." Savannah dipped her head, the bold question catching her off guard.

"What?" Ivy shifted on the rail, an impish smile lighting up her face. "Figured he would've by now, what with how much he likes you and all."

"That's a very private matter."

"I take it that's a yes."

"No."

"Then I guess I need to get busy and play matchmaker."

"Ivy." Savannah tried to make her tone serious, but a short laugh escaped.

"I'm good at matchmaking."

"Who says so?" Savannah busied herself with pulling the bottle topper off, turning her face, which was surely flaming.

"I had no trouble getting Flynn and Linnea together. And now I'm working on setting Dylan up with one of my friends who likes him and thinks he's real handsome. Might help him forget how Bethina hurt him so bad."

Savannah rinsed out the bottle. It was a good thing she

didn't encounter Ivy's meddling on a daily basis. She could only imagine how difficult that would be.

"Wyatt says Dylan's too wild and irresponsible to have another woman, needs to grow up first." Ivy lowered her voice, as though she expected the two men to come stalking through the barn at any moment. But Dylan hadn't been home when they'd arrived earlier in the morning. And Wyatt wasn't happy about the young man's absence.

"But now, Brody." Ivy hopped down from the rail. "I can see he's hankerin' for you in a bad way."

"We're just friends—"

"That's what everyone says when they're aiming to hide their real feelings."

"I'm not hiding anything." But even as the words slipped out, the untruth of them hit Savannah full in the face. She was hiding. From Chandler and Daddy. With every passing day, she expected some word to arrive from them. Since Flynn and Brody had easily pieced together her identity, she was waiting for others to do the same. But if anyone else had, they hadn't said anything to her. But that didn't mean they hadn't alerted Daddy yet either.

Her guilt pressed in tighter. Even if her parents knew where she was, she had to contact them soon. Write them a letter or send a telegraph and let them know she was fine. Would Daddy be willing to give her a few more weeks? Even a couple of months?

Maybe she could convince Daddy and Chandler to let her keep on doing her vet work after she got married. Could she gather the courage to ask them? She'd already hinted at it on more than one occasion to Chandler, and he'd always told her she'd be too busy with other things.

Perhaps she had to make her position clearer. That she didn't want to give it up. If Chandler agreed to it, would she be more inclined to go through with the weddin'?

Whatever the case, the South Park ranchers were beginning to trust that she knew what she was doing. They'd surely be happy to have her stay longer. Maybe until they found the experienced vet they were advertising for in Denver newspapers and in the East. Flynn was optimistic they'd be able to hire someone by summer's end.

If she stayed all summer, she might get her fill of being a vet and be ready to settle down as the proper wife and mother Chandler expected her to be. Even with the delay, Daddy and Momma would still have time to move east this year and allow Daddy to start his new ventures.

At a commotion out in the corral, Savannah glanced up again to see a petite young woman at the fence. She was holding a fair-haired infant on her hip and grasping the hand of a little boy who looked about the same age as Flora.

The little boy wiggled away from the petite young woman, ducked through the fence rails, and was on the other side before anyone could stop him. "Uncle Brody."

At the call of his name, Brody pivoted. A rare tender smile turned up his lips. He crossed to the boy, scooped him up, tossed him in the air, and then caught him.

The boy's laughter rang out.

"That's Ty," Ivy explained to Savannah. "Wyatt and Greta's boy. And then there's Astrid holding Ellie, who's Wyatt and Greta's baby girl."

Ivy had previously told Savannah about Greta's sister, Astrid, who had come to Colorado to fight against consumption, which had been slowly killing her. She'd turned into a healthy and strong fourteen-year-old, but Savannah knew that wasn't the case for everyone with consumption who moved to Colorado. Not all of the sick found relief or healing. Astrid was one of the fortunate cases.

When Ellie held out her arms toward Brody, Astrid relinquished the infant to him. He kissed Ellie's chubby cheek. As the girl wiggled and giggled, Brody lifted her more gently into the air above his head, clearly understanding that the infant wanted to be tossed up the same as her brother. He flew her around for a few seconds like a bird before he lowered her and kissed her cheek again.

He was one handsome cowboy, with those bulging muscles, broad chest, and big hands. Savannah's insides heated at the memory of being pressed against him, and getting to experience his muscles, chest, and hands for herself.

"Ain't Brody sweet?" Ivy whispered. "He's got a heart of gold beneath all that rubble."

"He sure does." Savannah loved seeing Brody like this, unguarded and real. The way he was meant to be. Since his talking about the war, he'd seemed less burdened, as if speaking of his experience had freed him from having to bear the horrors all on his own. She hoped he'd eventually be able to share more with her before she left. But she couldn't push him any faster than he was ready to go.

At Ty's tugging on his trouser leg, Brody hefted up the boy and held a child in each arm, listening to the little fellow rattle on about something all the while Ellie tugged at Brody's hat, pulling it down in a game of peekaboo.

Savannah couldn't hold back a sigh of pleasure. She'd never witnessed anything so adorable in her entire life.

"About that hankerin' . . ." Ivy's teasing tone drew Savannah's attention away from the corral and back to the interior of the barn. "I can see it ain't only Brody who's got it bad."

Denial rushed to the tip of Savannah's tongue. "No. Absolutely not."

Ivy studied Savannah's face. "You wouldn't be saying that so quick-like if it weren't true."

"I can admit, Brody's a very attractive man—"

"Then you are sweet on him."

"Just because I'm drawn to him doesn't mean anything."

"It means you're gonna marry him. Just like Sitting Bear predicted."

"No, I can't. I'm only here temporarily."

"You can stay permanently once you're married."

The conversation had spiraled out of control much too quickly. Before Savannah could find a way to snip it off, Ivy bounded across the haymow and through the open doors, tossing a mischievous grin over her shoulder.

"Brody, Savannah told me she thinks you're real attractive." Ivy's words carried through the spring morning right into the barn. "Said she's drawn to you."

Savannah spun toward the nearest calf, needing to hide. This was exactly what she'd hoped to avoid, having everyone think she was interested in Brody. Even if what Ivy said was true, that Brody McQuaid was the single most attractive man she'd ever laid eyes on, she couldn't allow anything to develop.

"Better get busy and ask her to marry you before she up and leaves." Ivy spoke loud enough for the entire ranch for miles around to hear.

Savannah shook her head and started toward the door. If she hid in the barn, she'd make it seem like Ivy was right.

She needed to go out there and set things straight—she had no intention of marrying Brody.

"I reckon with how pretty Savannah is," Ivy continued, "you'd make beautiful babies."

"Oh my." Savannah halted, fanned her face, and retreated to the far end of the calf pen as fast as her legs could carry her, mortification burning a trail through her. Brody's admonition for Ivy to "hush up" didn't make matters any better.

Thankfully, no one came into the barn as she finished tending to the sick calves. And thankfully, Ivy let the matter drop when Wyatt sauntered up to the corral fence and began discussing Hades and the bounty on the wild horse's head.

"You know I ain't got nothin' to do with that bounty." Wyatt had a hold of the back of his son's shirt as the boy attempted to rope the nearest horse. With his dark hair and eyes, Ty was a miniature version of both Wyatt and Brody and would grow up to be a handsome man just like his daddy and uncle.

Wyatt repositioned his son's hands on the rope, giving him a better grip. "Even if I don't agree with the bounty, I sure-as-a-gun can see why everyone's fixin' to send that stallion to the boneyard."

Brody had already handed Ellie to Astrid and was in the process of checking the horse's shoe. "The mustangs have as much right to this land—if not more—as the ranchers."

"Maybe. And maybe the same thing could be said of the Utes. But that ain't stopped more settlers from coming in."

Brody's back turned rigid, the sign he was growing agitated. Wiping her chapped hands, Savannah moved into the doorway, tempted to walk over to Brody and stand by his side so he'd know he wasn't alone in his battle to save Hades and the other horses. But before she could make up her mind, both brothers shifted their attention toward the west.

A rider was coming their way. The pace was unhurried, and the rider was singing at the top of his lungs.

Wyatt shook his head and muttered before he looked at Astrid. "Need you to take the young'uns in. Little ears shouldn't hear the jawing I'm about to give that scallywag."

Astrid managed to get ahold of Ty and started toward the house with the two children. Ivy had already explained that the large two-story home contained the original structure Wyatt and Judd had built from logs they'd cut and hauled from the surrounding foothills. The place was quaint and rustic with the newest wing having a large kitchen for Greta.

Several smaller log cabins rested on the opposite side of the yard, serving as bunkhouses for the cowhands who did most of the daily work of overseeing the cattle. Two barns and several other outbuildings, including a smithy, completed the ranch.

Wyatt and Flynn had clearly worked hard and done well for themselves.

As the rider drew nearer, Savannah could see the McQuaid family resemblance in the man's build and handsome features. This must be Dylan, with his hat askew, his shoulders slouched, and his garments unkempt. From the ruckus he was making as well as the liquor bottle he held, he'd had one too many drinks.

"Blast it all, Dylan!" Wyatt shouted. "I told you not to come home again drunk."

The young man held up the bottle in greeting, a charming grin making him almost irresistible.

"You told me not to come home at *night* drunk." Dylan

neared the corral, leaning precariously, hardly able to stay atop his horse. "And so here I am. It's morning."

Wyatt growled under his breath. "You know blamed well what I meant."

"Just trying to follow your rules, brother."

Wyatt's eyes narrowed darkly on his youngest brother. If Savannah had to guess, she'd put Dylan at nineteen or twenty years of age. From the few things she'd gathered from Ivy's ramblings, the young man had been hurt by a woman he loved and had taken to drinking ever since.

Wyatt crossed his arms. "You're late for work."

Ivy bounded toward Dylan and his horse, her pretty face tied up with worry. She reached her brother none too soon and braced him as he slid from the saddle.

"I'll head out right now and make it up to you by working into the night." Dylan pushed away from Ivy and started toward the corral but only made it two steps before he collapsed, unconscious.

Wyatt rushed toward his brother, as did Brody. Even Savannah hurried out of the barn, ready to be of aid. Brody, Wyatt, and Judd lugged Dylan to one of the bunkhouses.

Ivy slumped as she watched the men disappear inside. Savannah slipped an arm around the young woman and was glad when Ivy leaned in and rested against her shoulder.

"I hate seeing him this way." Ivy swiped at tears on her cheek. "I wish I could have the old Dylan back."

Savannah squeezed Ivy. "It's hard seeing the ones we love hurt."

"I need to do something to help him, but I don't know what."

Savannah wished she had some wisdom to dole out. But

the truth was, even when a person had the means to help a loved one, it still wasn't easy to follow through. She knew that firsthand.

Savannah swallowed past the tightness in her throat. She had the opportunity to bring her parents happiness. If only she could gather the strength to give it to them.

CHAPTER

13

As they rode away from Wyatt's ranch, Brody spoke sparingly. His brim was pulled low, shadowing his face. Even so, she didn't need to see his face to know he was bothered by everything that had happened with Dylan.

When she'd gotten word from one of the cowhands that Updegraff Ranch wanted the vet for a sow having trouble with farrowing, she'd offered to go on without Brody so he could stay at his brother's place as long as he wanted. But he'd brought around both their horses and now guided the way.

"I'm sorry about Dylan," she finally said. "He's having a hard time of it."

"Yep." Brody surveyed the open grassland, a herd of cattle far-off dots in the distance. "He fell in love with a woman who didn't love him back."

"I'm sure that's hard." She guessed it was hard on Chandler to love a woman who didn't love him in return. How had he handled her leaving? Hopefully better than Dylan was coping with his broken heart.

"Don't mind Dylan getting some of Wyatt and Flynn's attention. After causing my share of trouble, time for someone else to take up the job."

She couldn't tell if Brody was teasing or serious. She had the feeling it was a bit of both. "I can tell they're wonderful older brothers who truly care about you and your siblings."

"Wonderful?" His tone held a hint of playfulness, one she rarely got to hear but liked immensely. "There you go again thinking everyone's wonderful and good."

She couldn't contain her smile. "And what's wrong with that?"

"Nothin'." He tipped up his brim, giving her a glimpse of his eyes, which had turned a light, almost amber, brown. "Reckon you think Ivy's wonderful too?"

"Absolutely."

"Even when she spills your secrets and lets on about how attractive you think I am?"

"She's just teasing. That's all." Heat climbed up Savannah's neck and cheeks. She tilted her hat down, hoping Brody wouldn't see the color change.

"That's all?" His voice dipped a notch, which did something funny to her stomach. "Sure about that?"

Oh my. She had a sudden desire to fan her face and try to cool herself off. She had to figure out a levelheaded answer, something that wouldn't take the conversation to places it didn't need to go. "She misrepresented me. I was just watching you with Wyatt's little ones and thinking how sweet you are with them."

"Suppose *sweet* ranks right up there with *cute*?"

She laughed lightly at his reference to their conversation that day she'd watched Flora tuck him in for a nap. "I suppose it does."

They rode for several beats before he slanted her another look. "Word is Sawyer Marshall's searching for his daughter."

She reined in Molasses even as her heartbeat galloped far ahead. "Where did you hear that?"

"Wyatt." Brody halted his horse and crossed his hands on his knee. "Judd brought news back from town last night."

She stared down at her gloves, her thoughts spinning like a funnel cloud.

"Won't be long before he gets word that you're here." Brody's statement was quiet.

"I know."

"Reckon once he learns of your whereabouts, he'll come up and get you."

She nodded. All the more reason to write to her parents. She wasn't ready to leave. Not yet.

"Think he's still fixin' for you to marry Chandler?"

"Of course."

Brody was silent as though waiting for her to say more. But what could she say when she didn't know her own mind?

"Can see as plain as the sky you don't wanna marry him."

"You can?" She shifted, surprised Brody thought it was plain when she was so confused.

"Yep."

"I wish it was that plain to me."

"I can help make it real clear."

"How?"

He nudged his horse near enough that his thigh brushed hers. At the same time, he circled his fingers around her reins and drew Molasses even closer so their legs were pinned between the two horses. He slipped his other hand to her shoulder, then to the back of her neck.

Heat tingled down her spine at so intimate a touch. But she hardly had time to process the proximity when he leaned toward her, angled in, and captured her lips with his. There was no preamble and no preparation. Only power.

His mouth covered hers, fusing them so thoroughly and deeply she could feel his presence almost all the way to her soul. The delicate yearning inside twisted and turned as though weaving them together, leaving her with only one response—to kiss him in return.

She needed no more encouragement to bend in. He could have taken his hold away altogether, and she would have kept kissing him. In fact, she longed to lift her fingers to his face and let them explore at will.

But an instant later, his horse shied back, and Brody released her, leaving her breathless, her lips damp with wanting, her body aching for more.

Brody ducked his head, and his horse took another step away. His leg grazed hers again, the contact this time sending a charge through her blood, a charge that made her want to tangle both their legs.

She didn't understand all the emotions swirling through her, didn't know this kind of passion could exist between a man and a woman. A part of her could only take it in with a sense of wonder. Another part of her was frightened by the strength of her reaction.

When his eyes lifted to hers a moment later, the brown was as hot and dark as cane syrup. Her nerve endings tingled with an anticipation she couldn't explain. All she knew was that it had never been this way with Chandler or any other man. Never.

The surprise mingling with desire must have been written all over her face. He fidgeted with his reins, the makings of a smile curling at the corners of his lips. Had she given him the reaction he'd been seeking?

After several more seconds, he cleared his throat. "Reckon it's mighty plain now."

"What?"

"You don't have any feelings for Chandler."

"Oh." Her response was entirely too breathless, and the sound of it only made Brody's lips turn up even more.

He was right. In fact, had Chandler tried kissing her like this, she probably would have squirmed and broken the kiss as hastily as possible.

What was wrong with her that she couldn't have this kind of passion with a man like Chandler, who Daddy wanted her to marry?

"Guess you oughta send your father word about your decision."

"And what decision is that?"

"You ain't gonna marry Chandler."

She hesitated, and it was enough for Brody to mumble under his breath. Before she could attempt to explain her indecision, he'd already urged his horse into a trot, followed rapidly by a canter.

Releasing a pent-up breath of both desire and frustration, she started after him. She didn't owe him any kind of reasoning. This wasn't his business. In fact, after the talk with Flynn the other night, she shouldn't have let Brody kiss her. At the very least, she should have ended it right away.

The growing feelings for Brody would only make every-thing more complicated. And she didn't want to set off an ex-plosion, wounding everyone around her, particularly Brody. After the pain he'd already experienced in his life, he didn't need anything else to knock him down and hurt him.

The truth was, the best thing for both of them was to stay away from any hint of attraction. If only his kiss wasn't lingering on her lips and making her want to catch up with him and kiss him again.

⌒ॐ⌒

The pig strained, shuddered, then lay still.

On a bed of straw, the poor creature was young with her first litter. But something was obstructing the delivery, and she'd been struggling with the birthing for hours.

Savannah finished smearing oil onto her arms, stretched out on the ground, and then gently inserted her hand until her wrist and elbow disappeared inside. Her fingers came into contact with a tiny curled tail.

"The presenting piglet is transverse." She glanced up at the cowhand in charge of the livestock, Gill, a middle-aged man with sunken eyes, a shaggy beard, and clothes that hung on a skeletal frame.

"Knew something was blocking her." Gill looked like a twig that was frail enough to snap in two at the slightest gust of wind.

Savannah glided her fingers over the piglet, familiarizing herself with the position. This little baby was holding every-thing up. She had to draw the piglet out. Then the sow would be able to deliver the rest.

Brody knelt beside her. "What can I do to help?"

Gill lifted his boot, caked in manure, and rested it against Brody's arm. "Reckon you can help by staying away until she's done." The words were brittle, made more so as Gill shoved Brody hard with his boot.

Brody resisted the pressure and didn't budge. But from the corner of her eye, she could see his jaw flex.

"You're nothin' but a lowlife troublemaker." Gill pushed again, this time harder. "Go on. Get out of here."

"Brody's my assistant." Savannah started to withdraw and sit up, but Brody laid a hand on her shoulder and stopped her.

"I'll be alright," Brody said quietly. "Do what you have to for the sow. I'll be by the door if you need me."

She wanted to protest as he stood and brushed past Gill with heavy steps. But she kept her attention on the emergency at hand, unwilling to allow the sow and her piglets to suffer any longer.

With one finger, she worked the piglet's legs back until she could grasp both. She tugged, and it slid out. Lifeless.

"This one didn't make it." She placed it in the hay. "Let's pray the others aren't dead too."

She went back in and searched until she found another piglet. At the wiggle of a little body, she grasped the legs. It struggled, but then a moment later, she pulled it into the world.

The squirming pink creature stood, tottered, then wobbled toward the udder and began nursing. Within a few minutes, the sow's contractions became more powerful, and she soon delivered seven other piglets along with the afterbirth.

All the newborns wriggled their way, like the first, to the double row of teats and suckled while the mother rolled to give them better access. Savannah sat back on her heels and watched, wiping her hands on a rag towel while her heart swelled at the beauty of another miracle of birth.

From the corner of her eye, she caught a glimpse of Brody standing just outside the double barn door, leaning back, one knee bent and his boot propped against the barn wall, his fingers hooked in his belt.

He was a fine-looking man. Very fine.

And the way he kissed? Oh my. She could picture him bending in on his steed and taking possession of her mouth, could almost feel his mouth on hers again.

Gentle fluttering spread through her insides.

As if sensing his effect on her, he cocked his head in her direction. Seeing that she was finished, he shoved away from the barn and stepped inside.

She hoped he hadn't figured out she was thinking about their kiss. In fact, she had to forget it had ever happened.

"Thought I told you to get." Gill, crouched beside her, rose and stalked toward Brody, swiping up a shovel.

Brody halted. "Just checking on the progress—"

"Don't need a troublemaker like you here causing more problems."

What was Gill referring to? Brody taking a stand against the ranchers and defending Hades?

Brody eyed the shovel.

"Now, hold on, Gill." Concern drove Savannah to her feet. "Brody McQuaid is a good and kind man—"

Before she could find her footing, Gill swung the shovel directly at Brody.

"No!" She lurched forward.

Brody jumped away, narrowly missing the metal end.

As Gill lifted the shovel to take another swing, her breath got lost inside as a scream pushed for release.

Gill moved swiftly, but Brody blocked the shovel with one arm and twisted it from Gill's grip. The rail-thin fellow tried to hang on, but Brody was stronger, and the movement jerked Gill's arm.

A snap from inside Gill's body rent the air. He released a howl and fell to the ground, cradling his arm and writhing.

Brody stood above the man, the shovel gripped tightly, his chest heaving, his face a mask of fury.

Savannah prayed Brody wouldn't fight back, that he'd be able to control his anger this time.

Brody stared down at Gill, his nostrils flaring. Then he threw the shovel against the barn wall with a heave that cracked the boards. Without another glance at Gill, he stalked out.

Savannah wanted to run after Brody, didn't want to concern herself with the injured cowhand. But after determining that he had a broken radius, she did what she could to make him comfortable before finding Brody with their horses.

They mounted silently and began the ride to Flynn's. The whole confrontation hadn't been fair to Brody. Gill had been out of line. The broken bone had been an accident. And Brody had simply been defending himself and couldn't take the blame—if he was.

"Brody?" she said after long minutes of trying to decide how to talk about what had happened. "How are you feeling?"

He kept his focus ahead and didn't respond. The only indication he'd heard her was the twitching in his jaw.

"I'm sorry for everything that happened." The heaviness of the incident seemed to lace every word.

As if the sorrow penetrated his silent exile, he closed his eyes for several heartbeats before opening them and looking at her. "My ma's husband, Rusty, beat Flynn near to death with a metal rod."

Flynn's limp was hard to miss. Was the injury a result of Rusty's beating?

She didn't probe. Instead she waited for Brody to unburden himself in his own timing and in his own way.

They rode quietly for a few more minutes. "Heard Ivy screaming." Brody's voice was low and raw. "Thought Rusty was hurting her. Hated him and was just waiting for an excuse to kill him for all the ways he made my ma suffer."

He brushed a hand across his jaw, but nothing could loosen the tightness in his muscles.

She wanted to reach out and comfort him, but she held back, hoping his relief would come the more he shared.

"When I got to the barn and saw what he'd done to Flynn, I tried to kill the lowlife. But couldn't make myself pull the trigger."

More long beats passed.

"I was a coward—"

"No, Brody—"

"If I'd killed him, maybe Ma would still be alive."

"You don't know that."

"Told myself that by going off to war, I'd get the courage to pull a trigger." Brody's voice was hoarse. "Reckon I'd have no trouble killing that lowlife now."

She guessed this was something he'd never admitted to anyone except her, and she treasured that he trusted her enough to share it. "You're a sensitive man. That's what allows you to love your nieces and nephew so deeply. And it gives you the ability to calm the wildest of horses. But such a sensitive spirit can be easily crushed, like it was with Rusty and in the war."

His throat moved up and down in a hard swallow.

"Your spirit might have been crushed, but it wasn't destroyed. I see it. It's there, and it's beautiful. I just hope one day you can see it too."

He nodded but said nothing more.

CHAPTER

14

Brody's gut was sour enough to pucker a pig's mouth.

Didn't matter how merry a tune the fiddler was playing, how loud the caller was bellowing, or how fast feet were stomping—he was itching for a fight.

He hooked one heel of his boot against the chinking in the log wall and crossed his arms, trying to relax but guessing he looked stiffer than a coffin lid. Even though he tried real hard to focus on everything and everyone else, his attention shifted to Savannah, just like it had ever since the dancing had started.

For once she was hatless. And she was wearing a pretty dress. Her blue eyes sparkled as her partner swung her around. Her cheeks were flushed, her smile dazzling, and her laughter the sweetest sound in the barn. Every fella for miles around was waiting for a chance to dance with her, and she was giving them each a fair turn.

Problem was, anytime another man laid his hands on her, Brody wanted to haul off and wallop him.

He had half a mind to hightail it away from the annual dance held after calving season ended. Elkhorn Ranch wasn't far from Healing Springs. She'd be fine if he left, could ride home with Flynn and Linnea.

Beyond the wide-open doors, the dark starlit night spread out over the horizon. A few neighbors still congregated at the food tables set up in the ranch yard, but most had moved inside for the dancing.

He could slip away and no one would be the wiser. With as mad as he was getting, maybe it was for the best that he leave before he lost his temper and did something he'd regret.

The caller shouted out the final instructions, and the clapping and stomping only crescendoed. As usual, the men outnumbered the women, especially the single women. Some of the fellas wore white handkerchiefs tied around their arms to take the female part of the dance. They were *heifer branded*, as they laughingly referred to themselves. Even if they were good-natured enough about the lack of women, there was no denying the competition to twirl with a real woman, especially Savannah.

She'd posted a letter to her father on their last trip to town several days ago, the day after he'd kissed her. Right before she delivered it to the general store, she explained that she was asking her father for a little more time. Brody guessed it was her way of explaining that his kiss hadn't changed anything, that she was still confused.

No matter the letter, a powerful man like Sawyer Marshall wasn't about to let his only daughter gallivant about Colorado Territory any longer than he had to. No doubt the Cattle King would arrive in Fairplay by the week's end.

Which didn't leave Brody much time to convince Savannah

to stay. He suspected that was what kept him from running off from the dance.

As the music ended, the couples broke apart, and before Savannah had the chance to thank the fella she'd been with, another one cut in and took his place. As the newcomer's hands slid down her arms and then found her hips, Brody couldn't hold back a frustrated growl.

He pushed away from the wall and stalked right toward the man. Each heavy step against the packed dirt and hay echoed the heavy thud of his heart.

The past few days, he'd been consumed with wanting her, could hardly focus on anything else, even though he'd been busy helping the ranch hands brand their new calves and had spent less time with her. Even if she hadn't acknowledged her desire for him, he'd felt it in the kiss, had sensed it in the way he caught her watching him at times.

As he drew up to Savannah and her newest partner, he didn't bother with a greeting. He grabbed the man's flannel shirt, then shoved him aside.

Savannah's easy smile faded, and her eyes rounded upon the discarded dance partner stumbling into the wall.

The chatter around them faded, and the fiddler screeched to a halt.

"Wait your turn, McQuaid." The cowhand straightened. The thin, freckled face was familiar. The fella worked at Elkhorn Ranch, but Brody couldn't remember his name.

"You're gettin' too familiar with the lady."

"Just dancing is all." The cowhand advanced cautiously, as though he planned to put up a fight.

"Keep your hands off her." Brody positioned himself in front of Savannah.

"Or what?" The fella gave a pointed nod toward Brody's balled fists. "You gonna break my arm same as you did Gill's?"

Word had gotten around fast. No doubt Gill was twisting the story to make it seem like Brody had done the attacking and not the other way around. "Maybe I will. Or worse."

Savannah's fingers circled around his arm as though in warning.

He forced himself to take a deep breath. He didn't want to get into a fistfight tonight and ruin her fun. Swallowing his anger, he reached for her hands.

She was still watching him with big eyes.

He pinned a hard look on the fiddler. "Start playing."

The older cowhand nodded and then rapidly set his bow to the strings.

As the other couples took their places, Savannah leaned in. "Is everything okay?"

He situated one hand on her waist and the other at the small of her back before he tugged her closer. "Now it is."

She hesitated, then lifted her hands to his waist.

Even though her hold was light, his muscles tightened with need—the need to feel her fingers gliding over him, boldly exploring.

"You could have just asked for a dance." Her whisper contained chastisement but also a note of humor.

"Maybe." From the corner of his eye, he could see the other fella glaring at him and grumbling to his friends. Brody expected him to charge like an angry bull and was surprised when a moment later the man began to shoulder his way out of the barn.

The fiddle music rose into the air, and the caller made

the announcement of the first move. Within seconds Brody was dancing with Savannah. He didn't care that people were watching him with a little bit of fear in their expressions, especially the rest of the cowboys who hadn't yet danced with her. He hoped they'd gotten the message that for the rest of the night she was off-limits to everyone but him.

He couldn't talk to her over the music, but Savannah's eyes spoke loudly enough. She was glad to be with him. When one song ended and the next began, he only had to glare at the first man who approached, and the fella slunk away. After that, no one else dared to get near.

She made no mention of taking turns with anyone else, smiling her delight in the dancing. Though he couldn't make himself smile in return, his contentment at being with her swelled with each new dance, and he hoped she could sense his pleasure.

When the caller and fiddler took a break, Brody guided Savannah outside to cool off in the rapidly dropping temperature of the May night.

They helped themselves to cider before wandering along the corral fence. He wanted to say something—anything—to convince her to stay the whole summer, regardless of what her father might say.

He took a drink of the spicy cider, letting it burn down his throat.

"You're a very good dancer." She leaned against the rail.

He wasn't all that good. But she was being polite, like usual. Problem was, he didn't want her pity at that moment. He wanted her passion. He wanted her to stop seeing him as weak and wounded and instead view him as strong and capable.

Maybe he had to stop seeing himself as weak and wounded first if he wanted others to do the same. He swigged more cider, then tilted his head and studied her. "You're the most beautiful woman I've ever met."

She paused with her mug halfway to her mouth.

Had he said too much? Been too lavish? "Reckon if you pay me a compliment, then I oughta pay you one in return."

"I think your compliment is nice enough to count as two."

Immediately, she put him at ease with her sweetness. How was she able to do that? Make a bumbling fool like him feel as though he were a prince?

"You're not only beautiful, but you're the smartest and kindest person I know."

"Brody McQuaid. I do believe you're trying to charm me."

"Is it working?" The flirting was getting easier every day.

"It might be."

"Then maybe I can charm you into staying on at the ranch for the rest of the summer."

She focused on her mug of cider, swishing it around before taking a sip.

"You're a real talented vet." That same sense of urgency he'd been feeling earlier drummed within him. "Don't see why you couldn't stay on awhile longer."

She swallowed her mouthful. "I'd like to. . . ."

"Then tell your father not to come up. Tell him I'll bring you home at the end of summer . . . if that's what you want."

She sighed. "He might give me a few more weeks, but I don't think he'll wait for the summer's end."

"He will if you tell him to."

"You don't understand."

"Explain it."

She lifted her mug for another drink and took her sweet old time finishing. Finally, when she didn't have anything to hide behind, she met his gaze. Her blue eyes were sad and serious. "Daddy made investments in the war efforts that didn't pay out. Now he's land rich, but he's struggling to make up for all he's lost."

"Lots of people struggling." He'd heard the reports of just how bad it was in the South with efforts to rebuild all that had been destroyed by the Union army. They'd gotten news that the Reconstruction Act had been passed earlier in the spring, dividing the South into military districts, sanctioning the southern states until they agreed to ratify the Fourteenth Amendment and give equal protection to former slaves.

A part of Brody argued that the South got what they deserved. But another part of him knew that a whole lot of innocent folk were hurt in both the North and the South.

"Chandler's family isn't struggling." Her words were soft but hit him like the whack of a bucking bronc.

"So he's offering your father money." He suddenly despised Sawyer Marshall for involving his daughter in the deal, especially since Savannah was born to help. Brody'd only known her for two weeks, but even he could see how easy it would be to manipulate someone as caring as she was.

"Daddy wants to invest in railroads again."

"So he's bargaining you."

"No, Brody. It's not like that. With the weddin', Daddy's giving Chandler the deed to the ranch, and in return, Chandler is giving Daddy the means to invest." Pale strands of Savannah's hair that had come loose during the dancing now glistened in the moonlight. "Daddy and Chandler would never force me to do anything I don't want to do."

"Reckon Chandler ain't gonna hand over the money your father wants for investing, not without a marriage." He knew the way Chandler worked. The fella drove a hard bargain and was known for doing whatever he had to in order to make a profitable sale—sales that undercut his competition and capitalized on the Double L's hold on the eastern beef market. There was no way no how a man like Chandler would give something for nothing.

"Without Hartley, Daddy needs to make sure the ranch is in good hands." Savannah's expression was earnest with the desire to defend her father. "And he knows Chandler will take good care of it."

Brody's muscles were prickling like porcupine quills. "He could sell the ranch to someone else."

"He's considered it, but he'd likely have to parcel it off to smaller ranchers and wouldn't get the return he needs, at least not enough to invest in railroads as well as buy a home and start over in Atlanta."

"Guess he'll have to stay and make the best of it."

"It's not that easy. Momma hasn't been happy in the West. Daddy doesn't want to be out here anymore either. Not since Hartley died. And I don't want to let them down. Especially when they have this opportunity to start over again in the East."

Brody had the sudden urge to hit something. Hard. "You ain't responsible for making your parents happy."

"But I want to help them—"

He slammed his hand against the top fence rail.

Savannah jumped, her eyes widening.

"You can't help everyone." The words came out harsh.

"I can try."

He wanted to bang the rail again, but he held himself in check, staring straight ahead, not seeing anything but a haze of frustration. He was aiming to keep his anger under control, but that was turning out to be a whole heap harder than he'd realized.

She tentatively touched his arm. "Let's not talk about it anymore, okay, Brody?"

He faced her and boldly covered her hand with his. From the despair in her eyes, he realized she was as torn up about the predicament as he was, maybe even worse. After all, it had driven her away from her home and the wedding.

"Won't say no more about your staying on." He slid his fingers through hers slow and gentle. "But I aim to convince you one way or another."

As he caressed down her fingers and then back up, she drew in a breath. He liked knowing his touch affected her as much as hers did him. With her standing only inches away, he wanted to trace the lines of her beautiful face, which he'd sketched in his notepad half a dozen times.

If he touched her face tonight, he wouldn't stop with the tracing. He'd kiss her. Now that he'd gotten one taste of her, he longed to go back time after time. He doubted he'd ever get enough.

But with the other revelers standing around the barnyard and corral, including his family, he wasn't about to give them a show. No doubt they'd all already guessed the direction he was going with Savannah. It was pretty hard to hide his feelings about her, especially from Ivy. She'd tease him mercilessly if she caught him kissing Savannah.

He intertwined his fingers with hers, locking their hands together, and then rubbed his thumb across the pulse at her wrist.

She sucked in a second breath. "Brody." Her whisper of his name was more plea than rebuke. "You can't."

He brushed her pulse again.

She leaned in closer.

"Can't what?" he whispered, drawing a line with his thumb to her palm.

"We can't do this." She made no move to extricate her hand from his caresses. "You have to stop. . . ."

"You ain't engaged to Chandler, are you?"

"No, but—"

"Then from where I stand, you're free for the taking."

"Not really."

"We'll see about that."

Before he could convince her any further, Ivy was calling to Savannah and jogging toward them. For once she'd worn a pretty dress and shoes. But from her flushed face and the bits of hay sticking in her hair, it was easy to tell she'd been rolling around and getting fresh with someone. Wasn't she too young for that?

Brody frowned. The girl ran all over God's green earth with no one keeping an eye on her half the time. Why weren't Flynn and Wyatt doing a better job raising her? He shot a glance in their direction, but they were occupied talking with neighbors they saw infrequently and enjoying the break from the constant stress of ranch life.

Of course, he hadn't exactly made things easy on them, causing them a whole lot of worrying. And now Dylan was giving them a run around with his drinking and wild living.

Maybe he couldn't come down so hard on them for neglecting Ivy. After all, he was old enough to pay her attention too. But the truth was, he'd been so focused on himself and his own hurts that he hadn't taken the time to think about others, including Ivy.

Yep, he'd lived through hell and still did at times, but that was no excuse for being so blamed selfish. Because that's what he'd been. Selfish.

CHAPTER

15

"You have to come help." Ivy's face was creased with distress. "I found some abandoned kittens. They're weak and dying with no momma in sight."

Savannah tugged her hand free from Brody and hid it behind her back, praying Ivy hadn't seen their interaction, which had somehow grown more heated with every passing second. Even now, her insides were sparking with flames higher than the bonfire someone had started a short distance away from the barn.

How could Brody set her ablaze with just the merest of touches? In fact, he didn't need to touch her, only had to look at her in that unguarded way that revealed his wanting. And her insides turned to liquid. At least, that's what had been happening since their kiss. Most of the time his glances were brief but intense. But on several occasions, his perusal had been bold and inviting, melting not just her insides but her whole body.

"Please, Savannah." Ivy halted in front of her, breathless. "You have to save them."

"Save who?"

Ivy's brows shot up, and her eyes bounced back and forth between Brody and her. "The kittens?"

Too late Savannah realized her blunder. Ivy was already scheming enough and didn't need to know exactly how much Brody rattled her. "Yes, the kittens. Of course." Before Ivy could make an embarrassing comment, Savannah linked her arm in the girl's. "Take me to them."

Ivy half dragged her across the yard and into the barn, chatting all the while about how she'd already checked and learned that none of the ranch hands had seen the mother cat for a few days and that most likely she'd been killed by a fox while out hunting.

With most of the folks outside, the barn interior was quiet, except for the fiddler tuning his instrument for the next round of dancing. The oil lanterns hanging from the rafters were brightly lit and would remain that way all night. She'd been to enough barn dances to know that everyone wanted to make the most of the occasion, since the social gatherings were so few and far between. The festivities would last well into the early morning, leaving only enough time for guests to get home and start chores.

She followed Ivy into a dark rear stall, then paused. What had Ivy been doing in this part of the barn? Before Savannah could come to any conclusions, Ivy pulled her down to the corner and the nest where four kittens lay curled together. At their approach, the creatures stirred, clearly hungry but also very weak.

Savannah knelt in front of them and stroked each one.

With eyes still closed, they were entirely helpless, likely a week or so old. And they were in desperate need of nourishment.

Brody crouched beside her. "Don't think they're gonna make it." His tone was grave. After growing up on a farm and seeing lots of newborn kittens, no doubt he had just as much experience with them as she did and could easily diagnose the direness of the situation.

Even so, she wasn't ready to give up on the creatures without making an effort. "We can try to save them."

Ivy, standing a few paces behind, nodded and released a relieved breath.

Savannah leveled her most serious gaze at the young woman. "It won't be easy, and I'll need you to gather a few things."

With the help of one of Elkhorn Ranch's cowhands, Ivy returned in no time with the supplies. Savannah set right to work and Brody did likewise, and within minutes they were each feeding two kittens warm goat's milk through pinpricks in the fingers of leather gloves.

Though the creatures were ravenous, she made them go slow and encouraged Brody to do the same, gently rubbing and nurturing the tiny babes while they ate. When they were finished, she positioned them together in the nest. One of the three was still sluggish, and she continued to massage it, hoping the milk would revive it but fearing they were too late.

"They'll need to be hand-fed every few hours." Savannah glanced up from where she sat in the hay to find Ivy tucked against a young cowhand. He'd wrapped his arm around her, and she leaned against his shoulder.

Savannah paused, surprise coursing through her. She

hadn't known Ivy was courting anybody. And even if she was, a lady needed to use restraint. Her momma had always said a woman couldn't give away her favors so easily. A man wouldn't learn to cherish what he got freely but would prize what he worked hard to earn.

Brody's attention had shifted to Ivy, too, and at the sight of her cuddling up to the cowhand, he stiffened and climbed to his feet.

Savannah rose next to him, captured his hand, and tugged him back before he could barrel forward and beat up the fellow. He stared down at their intertwined fingers.

Before either of them could figure out how to handle Ivy and the situation, another of Elkhorn's ranch hands appeared. Even in the low lighting at the back of the barn, she recognized him as the man Brody had fought in town last week. Jericho.

His gaze glossed over her and Brody before locking in on the cowhand embracing Ivy.

"Hank." Jericho folded his arms over his chest. "Thought I told you to stay away from Ivy."

Alarm flashed across Hank's face, and he started to extricate himself from Ivy.

She clung to him, not letting him get away, even as she lifted her chin and glared at Jericho. "We don't need you telling us what to do, like you're our pa."

The muscles in Jericho's jaw flexed, and his eyes flashed. "If you're behaving like a child, then you're forcing me to act like your pa."

Before anyone could speak another word, Ivy rose on her toes and planted a kiss against Hank's lips. The contact was brief, but while she did so, her gaze never left Jericho's, almost as if she was taunting him. As she finished, she smirked. "A child don't go around kissing men."

"You're impossible." Jericho jerked Hank from her and shoved him down the aisle. Then he spread his feet and blocked Ivy's path, preventing her from going after the fella.

Hank scrambled to leave, tossing a frightened look over his shoulder as he stumbled away.

Ivy watched the ranch hand indifferently before glaring at Jericho, a glimmer of hurt in her eyes.

"When are you going to grow up?" His voice was terse.

"I am grown up. When are you gonna finally realize it?"

Savannah didn't move and neither did Brody. An internal warning told her she needed to stop holding his hand, but when Brody's fingers tightened around hers, she let the thought fall from her mind.

Jericho's gaze swept over Ivy's face. For an instant something flickered in his eyes. Was it interest? Attraction? Before Savannah could analyze it, he scowled. "You're not grown up yet. You toying with Hank just proves it."

"I wasn't toyin'—"

"He's not your type, and you know it."

She fisted her hands on her hips. "And who exactly is my type?"

Jericho pressed his lips together. He seemed to be trying to come up with an answer, then released a taut breath. "You're still just a girl, too young to have a man. So stop trying."

"I'll be seventeen in a few months." Her shoulders were rigid.

"Like I said, too young."

Savannah waited for Ivy to spout off something else. But

she stared at Jericho a moment longer before she pushed past him and stalked away.

After she was gone, Brody expelled a breath.

Jericho didn't move, except to close his eyes, as though fighting back an urge to go after her.

"Thank you," Brody said.

Jericho opened his eyes and glanced into the stall, almost as if he'd forgotten the two of them were there. "Tell Flynn he needs to keep a better eye on that girl, or she'll stain her reputation."

"Reckon it's past time for me to help keep an eye on her too."

Jericho's response seemed to die, and he stared at Brody as though seeing him for the first time.

Brody's fingers twitched within Savannah's, and she pressed gently, hoping he could feel her encouragement for his kind offer.

The fiddle music filled the barn into the rafters. The laughter and talking and clapping had grown louder. Jericho glanced in the direction of the open haymow. "I need to keep an eye on things."

Brody cocked his head toward the kittens. "We'll be taking the kittens to Healing Springs if that's alright with you."

Again Jericho paused and studied Brody.

"Once they're bigger and eating on their own, we can bring 'em on back if you want."

Jericho shrugged. "If Ivy wants them, she can have them."

Savannah guessed Elkhorn Ranch already had plenty of cats. From what she'd seen, Healing Springs did too. But a few more wouldn't hurt.

Jericho touched the brim of his hat before starting down

the row of stalls toward the dancing. He only went a few feet before he stopped and faced them again. "If you want to save the wild horses, then maybe you should consider driving them west. Lots more land there without any cattle."

Was Jericho holding out a peace offering? For a man bent on seeking revenge for his brother's death, it was a kind suggestion.

As though recognizing the same, Brody nodded. "Much obliged."

"Either way, I'm planning to bring down Hades."

"Figures." Brody's voice lacked the usual anger. "And you should know that either way, I'm aiming to save him."

Jericho held Brody's gaze a moment longer. But his expression was void of anger, too, and Savannah prayed that meant the two had come to an understanding.

After Jericho left, Brody stared past the rows of stalls. His brow was furrowed, and Savannah wished she could see inside and understand this complex man.

For someone who tenderly helped nurse motherless kittens and fought to save a wild old horse, how had he been able to survive the brutality of the war without going mad?

His offer to invest in Ivy was a good sign, wasn't it? And this tentative peace with Jericho was also progress.

He'd made significant strides over the past two weeks since she'd arrived, becoming more talkative, more self-controlled, and more aware of others. She didn't know if she was working her healing touch on him, or if he'd simply come to a place where he was ready to move forward. Whatever the case, she couldn't go home yet, not when she still could facilitate more growth.

"Tell your father not to come up. Tell him I'll bring you

home at the end of summer . . . if that's what you want."
Brody's words from earlier reverberated through her. She'd
asked Daddy to give her a few more weeks. Did she dare write
again and ask him for the whole summer? She'd already de-
layed his departure to Atlanta. Doing so longer wouldn't hurt
anyone too much, would it?

She released a sigh and let go of Brody's hand. She returned to the kittens and stroked the runt's tiny body. "I
think I should take the kittens to Healing Springs before
they're due for the next feeding."

"I'll help you."

"But I don't want you to have to leave the dance."

"I won't mind none." He reached out his callused finger
and rubbed the head of one of the kittens.

"These kinds of events don't happen often—"

"Only reason I showed up was to keep my eye on you."

"You didn't come to dance?"

He didn't take his attention from the kitten. "Wasn't planning to until I saw all the fellas puttin' their hands on you."

"They had to in order to dance."

"Didn't like it." His voice was low, and when he glanced
up, his eyes were darker than midnight.

He'd been jealous. The realization sent pleasure through
her. And oh my. She could easily get lost in those beautiful,
soulful eyes. But she couldn't. Wouldn't.

She dropped her gaze. "We should find a basket for the
kittens. That would make it much easier to transport them."

He didn't say anything, almost as if he was waiting for her
to acknowledge what was happening between them. But she
kept her head bent. Finally, he rose. His footsteps crunched
in the hay as he walked away.

As much as she liked the sparks that flew back and forth between them, she pulled in a deep breath and tried to dampen them. Lightning, while beautiful, was dangerous and capable of great damage. She couldn't let it sizzle, for both of their sakes. But the longer she stayed with him, the harder it was getting to put out the fires.

CHAPTER

16

Brody shook hands with the teamster before giving the mustang a final pat.

As he started to cross Fairplay's dusty Main Street, he pocketed the handful of silver dollars inside his vest. The earnings from the mustang would put Savannah's mind at ease. She'd been trying lately to pay him for the mustang they'd rescued her first day in Fairplay, but he refused every time.

Now he could prove he'd made back what he'd paid Lonnie Quick plus a couple dollars more.

The morning sun was high and bright and the street busy with stagecoaches and teamsters getting ready to head up into the passes on their way to the Front Range. The mustang would do well now that she'd been thoroughly gentled. It helped that she had a good owner now too. Brody had sold to the fella before and knew he treated his horses with dignity.

The front door of Hyndman Bro's General Merchandise opened, and Elmer stepped outside. Brody dodged a horse and rider and veered toward their mounts tied to the hitching post in front of the store.

Elmer had offered to ride with him to town to get the mail for Linnea, who was constantly in contact with her grandfather and other family back east. Elmer had also picked up some nails and wire for Flynn to use on repairing fences.

Since the calving and branding season was over and the weather was warming up, they'd start repairing the fences next on the never-ending to-do list. Most of Healing Springs' fences were made from aspen trees a few inches in diameter that were stacked in a zigzag pattern. The aspens were plentiful enough. But they'd learned to reinforce the fences by nailing them in some spots and wiring them in others.

Brody unwound his lead line as Elmer tucked his supplies into the saddlebag. "Heard tell Hades been spotted moving southwest of Fairplay."

Brody paused. "Reckon there'll be a bunch of fellas on his tail in no time." With the bounty still out on Hades, plenty of men were itching to put a bullet in the horse's head.

For the past couple of days since the dance, Brody'd been aiming to take Jericho up on his advice and start driving the mustangs farther west. He'd heard the Arkansas River Valley around Buena Vista was open pastureland. The route over the Mosquito Range to get there would be difficult, but already the miners up in Stubborn Mule and Happy Jack mines had cut a trail they could follow.

The first band he planned to move was Hades's. Looked like he needed to do it today before word of the stallion's location spread.

He should've made the effort sooner. Trouble was, he didn't want Savannah leaving while he was away. Hated the thought of coming back and finding her gone. But he couldn't put the task off any longer. "Best head on out this morning."

Elmer finished buckling his bag. "Told Flynn I'd deliver the supplies over to Wyatt's place. But once I'm done, I can ride along if you want the help."

Acceptance was on the tip of Brody's tongue, but he shook his head. "Much obliged. But Ivy and Dylan can come with. I'm due to spend some time with them."

Elmer tipped up his battered felt hat, and his ebony eyes met Brody's and radiated encouragement. "Reckon they'd like that."

Brody nodded. The trip would be a good way to start paying them both some long-overdue attention.

"I can take 'em word."

"I'd be obliged. Tell them to hustle over. The sooner we can get going, the better."

Elmer mounted. Before Brody could do likewise, a commotion outside Cabinet Billiard Hall drew his attention. And immediately set his blood to percolating like coffee in a tin pot on high flames.

"Let them go!" Brody started to stride toward the group of men surrounding Sitting Bear and his nephew, Tall Arrow. Even though no one was touching the pair, Sitting Bear's deadly expression said it all—he hadn't done anything wrong and the fellas were provoking him anyway.

Before Brody could make it more than two feet, Elmer kicked his horse forward, blocking Brody's path. Brody growled and tried to round the horse, but Elmer shifted into his way again. "Don't want you getting locked up today and ruin your chance of driving those mustangs."

Brody blew out a frustrated breath. After he'd broken Gill's arm and thrown the fella around at the dance, tongues were wagging about the need to lock him in the town's makeshift jail next time he got into a fight.

Brody bunched his fists, fighting against the urge to plow forward and punch the scallywags away from Sitting Bear and Tall Arrow. No doubt Sitting Bear had come to town to communicate with officials regarding the upcoming negotiations set to take place in Washington, DC. He was one of the only Utes who could speak fluent English after having lived in Denver for a while. Over recent years, he'd returned to the high country to safeguard the interests of the Ute tribes.

The first time Brody had encountered Sitting Bear, he'd been frightened, had heard Wyatt's tales of the hostility with the Utes during his early days in Colorado. But while Brody was in the middle of working with a particularly difficult mustang, Sitting Bear had walked right up to the wild horse and gained its trust within minutes.

That's all it had taken for Brody to know the man was a friend and not a foe.

Now after two years of Sitting Bear's help training the mustangs, Brody knew of no better man. And he aimed to repay him any way he could.

Elmer put a steadying hand on Brody's shoulder. "Sometimes conflicts can be solved with words, not fists."

Brody rolled his stiff shoulder, flinching at the residual pain from his battle wound. He uncoiled his fingers and shook them. Then he rounded Elmer's mount.

"Let Sitting Bear and his nephew be on their way." His voice carried across the street. It contained all his anger and frustration . . . and hopefully a warning that these fellas wouldn't ignore.

Lonnie Quick, foreman of Stirrup Ranch, stepped forward. His bulging lip curled up into a half smile, revealing his cracked tooth and teeth darkened by chewing tobacco. "Well, if it ain't the king of the lowlifes himself."

Hot, angry words swelled up and pressed for relief, but Brody stuffed them down. "You ain't got no right to harass Sitting Bear, not when he ain't done nothin' wrong."

"He's here," shouted someone else. "No telling what kind of trouble he's gonna cause."

Sitting Bear and Tall Arrow used the interference to slip past the men and quickly headed between the buildings toward the alley.

Brody had to keep distracting the men so the two could get away. "Sitting Bear is working with the government toward peace. If you don't leave him alone, you're gonna cause more problems. That what you want?"

Sitting Bear disappeared around the corner into the alley, and Tall Arrow was fast on his trail.

Quick spat out a stream of tobacco. "This here land don't have room for the Utes and all their demands."

"This was their home first." Just like it was home to the mustangs before the cattle industry had taken off.

"They think they own the whole blamed West," shouted someone else. "And they don't."

Quick wiped a sleeve across the spittle on his lips. "The government's paying them—"

"Not enough," Brody interrupted, "and you know it."

"It's more than they deserve."

The heat started to bubble inside Brody again, but Elmer

shifted his horse, as if to send Brody a silent message to be careful.

Brody had to get out of town fast, before he said or did something he'd regret. He grabbed his saddle and hoisted himself up. "Stay away from Sitting Bear and his family." Brody tossed a glare at the group of fellas and let it fall on Quick. "You give him a hard time again, I'll string you up."

The fellas guffawed and tossed more taunting comments Brody's way, but he urged his horse down the street, forcing himself to ignore the calls. He had to use every bit of will-power within him to nudge his horse into a gallop instead of tugging at the reins, riding back, and swinging his fists.

When he arrived at the ranch, Brody took care of feeding and watering the wild mustangs. After finishing his work and packing, he headed toward the house, wishing the choices weren't so complicated and hard for both the wild horses and the natives.

He threw open the kitchen door and stopped short at the sight that met him. Flora was sitting on Savannah's lap, feeding a kitten goat's milk through a tiny bottle contraption Savannah had created. Their heads were bent together, Savannah's long blond hair mingling with Flora's curly red.

Heaven help him. They were so pretty, especially Savannah with the way she gently stroked Flora's hair and so tenderly murmured words of encouragement. His breath got lost somewhere in his chest just looking. He couldn't imagine anything prettier, except maybe Savannah with her own little girl. She'd make a good ma.

Trouble was, he was the only one he could imagine her

being with. The thought of her wearing any other man's brand—including Chandler Saxton's—boiled his blood.

Both Flora and Savannah glanced in his direction, their eyes bright, their cheeks flushed.

"Uncle Brody!" Flora whispered in a half yell. "I'm feeding the kitties."

Vesta paused in kneading the bread and glared at him. "You gonna stand there all day, letting in every fly on the ranch?"

He closed the door behind him, even though the flies wouldn't be a problem until after the last frost. He'd learned soon enough his first spring in Colorado that snow could fall any time in the spring. Last year, they'd had close to a foot near the end of May. Even though it didn't stick around long in the lower elevations, it made for a shorter summer.

As he started to cross the room, Vesta stopped him with a jerk of her head toward the washbasin on a stand next to the door. He veered toward it and plunged his hands into the icy water.

"This one here's Tiger." Flora's whisper was still loud enough to wake the dead.

"Tiger?" He scrubbed away the grime of the barn. "That's a real fine name."

"Vannah let me name the kitties." Savannah's name was a mouthful for Flora, and *Vannah* was the best the little girl could do. "He's Tiger 'cause he's striped."

As he shook the water from his hands and reached for the towel, Savannah watched him with those eyes of hers that were as warm and blue as a columbine in a mountain meadow. The moment he shifted his attention to her, she focused on Flora, pressing a kiss against the child's unruly, runaway curls.

Since the dance, Savannah had been doing her best to hide from the attraction between them. And he'd been doing his best to make sure she could see it.

Trouble was, she'd kept herself busy. When they weren't out on one of her calls, she'd worked around the clock feeding the kittens. The runt hadn't made it past the first night, but the other three were gaining weight and growing stronger each day.

"This one's Snowball." Flora pointed to the kitten with white fur. "Then here's Mittens."

"Because she looks like she's wearing mittens?" he asked as though it wasn't plainly obvious from the dark paws.

She beamed at him. "That's what Vannah said too!"

"Because she's real smart." He let his tone turn playful, hoping Savannah would reward him with a smile.

When her lips started to curl upward, his heart flopped in his chest.

He finished drying his hands and tossed the towel near the basin. "And teaching you to help feed the kitties, why, that's about the smartest thing she's done yet."

Savannah's lips rose even higher, making his heart tumble again.

"Come and say hi to Tiger, Uncle Brody." Flora dangled the tiny tomcat out toward him.

Brody crossed to where Savannah had positioned the kittens' crate near the stove for warmth. Vesta had been about as happy to have the cats in the house as a hen meeting up with a pack of coyotes. But all it had taken was Flora's joy at the sight of the tiny creatures to smooth down the housekeeper's ruffled feathers.

Brody rubbed the tomcat.

"You gotta talk to him gentle," Flora whisper-yelled again.

"What do you want me to say to the critter?" He imitated her whisper.

"Say hi."

He scratched under the kitten's chin. "Howdy-do, little fella."

"Gentle, Uncle Brody."

"Hi there, Tiger." He lowered his voice even more, and it came out a high squeak.

"Oh, saints have mercy." Vesta rolled her eyes and shook her head, but a rare smile creased her face.

Savannah covered her mouth, but her eyes sparkled with mirth.

"Go ahead," he teased. "Laugh. I don't mind none. I'm proud to be a softy."

She dropped her hand and released her laughter. Soon Flora was laughing too. And Brody could only grin like his head was full of collards instead of brains.

How had he survived before Savannah came into his life? Had he really lived? Or had he only been existing? This was what he wanted—more of her, more time together, more laughter, more love. No doubt about it, he was a goner. So far in love with this woman it defied reason.

As though she sensed the train of his thoughts, her laughter tapered, and she ducked her head, focusing on one of the kittens.

He'd kept his word and hadn't said any more about her staying on in South Park. But he'd been trying everything else to convince her not to leave. He'd offered to teach her more of his mustang training techniques. He'd been putting out the word as best he could about her veterinarian skills, hoping she'd realize how needed she was. He'd also been flirting with her whenever possible—like now.

But none of it seemed to be working to change her mind. Not yet. With each passing hour and day, he kept expecting that every horse and rider who appeared on the horizon was her father coming to fetch her. And the knot inside him cinched tighter. Maybe he'd have to find a way to kiss her again and prove what was developing between them was real.

The front door banged open and footsteps slapped in the hallway. An instant later, Ivy barged into the kitchen. "Me and Dylan are ready to go." With her dark brown hair tucked under her wide-brimmed hat and her wearing a pair of Dylan's old trousers and a baggy coat, she resembled a regular cowhand. Of course, her features were too pretty and feminine and would give her away quicker than the flick of a quirt. But Brody figured she was safer this way, especially from the unwanted attention from cowhands like Hank.

"Where you goin', Uncle Brody?" Flora took Tiger from his hands and cuddled him in her arms like a baby.

Savannah's questioning gaze was upon him.

Ivy crossed to the table and swiped up a warm biscuit. "We're gonna drive Hades and his band up the Mosquito Range. It's gonna be real fun."

Still holding one of the kittens, Savannah stood. Her eyes took on an excited glimmer.

Was it possible she'd consider tagging along? It would be some rough riding, long hours in the saddle, and camping out under the stars. But if she helped, he wouldn't have to worry about finding her long gone when he returned.

"You interested?" He tried to keep the eagerness out of his tone. Didn't want to scare her from going.

She started to nod but then stopped herself. "How long will it take?"

"We're not traveling too far. Once we drive the herd over the range, they'll head down to the lower elevations on their own. But it still could take a few days."

She seemed to mentally calculate the passing of time, likely trying to decide if she'd be back soon enough so that she wouldn't have to make her father wait.

The Cattle King deserved to wait after manipulating his daughter into marrying the man of his choice, one who would bail him out of his financial woes. In fact, if Brody took his sweet ol' time driving the horses, maybe Mr. Marshall would get tired of hanging around and would return home without Savannah.

A gut instinct warned Brody that wouldn't happen, especially if her father was desperate. But at the very least, having Savannah ride along would give Brody more opportunities to convince her to stay.

"I'd love to go—" Savannah glanced to Ivy and then back at him—"if you're sure you won't mind me accompanying you."

"Reckon Brody won't mind one little bit." Ivy flashed a smile through her mouthful of biscuit.

A flush moved into Savannah's face.

"Could use the help." He spoke rapidly before she changed her mind.

Ivy gave a nod toward outside. "Especially because Dylan smells and looks like he bedded down in a whiskey bottle."

Brody stifled a sigh and hoped he wasn't making a mistake in bringing his brother along. He reckoned getting the kid away from the saloons for a few days might help sober him up. But with the difficult terrain up in the mountain passes, Dylan needed to be alert.

Savannah placed the kitten back into the crate and turned to Vesta. "Vesta, would you be so kind as to pack provisions for us to eat?"

Ivy gave a squeal of delight and hugged Savannah. As a secret thrill wound through Brody, he wished he was at liberty to wrap Savannah in his arms too.

Elmer and Vesta agreed to help Flora feed the kittens while Savannah was away. Vesta jabbered on about it like a cranky old goose, but she was wrapped around Flora's pinky and would do about anything for the child.

Within the hour, they were on their way. Ivy charged ahead, and Dylan lagged behind, as hungover as Ivy had indicated, if not more so. Brody rode in companionable silence next to Savannah. The fact that she had such a soothing effect on him was unnerving, but he didn't want to think about it, just wanted to soak her in, even if only for a little while.

Southwest of Fairplay, they spread out to search for Hades and his band. They tracked the mustangs for several hours before they started driving the wild creatures toward the western range. They spurred the horses onward for many miles before ending the pursuit.

Eventually Hades led his band to a secluded mountain pasture for grazing and resting. The night air was colder in the higher elevation, and the patches of snow had grown thicker and more difficult to traverse. But they found a dry spot not far from the mustangs, built a campfire, and had a filling meal from the bounty Vesta had packed.

Dylan was testy and fell asleep soon after they finished their supper. But Ivy was as talkative as always, spinning yarns and entertaining them until her yawns slowed her prattling to a crawl.

When they spread out their blankets around the fire, Ivy winked at him. "You wanna sneak in a kiss or two goodnight with Savannah, I promise I won't tell no one."

Savannah, already tucked deep in her bedroll, grew motionless.

Brody couldn't deny he'd been thinking about trying to work in a kiss with her one way or another on this trip. But he wasn't about to admit it. "Hush up, Ivy."

She laughed, as if getting the exact reaction she'd wanted. Then she rolled over and fell asleep in the next instant.

Brody situated his head on his arm and peered through the dancing flames toward Savannah. The light from the fire glowed upon her beautiful features.

She was watching him. Was she looking at his mouth? Thinking about Ivy's suggestion and what it would be like to kiss him again?

A moment later, she shifted her gaze, locking eyes with him. The desire there curled up as hazy and thick as the smoke rising from the fire. It fanned the flames already at a low burn inside him.

He forced himself not to move. In fact, he closed his eyes, knowing he had to block out the wanting before he let himself act on it. He couldn't kiss her here. Now. Not when he'd be all too tempted to let it lead to more.

He could feel her studying him, the heated tension lingering between them, until the chill of the night settled around him, cooling him off. When enough time had passed, he lifted his lashes to find her asleep and breathing as evenly as she always did.

He released a tense breath and prayed for patience. He hadn't uttered many prayers in recent years, not since all his prayers during battle had fallen on deaf ears. But tonight, he wanted to pray, wanted to find a way out of all his horrors so he could be worthy of a woman like her.

If only he didn't have the doubt that he'd never be the man she needed. . . .

CHAPTER 17

After two full days and half of a third day in the saddle, Savannah was sore but more alive than she'd ever been.

Cresting the rocky peak that rose above the tree line, she paused and drew in a deep breath of the thin mountain air. Her lips were cracked, her mouth dry, and her head light, almost dizzy. But the view was spectacular. Dark pine covered the mountainside and spread down into the Arkansas Valley far below with its pastureland beginning to turn a light green. A river wound through it, the rapids a foamy white with the melting spring runoff.

"Words can't begin to describe this." She felt as if they were at the top of the world, the beauty of the Rockies stretching out as far as they could see. They were so high they could almost reach out and graze one of the many wispy clouds above them.

Brody rested his reins and hands across his thigh, as comfortable on the jagged, snowy peak as he'd been during the ascent. The slush and the mud had made the way difficult and even treacherous at times, but somehow he'd blazed a trail to the summit.

"Thank you for bringing me here." She'd wanted to ride up even though it was out of the way and had been grateful when he'd suggested it.

Her gaze alighted on the mustangs now grazing in an open grassy area beneath the snow line, already well on their way down the slope leading to the valley below. "There they are." She pointed, directing Brody's gaze to a majestic sight.

His attention shifted to the herd, to Hades standing slightly apart from the rest, his blond-bay mane flowing in the mountain breeze, each scar in his painted coat highlighted by the sunshine, his muscles taut and ready for flight.

She'd grown to admire Hades's resilience, strength, and perseverance. He cared about his band, his mares and foals, and led them with dignity. And now he turned his head in their direction. He nodded, as though communicating with them. Did he know they'd chased him only because they wanted to save his life? Did he realize the fear of the past couple of days would lead to his freedom?

Maybe he'd never understand what they'd done, but she liked to think he was thanking them for their efforts anyway. Was that the way God was with His children? Did He drive them through difficulties, up steep mountains, because He cared and was leading them to better pastures? Even when they didn't understand what He was doing, maybe He was asking them to thank Him regardless.

"We can get down, sit a spell, and eat." Brody's voice contained a hint of shyness.

Her stomach chose that moment to grumble with hunger. After the quick breakfast they'd had earlier, she'd worked up an appetite. And now that they'd driven the mustangs over the Mosquito Range, their mission was complete. Brody had explained there was always the chance the mustangs would make their way back into South Park. But he expected they wouldn't make the hard climb, not as long as the grass was plentiful in this new valley.

She glanced around at the slushy, rocky peak. Where would they be able to sit? The snow was wet, and they'd had to tie stockings on each of their horses' front hooves to keep them from icing up and slipping.

Brody had already dismounted and was flapping open a piece of canvas and laying it over the snow. Then, as though reading her mind, he pulled a woolen blanket from his saddlebag and unfolded it over the canvas.

"Won't Ivy and Dylan be waiting for us?" she asked.

He ducked his head. "Naw, told them to ride on ahead to the spot where we camped the first night."

"That far?"

"Trip down goes faster. We'll meet up with them later after our picnic."

"Picnic?"

"Yep. The food might not be much, but the view'll more than make up for it."

Had Brody planned a special picnic for just the two of them? Her stomach suddenly twirled with strange butterflies.

No wonder Ivy had been grinning and winking when she and Brody had headed toward the peak. Ivy had known Brody intended to make it more than just a simple detour.

Dylan hadn't said much most of the trip except to grouse and grumble. Brody had the patience of a saint with the young man. She sensed he was attempting to reach out and be there for Dylan, even if only as a silent and steady companion. He'd also made more of an effort with Ivy, which the girl soaked up faster than dry ground after a rainstorm.

He approached and held out a gloved hand.

When Savannah hesitated in accepting, he finally met her gaze. In the sunshine, the dark brown of his eyes had turned lighter like honey and just as sweet. Even though the usual warning clanged inside, the one that told her she couldn't encourage anything between them, she wanted to turn it off for the afternoon.

Of course, the sparks were always there with Brody. It didn't matter how hard she worked to stamp them out, they cropped up in the most unexpected moments, like when their hands brushed in reaching to fold up a bedroll, or when they shared a smile over something Ivy said, or as she awoke in the morning to find him already making the coffee.

But soon enough they'd be back at Healing Springs Ranch. No doubt her daddy would be there waiting and ready to take her home. And the truth was, she wasn't any closer to coming up with a solution for her future than she'd been two weeks ago.

She hoped she could convince Daddy to let her stay longer, to give her a little more time to think over the matter . . . and enjoy being a veterinarian. But if he insisted she leave, she'd have a hard time saying no to him. She always did. So it was possible she'd only bought herself a few more days.

Why shouldn't she enjoy a picnic? Especially since this might be her last time alone with Brody?

Throwing caution aside, she placed her hand in his. And as he helped her down, she nearly brushed against him as she slipped in the snow. His hands quickly settled upon her hips as he steadied her. The contact immediately made her all too conscious of his masculinity in every nuance—the smoky scent of his leather coat, the thick sturdiness of his fingers through his gloves, and the broad steadiness of his arms on either side of her.

Thankfully, he didn't hold on for long. She wasn't sure she could have resisted if he'd decided to tug her close. Instead, he took her elbow and guided her to the blanket. When she was seated, he draped another blanket around her, then lowered himself next to her with one of the food packs.

As she breathed in another lungful of the crisp air, she focused on the view again, taking it all in. Not many men would think of having a picnic at the summit of a mountain. Brody was special to plan this for her.

He pulled out the few food items left—a couple of biscuits, Greta's jam, beef jerky, and a handful of dried currants. They ate and watched the mustangs, and they shared sips of water from his canteen. This was just one more memory with him she'd never forget.

He was a man she'd never forget.

"This is amazing, Brody." She handed the canteen back to him and wrapped her blanket more fully around her. "Thank you."

His focus was on the horses again, almost as if he was memorizing them. He reached into his coat pocket and pulled out a notebook and pencil. He twisted the pencil in his fingers for a moment, then opened the notebook and flipped through the pages. As he came to the last one, he stopped and held it out to her.

She took the book and studied the drawing of Hades and one of his mares, the pure white one with a star on her temple.

The likeness of both horses was perfect, the setting lightly sketched behind them.

"You drew this?" She couldn't hold back her surprise.

"Yep." He angled his head down, hiding his face beneath the brim of his hat.

"This is incredible." She examined the sketch again. "You're incredible."

"You'd probably say that to Flora with one of her drawings."

She laughed. "I suppose so. But of course, hers couldn't begin to compare to this. It's gorgeous."

He began to tug the notebook away from her.

She refused to relinquish it. "Brody McQuaid. You astonish me more every day."

He shrugged. "Reckon I've buried a lot of myself and am dusting off the ashes so I can see the beauty again."

At his reference to her words of encouragement from previously, a fresh sense of amazement wafted through her.

"Haven't sketched since the war. Never thought I'd want to again." His admission was soft. "But with you always seeing the good in everything, guess I can't help seeing some of it too."

Her chest tightened with emotion, and she whispered a silent prayer of gratitude that Brody was beginning to heal.

She turned the page in the notebook, opening to a clean white sheet. Then she handed it back to him. "I think you're itching to draw the horses and the scene around us, and I can't think of anything I'd rather do than watch you."

He fidgeted with his pencil. "You sure?"

"I'd love to watch you as long as I won't make you nervous."

"Naw. You don't make me nervous." His gaze lingered over the landscape, as if he was already penciling it in his mind. "You bring me peace."

"I do?"

"Yep." He lightly drew a line on the paper.

He never flattered her like other men did. Instead, he was honest, not afraid to tell her what he thought, even if it was something she might not like hearing. It made his compliments—like this one—all the richer.

He started sketching more rapidly. Since the notepad wasn't overly large, only the size of a journal or book, she sidled closer to get a better view.

Hades took shape. But Brody didn't stop there. He drew the whole herd grazing on the mountainside, bringing them to life and accentuating their glory. When he finished with that, she marveled over it, then flipped it over so that another blank sheet faced him.

His pencil flew over the new page, this time capturing one of the foals staying close to its mother. Brody exquisitely rendered the tenderness of the pair. As he finished each drawing, she turned the page for him, hoping he knew it was her way of asking him to keep going. She loved observing him at work, the keenness of his gaze, the concentration etched into his features, the swiftness of his fingers, and the beauty he was able to create.

She wasn't sure at what point she'd laid her head against his upper arm. But he hadn't minded, had kept right on drawing. Next to Brody on the mountain peak, peace settled around her too. And a part of her wanted to stay in this place with him forever.

As he added a final shadow to a drawing of a mare rearing

up on her hind legs, she sighed her contentment. "It's perfect, Brody. Absolutely stunning."

He smiled, and, as usual, the rare sight brought a hitch to her breathing. "With all your compliments, my head's bound to get bigger than a melon."

"I doubt that."

He took out his small hunting knife and carefully shaved the end of his pencil to give himself more lead.

"If you displayed these drawings, maybe sold them, they could create more compassion and interest from others in saving the wild horses."

He paused his sharpening. "Maybe. But I ain't sure if I'm ready for that. If I'll ever be."

She squeezed his arm. "If and when the time is right, I think you'll know."

The muscle in his bicep was hard beneath her fingers, and she couldn't keep from circling her hand wider and letting herself get a fuller feel of him. The moment she did, however, his posture shifted, and he leaned back just slightly.

She glanced up to find that his attention had moved away from the sketch pad and now focused on her face. Something in his eyes said he was mentally drawing her.

"Can you draw people as well as animals?" She tried to keep her voice light, but having his full scrutiny made her suddenly breathless.

"Yep." His gaze traced the shape of her face.

"Would you like to draw me?" The words were out before she thought about what she was saying.

"Already have."

"You have?"

"Lots." Instead of ducking his head at the admission, he continued to boldly explore her features.

Oh my. She was tempted to press her hands to her rapidly heating cheeks but refrained.

"But I'll gladly do it again." He poised his pencil. "Ain't never gonna get tired of drawing you, darlin'."

She loved the way *darlin'* rolled off his tongue, as though she was truly special to him. Was she?

His gaze darted from the paper to her face, and his pencil began to fly.

"What should I be doing?" She smoothed a hand over her flyaway strands. She likely had a hat mark in her hair from wearing the thing almost constantly during their trip, even though she'd taken it off when she'd first started watching him draw, needing to get a better view.

He moved the lead effortlessly. "Why don't you look out at the view."

Trying to do as he said, she angled her head.

"Just be natural."

"Alright." She should have groomed herself better that morning or perhaps changed her bodice.

He paused.

She didn't move her head but attempted to peer down on what he was sketching. "How's it coming?"

His fingers brushed against her shoulder, sending tingles over her skin. She barely had time to react as he reached for the leather strip holding her hair in place. Before she knew what he was doing, he loosened the knot and her hair fell free. The mountain breeze immediately picked up the strands, twisting and twirling them.

"There." He returned to his sketch. "That's natural."

She resisted the urge to gather her hair back up and tried to concentrate on the scenery. But the longer he studied her as he drew, the harder it became to think of anything but him. Her insides tightened with a growing need she didn't understand.

When he finally lifted his pencil and tilted his head to examine his drawing, she allowed herself to look at it too.

"Brody McQuaid." She tried to make her voice stern while tightening her blanket about her to ward off the chill of the wind. "Don't you think you made me a bit too pretty for the circumstances?"

He watched her and turned to another blank page. "Don't move."

She held herself motionless.

Again, he sketched in quick, deft strokes, glancing up and then down, his beautiful eyes taking her in.

"You need to be realistic, Brody. Draw me like I really am."

"I am."

She glanced down. "Let me make sure."

He hid the pad against his chest and smirked. "Be patient."

She gave him a censuring look.

His smirk turned into a small smile. "Perfect."

After several more minutes, she wanted to toss off the blanket, even though the sun had disappeared and the air had grown colder. Under his intense scrutiny, she guessed her cheeks were flushed, attesting to how much he affected her.

"All done." His expression radiated satisfaction, before he turned the pad to face her.

He'd captured her to perfection, her eyes upon him and filled with humor, a slight smile, wind tossing strands of her hair while she clutched the blanket close.

"Somehow you manage to flatter me even when I'm in such disarray."

"Ain't flattery." He reached up, caressed a strand of hair, and grazed her collarbone.

She sucked in a breath.

His fingers skimmed the delicate bone until he reached her neck. Then he grazed upward, following the path of her rapidly beating pulse. His touch paused, and his eyes darkened. "You're beautiful. Could draw you every day and never get tired of it."

Her voice got lost inside.

When he resumed his tracing, he slid his fingers to her jaw and drew a line all the way down to her chin. As his thumb brushed against her bottom lip, she trembled, the wanting inside her suddenly irresistible.

His attention had shifted to her mouth. He traced her lower lip as though his finger was his pencil and he was shading it just the way he wanted.

"Brody?" She hoped he could understand her plea. She needed him to stop. Their interaction was making her feel things she shouldn't.

"What is it, darlin'?" His husky tone told her he was feeling things too.

"You shouldn't be—"

His fingers glided over her upper lip, cutting off her breath.

She closed her eyes to fight off the pleasure and to control the gasp that needed to be released. In the next instant, the stroke of his fingers fell away, and before she could protest, his lips took their place.

Warm, sweet pressure. It wasn't hard or demanding like

his first kiss. This was soft and velvety, allowing her every opportunity to pull away, stand up, and put an end to it.

But something in the taste of his mouth mingling with hers was intoxicating. It only drew her in and made her crave more. She lifted her hand to his cheek, letting her fingers slide across the scruffy stubble and pressing her mouth into his fully.

As she opened up to him, he must have taken that for the invitation he'd been waiting for, the declaration that she wanted his kisses every bit as much as he wanted to give them. His arms came around her, picking her up and situating her on his lap, and at the same time, he took full possession of the kiss, deep and consuming.

She could go on kissing this fine-looking, kindhearted, sensitive man for the rest of her life. She didn't want to stop, didn't want to do anything else, didn't want to come back to reality.

But all the warnings she'd been whispering to herself, including Flynn's, rose louder with each passing second.

She had to be careful, had to break away, had to control her longing.

A cold gust slapped her. She pulled back and turned her head away, needing to prevent him from kissing her again but too weak to stand up and get on her horse the way she knew she should.

His hands against her back were taut, and his exhalations against her temple were ragged.

This man . . .

She closed her eyes tighter as if that could somehow block out the rush of emotion that swelled. How had she developed such strong feelings for Brody in so short a time? When the day came to go home, she didn't know how she'd be able to ride away and leave him behind.

She couldn't let Daddy down, but the honest truth was that she couldn't marry Chandler. Maybe she'd known it all along. Maybe that's why she'd had to run away—so she could figure out how to tell Daddy without causing him more grief.

Brody seemed to be waiting, as though he sensed her inner turmoil. As much as she longed to kiss him again, doing so would communicate to him that he was right, that she wouldn't marry Chandler, that she was ready to pursue whatever was happening between them.

Was she really ready? Could she so easily toss aside her daddy's feelings and plans for the first man to turn her head and stir her heart? What about sacrifice and honor and family loyalty?

"Brody," she whispered.

"Yes, darlin'?" His response was laden with deep emotion she didn't want to analyze.

"I just don't know what to do."

CHAPTER

18

Savannah might still have doubts, but at least she wasn't saying no anymore. That was a heap of progress.

Brody nuzzled his nose into her neck, and she nuzzled his neck back. She was changing her tune from the barn dance, when she'd insisted she couldn't go against her father's wishes. All she needed was a little more nudging, a little more gentle persuasion, a little more letting her feel everything growing between them.

He could kiss her again. He'd felt her response in the sweet melding of their mouths. Showing her the passion that easily ignited between them was a surefire way to convince her to give them a chance.

His fingers splayed across her lower back. With her weight on his outstretched legs, he had the urge to lie back and pull her down with him. But something inside warned him that if he lay beside her, he wouldn't be getting up for a while. A whole lot of kissing would lead to places that weren't meant to be visited until he made sure he had his loop around her.

Could he make her his wife? Was that really a possibility? He was working on fighting his demons, wasn't he? He was trying to move out of the darkness he'd been in for so long. Maybe that meant he'd have a better future after all.

He pressed a kiss to her hair and breathed her in. Whatever the case, she deserved someone to cherish her, not use her. And he'd prove himself more of a man by exercising self-restraint than by getting carried away.

He sat still for a moment, trying to steady his wildly thudding heartbeat and cool his overheated blood.

"I just don't know what to do, Brody," she whispered again, this time resting her head on his shoulder.

He brushed her hair down, relishing the silky strands cascading through his fingers. "Once heard it said, 'When the time is right, I think you'll know.'"

"Those are very wise words." Her voice contained mirth.

"Yep." A cold drop hit the back of his hand. Then two, three, and more. He shifted, and the moisture and wind pelted his face, stinging him. Was it rain or snow or both?

"We best be going." The sky that had been mostly clear and blue at the outset of their picnic now teemed with thick, dark clouds.

Savannah glanced to the clouds and shivered as the wind and precipitation buffeted her too.

As much as he wanted to have more time alone with her before rejoining Ivy and Dylan, he guessed the sky was gonna let loose any time. And with the dropping temperatures and increasing wind, today wasn't the day to be riding about soaking wet.

He helped her to her feet and then glanced over the eastern side, trying to remember everything he'd ever heard about this part of the Mosquito Range. Were there any nearby caves where they could take shelter until the rain passed over? An abandoned mine? A current claim? Even an old trapper's hut?

The rainy snow came down harder, and the wind flung ice pellets like tiny bullets. Savannah turned her back to the mixture, pressed her hat onto her head, and then curled the woolen blanket about her more securely.

He swiped up the remainder of their picnic. "Ready?"

"No, but I guess we don't have a choice, do we?"

As they made their way toward the horses, their footsteps crunched against the ground.

The precipitation was turning to ice even as it fell, coating everything much too quickly. The terrain would be dangerous for them and their horses to attempt to ride down. They would have to go out on foot and lead their mounts for a ways, at least until they got to a low enough elevation where the rain wasn't freezing.

"We're gonna walk for a spell." A gust almost wrested the canvas from his grasp. He fought against the wind and draped the canvas over Savannah. She was already shivering hard.

Shoving the rest of their supplies into the pack, he scanned the heavy clouds rolling toward them. How had he not noticed the oncoming storm?

He wanted to blame the fact that the weather on the peaks could change in the blink of an eye, wanted to curse the temperamental mountains.

But the truth was, he'd gotten distracted while he was drawing and then afterward when he was kissing Savannah. He hadn't been paying attention to anything but her, and now she was gonna suffer for it.

He was a blamed fool. He might not have lived in Colorado long, but he should've turned back right away when they reached the peak. Should've found a lower elevation for their picnic.

Now the only thing he could do was locate a place to wait out the storm. But where? He wasn't familiar with this area the way he was with South Park and the foothills surrounding it.

He gauged the distance off the barren peak. They had several hundred feet to go before reaching the tree line. Even the protection of the evergreens would be better than being caught out in the open.

"Follow me," he called over the pelting and gusting.

She nodded and led Molasses gingerly over the crusted snow.

A second later, Brody slipped and almost fell. As he straightened, he held on to his gelding's lead line to keep from landing on his backside. What if they couldn't make it down?

Suddenly the urgency of their situation hit him. Being cold and wet was the least of their concerns when their lives might be at stake.

He paused, extricated his spyglass, and examined the surrounding area for any sign of a place they could take shelter. The ice landed on the spyglass and froze to it immediately. As droplets hit the lens, he dried them and resumed his scrutiny.

From what he could tell there was a gulch to the south. Which meant there were likely miners or the remains of a mining camp. If he could get them to the gulch, at the very least they'd be out of the worst of the wind and precipitation.

He angled toward the south, taking one careful step down the slope at a time, making footholds that Savannah could use. Even so, frustration burrowed deeper, especially as Savannah huddled beneath the canvas, shaking.

"We have to keep going down," he shouted above the wind, now roaring against them, threatening to blow them off the mountain.

She nodded.

Their pace was painstakingly slow, but he didn't want to push too fast and chance injury to themselves or the horses. He kept one eye on the icy path ahead and one on Savannah following behind. As she struggled to maintain her balance, he wanted nothing more than to pick her up and carry her, but doing so would only put them both at greater risk.

They were only halfway across the barren open peak when large, heavy flakes of snow began to mingle with the ice pellets. Within minutes the snow was falling thick and fast. The wind blew it into his face, and he could hardly see where he was going.

The conditions were deteriorating even more. What if he took them the wrong direction? Got lost? Lead them toward a cliff?

The scenarios ripped through his mind. And the anxiety squeezed hard, the same anxiety that had taken up residence during the war. Without the heavy crushing in his chest recently, he'd hoped the unwanted companion had moved on. But with the unfolding nightmare of their situation, his worry pounded harder, taking him back to the battlefield so that for several strange seconds, the snow became ash and the wind became the howls of the wounded.

He wiped at his eyes and brought the snowy range back

into focus. He couldn't allow himself to fall apart now, not with Savannah relying on him. But again, his head filled with the cries of his comrades lying around him, hands reaching out, begging for him to save them.

He'd failed once. What if he failed again?

As he took another step, his body trembled, so much he had to pause and take a deep breath. He wasn't on the battlefield anymore. Wasn't at the mercy of his enemy. Instead, he was with Savannah. Sweet, tenderhearted, helpful, kind Savannah.

South. He had to get to the gulch in the south.

The snow thickened and turned blinding. With each step, he had to rely on an innate sense of direction and pray he wasn't wrong. He secured his belt to Savannah to make sure they didn't get separated. Though he could feel her shaking, she didn't utter one word of complaint and stayed right behind him.

Finally, after what felt like hours, his fingers connected with a branch. They were reaching the tree line and would soon be in the thick of the growth with some protection. Even so, after the past hour, he guessed at least four inches of snow had fallen. The accumulation covered the icy layer, but it was dense and slippery and posed a hazard of its own.

He led them into the tree cover, but the heavy, wet snow bent the branches low. Not only did they have to push past the loads, but their feet stuck in the increasingly deep drifts. Didn't take long for his shoes and stockings to be thoroughly sodden and his feet to ache from the cold.

He halted and reached back for Savannah. "Time to get up on Molasses."

She nodded wearily, her teeth chattering so that she couldn't speak.

As he lifted her into the saddle, he struggled to maintain his grip. His leather gloves were saturated and his fingers stiff. When she was situated, he tried to reposition the canvas over her, but it hadn't done much good since she was soaked through to the skin.

Regardless, he covered her as best he could, his heart thudding out a warning. The temperature had dropped dramatically from what it had been during their picnic. And now they risked becoming frostbitten or worse.

He wanted to mount his horse, too, and move swiftly, but he had to get them to leveler ground first. He hiked carefully, leading both horses along the tree line to the south to the gulch he'd spotted. But as with everything in the mountains, it was farther away than he'd anticipated.

With the ever-increasing snowfall, he trudged on, pushing through the deep layers. Once they were lower, he mounted his horse. Even though the creatures couldn't go fast, at least he was no longer expending energy he'd need for their survival.

He kept close track of the passing of the afternoon and the nearing of evening. If he couldn't make it to the gulch soon, he'd have to stop and create some kind of shelter. In fact, with every glance behind him at Savannah and her continually drooping shoulders, he considered halting and trying to warm her. Problem was, the ground was too wet to start a fire, and with the coming of the night, they would need the heat to survive.

Darkness was settling when they reached the gulch. As they made their way up a winding creek, the natural rock formations cut down on the blowing. But the snow still fell rapidly, and its depth proved difficult even for the horses.

All the while they slogged forward, he scanned the rocks, looking for an alcove, cave, niche—anything that was dry.

With every bend of the gulch, the despair inside, which had been growing all afternoon, turned into a monster, tearing him apart inside. Death and destruction taunted him with all the memories he'd tried to suppress.

"No!" The word tore from his throat, raw and anguished. "No! We're not dying here."

Behind him, Savannah stirred but didn't have the strength to raise her head or encourage him with something wise and positive like she usually did.

Her damp hair hung in loose waves coated with snow and ice. Her garments, stiff and frozen, clung to her. The tarp draped over her was layered with snow. And at some point, she'd wrapped her reins around her wrists—likely to keep from falling off.

"Savannah, stay with me." His voice was sharp, desperate. *Stay with me.* How many times had he said those same words to men on the battlefield? It hadn't worked. They hadn't stayed with him. Even Newt—who'd vowed to make it—hadn't stayed with him when they'd been lying in the hospital after Andersonville.

Brody's horse struggled up an embankment and almost collapsed in what had to be two feet of snow. "Come on now." At his gentle encouragement, the gelding steadied his footing and kept going. As Brody reached the level crest, his heart bucked in his chest.

There, sheltered against a ravine wall, was a log shack. The lone window was shuttered. The place was dark, without a curl of smoke coming from the pipe in the snow-laden roof. And a chain was wrapped around the door handle.

He guessed that whoever had claimed the land had gone down to the lower elevations for the winter and hadn't yet returned to resume mining. Even if no one was here to help them, it was still a dry place.

His relief made him suddenly weak, but he pressed on until he reached the shack. With the need to get Savannah warmed up, he couldn't waste time breaking the chain. Instead, he used his knife and the barrel of his rifle to pry away the boards in the window. Once he freed the slabs of wood, he dragged over a stump from beside the door that served as a chair. He used it to climb through the window. Once inside, he located a bench, pulled it over, and went back out for Savannah.

Only half-conscious, she slid off the horse and into his arms. He struggled to carry her in the snow but made it to the window. She roused enough to help as he hefted her through. When he was back in the cabin, he fumbled in the dark to find the stove. The shack was tiny, no bigger than the upstairs bedroom in Flynn's house. But whoever owned it had left a pail of shavings, a few logs beside the stove, and matches.

He could hardly get his fingers to work as he built the fire in the cold stove. Behind him, sitting on the bench, Savannah didn't move.

"Come on, come on." He finished stacking the twigs, then struck the match.

Within a minute, he had a flame started. Though he was tempted to dump on more shavings and a log, such haste would only dampen the sparks and he'd have to start over. Instead, he added more fuel slowly until a sturdy fire rose to life.

The flickering light illuminated the interior, showing a tidy place consisting of a bed built into the wall, a barrel with a board across the top forming a table, a few pots and pans hanging from one wall, and an assortment of other necessities, including an ax and shovel.

Savannah was watching him. "You did it." Her voice was weak but relieved.

"We gotta get you warmed up." He grabbed the blanket from the bed. "Can you get out of your wet clothes?"

She tried to push herself up but didn't make it more than a few inches before she collapsed on the bench. "I'm sorry, Brody. . . ."

He crossed to her. "I'm gonna have to help you." This wasn't the time to worry about modesty, not when she was at risk for chilblain or frostbite.

He settled her in front of the open stove and then knelt in front of her and made quick work of taking off her boots and stockings. He wrapped her feet in the blanket and rubbed them, trying to bring life and heat to them.

After a few minutes, he helped her shed her coat and gloves, blowing heat onto her fingers and holding them closer to the stove. She could only watch him listlessly, hardly able to hold her head up.

The angst inside drove him, and he started on her bodice. He had to get her warmed up faster. He peeled it away from her arms and dropped it on the floor and did the same with her split skirt and the trousers underneath. Wearing only her chemise and drawers, she was as pale as a corpse. He'd seen enough to know.

He hesitated at the thin shoulder straps of her chemise. It was damp, too, but he suspected she'd be mortified if he bared her completely. For now, he'd leave her in the under-garments and attempt to warm her despite their dampness.

Wrapping the blanket around her, he briskly began to rub her. He stopped to add more fuel to the fire and then rubbed her again up and down her arms, her legs, her back, and shoulders. The crackling of the wood taunted him that they'd soon exhaust the small supply and that he needed to get more and dry it before it was too late.

As much as he regretted having to leave Savannah, he bundled her in the blanket and laid her in the bed. Then he headed out through the window into the darkening shadows of the evening. He explored the surroundings and discovered a lean-to behind the cabin. It contained more cut wood, enough to get them through a week, if used wisely. While the quarters were tight, he led both horses underneath and out of the snow. He hurried through the unsaddling and grooming, anxious to get back to Savannah.

Somehow in all the work, his limbs started to thaw so that by the time he finished he'd warmed up—all except his cold toes. He checked on her to find that she was huddled under the blanket and asleep. Though he wanted to do more to warm her, he had to make sure they were supplied for the coming night with both water and wood, especially since the snow wasn't letting up. By the time he gathered what they needed and boarded the window, the blackness of the night was heavy upon them.

Without a lantern, the only light came from the stove, and he used it to scour through the shack, taking better stock of the few supplies left behind—a pair of hand-hewn snowshoes, several steel traps, and mice-eaten blankets in a crate underneath the bed.

After setting snow to melt in a pot on the stove, he shed his own clothing and laid the garments out alongside hers to dry. He wrapped himself in a blanket and stoked the fire. When the water was steaming, he poured a mug and took it to Savannah.

Sitting beside her in the box frame with a thin, straw-filled mattress, he gently shook her. "Got some hot water."

She stirred but didn't make an effort to sit.

"Wake up, darlin'," he pleaded with her softly.

"I'm so cold." Her breathy whisper was followed by her teeth chattering.

He set the mug aside and gathered her into his arms. Her skin was clammy and pale and still frigid. He settled her closer, wrapping his arms around her fully and wishing he could transfer every ounce of his own heat into her body.

She trembled, and he embraced her tighter, a fierce possessiveness taking hold of him. He wasn't willing to lose her. Not now. Not after all the loss he'd already experienced.

This time, he wasn't gonna sit around helplessly. He'd do everything he could to keep her alive, even if it cost him his own life.

CHAPTER

19

A chill slithered over Savannah's skin—a deep chill that seeped through her flesh all the way down to her bones.

A pounding from somewhere broke through her frozen world. She tried to motivate herself, tried to climb out of the frigid lake where she was drowning, but she couldn't seem to grip the edge.

More pounding echoed around her. It filled her head and jarred her body, wakening her from the icy abyss.

Where was she?

She pried open her heavy lids to find herself in a dark room, a shelter of some sort. Gray light streaked past broken boards propped in the window. At the sight of snowflakes falling in a fast flurry through a gap in the boards, the memory of the previous day rushed back—the picnic with Brody on the mountaintop, the snowstorm blanketing them, the slippery descent, the hours of torturous riding.

At some point he must have discovered this cabin. She had

a brief memory of him helping her inside, but beyond that everything was a blur.

She opened her eyes wider and took in her surroundings: a log structure with sound chinking, a sturdy roof, a small cast-iron stove in one corner, a makeshift table in another, and the bed. Aside from a few cooking items and tools, that was it.

Banging rattled the cabin again, and this time she realized it was coming from the door. Was Brody locked out? Was he attempting to get her attention?

She pushed up to her elbows, but the movement sent trembles across her body and through her limbs. The long hours in the cold had weakened her.

At another crashing that rocked the cabin, the door burst open and banged against the wall, a broken chain dangling from the door handle. Snow swirled inside along with a gust of bitter air. It swept around her, and she clutched at her blankets, drawing them closer.

In the next instant, Brody stepped inside, an ax in one hand and a shovel in the other. His coat and hat were covered in a dusting of snow, but he appeared to be dry and safe.

She sagged back into the bed, relieved to see that he was faring better than she was.

As he kicked the slush from his heels, his gaze darted to her. His eyes were dark and anxious beneath the brim of his hat. Upon seeing her awake, he paused. "Hey there."

"Where are we?" Her voice came out scratchy.

"A deserted miner's cabin."

How had he managed to find it and bring them here? In doing so, he'd surely saved their lives. "What about Ivy and Dylan?"

His expression remained grave. "Hopefully they were down far enough and beat the storm."

"Let's pray so." She shuddered.

At the sight, he shoved the door closed, set aside the tools, and crossed to the stove. He poured something from a pot into a mug and then approached her.

She wanted to tell him he didn't have to serve her, but she was too thirsty to protest.

He perched on the edge of the box frame and held out the mug. "Hot water."

She fumbled to sit up.

He lifted her just slightly and pressed the mug to her lips.

She breathed in the steam and sipped slowly, letting the warmth cascade through her.

He watched, weariness creasing his handsome face.

When she'd managed several swallows, her lashes fell, exhaustion overcoming her. He gently lowered her and started to rise.

She forced her eyes back open. "Thank you, Brody. You saved my life."

"Hope so."

"I'll be fine."

"You sure?" He hovered above her.

She nodded. Again, her eyelids were too heavy to keep open, and she let herself return to the abyss.

❦

She wasn't sure how long she slept before waking from dreams filled with snow and ice. Brody wasn't inside the cabin, and the light that pierced through the boarded window told her the day hadn't yet passed. Though she couldn't stop shivering from the cold, hunger bothered her more, gnawing at her stomach and prodding her with the urgency of their situation.

They were stranded high in the mountains in a spring snowstorm. How much snow had fallen? If it had accumulated all night and throughout the day, they could easily have two feet, if not more.

That meant they were trapped. For days. Maybe even for a week or two with only a few food provisions left in their pack and until the snow melted enough that their horses could travel through it. If the horses survived. With the heavy accumulation covering everything, the poor creatures wouldn't have anything to eat either.

Where was Brody?

She tried to sit up, but she didn't have the energy. Instead, she lay listlessly, covered under what appeared to be half a dozen blankets—the ones they'd brought for bedrolls that had dried and then apparently some that had been in the cabin.

Her wet clothing? She brushed her fingers over her bodice but found she was wearing only her chemise and drawers, which were damp. She couldn't remember shedding her outer garments, although it was likely. Hopefully Brody hadn't needed to undress her. The very thought sent a flush through her.

She had to remain grateful. They were out of the elements. She was safe inside. And Brody was unharmed.

Brody. Dear, sweet Brody, who was doing everything he could to keep her alive.

As grogginess overtook her again, her mind wandered to those blissful moments on the mountain peak when they'd kissed. His kiss had been so full of passion and emotion. Just the memory of it stirred longing inside her to be with him, by his side, and in his arms. If she had him, then no matter their fate, she'd have enough.

◦⌒❧⌒◦

Gentle but callused fingers brushed her face. Brody's.

She awoke to find him crouched by the side of the bed. He wasn't wearing his coat or hat this time, giving her a better view of his face and the worry still etched there.

He held up the tin mug, steam rising from the top, and slipped his arm behind her, helping her up enough to drink again. This time she sipped more, relishing the warmth as the liquid went down. Though she couldn't shake the cold, she wasn't as chilled to the bone.

As he set the mug down, he lifted a biscuit slathered with jam to her lips. If she remembered right, it was the last biscuit along with a few pieces of beef jerky—enough for their picnic and not much more.

Ivy had been carrying the main food pack with provisions for the return trip. Savannah was glad it had worked out that way. She didn't want Dylan and Ivy to have to go hungry and suffer more than necessary.

Same with Brody. But he was obviously planning to feed her the remaining food and would likely leave nothing for himself.

"No," she whispered. "You have it."

He pressed it in closer. "Naw. I'm fine."

She shook her head and closed her lips.

"Come on now, darlin'. You need the energy."

She turned her head away. "I want you to have it, Brody."

"No way, no how." His tone turned almost harsh, and it drew her attention back to his face. "Can't tell you how many people I had to watch starve while I was in . . ."

He stared at a spot above her head as though seeing into the past. Was he thinking about his time in Andersonville Prison? Since the time she'd comforted him during his nightmare, he hadn't talked any more about the war or his experiences. She sensed he didn't want to now either. But in this small way, he was sharing what he could.

The muscles in his jaw flexed. She wanted to stroke his cheek and assure him everything was fine, that she wouldn't starve. But how could she say that when she didn't know how they would get out of this predicament?

After a moment, he swallowed hard and let his gaze return to her. "Ain't gonna let you go hungry."

"I don't want you going hungry either."

"There were a few traps, and I set 'em out with the last of the beef jerky as bait." He nodded toward a pair of snowshoes leaning against the wall near the door. Snow stuck to the wood and was dripping onto the rough-hewn plank floor.

"Do you think they'll come out?" Up so high, they'd only seen a few birds and squirrels and not much else. From what Ivy had explained during the hours of conversation on the ride out, most of the mountain animals went into the lower elevations during the winter and hadn't yet returned.

"It's finally stopped snowing." He glanced at the window. Darkness was falling. "If any critters are in the area, they're gonna come out soon enough searching for grub."

If. She held Brody's gaze. The heartache in his eyes told her more than his words had of the horrors he'd witnessed in Andersonville. She couldn't put him through such horrors again with her. She opened her mouth and looked at the biscuit.

He held it out again. This time she took a bite, and the tension in his shoulders eased.

She chewed, then forced it down even though it stuck in her throat. "How are the horses?"

"Shoveled a spot of grass for them." He inched the biscuit into her mouth, making her take another piece.

With as much snow as had fallen, she could only imagine the work he'd gone to in shoveling a small area. While something, it wouldn't be enough to sate the ravenous appetites of the horses for long.

From the wood piled up next to the stove, she guessed he'd also been out gathering fuel. He had to be tired from all his hard work. And hungry.

She swallowed the mouthful of biscuit. "Please have the rest, Brody."

He shook his head, his expression hardening. "I know I can survive. I've already done it once. But you . . ."

"I'll manage—"

"Please, Savannah." His tone dropped to a whisper, a desperate whisper. "I've lost too many people I've loved. And I can't lose you."

Her insides quivered. Was he telling her that he loved her? Was that even possible yet? Of course, they'd spent countless hours together over the past two weeks riding to different ranches on her vet calls and also taming the mustangs. In fact, they'd rarely been apart. The attraction was definitely there. But love?

Whatever the case, he clearly cared about her. And she cared about him too. If her eating the biscuit would make him feel better, then she had to do it, even though she wanted to share it with him.

She took another bite, and while she chewed, he smoothed back her hair. The motion was soothing. And from the loosening of his features, she guessed touching her comforted him as well.

She wanted to know more about this complex man and his pain, but she hesitated. She'd never pushed him to share beyond what he wanted. Was it time to encourage him to open up more?

He offered her another piece of biscuit, but she asked him a question first. "Tell me more about your pa. Was he one of the people you loved and lost?"

He paused in caressing her hair and was silent for a long moment as though he had no intention of talking about it. Finally, he nodded. "Pa loved horses. Had a special way with them. Reckon I got my love of horses from him."

"Did he tame them too?"

"Yep. Every farmer in southwestern Pennsylvania knew who to go to with an unruly horse. Wasn't a broke, wild, or obstinate horse he couldn't gentle."

She could just imagine Brody as a dark-haired, dark-eyed boy following his father around, watching and learning from him. "How did he die?"

"Heart attack. Healthy as ever one day. Gone the next."

"You must have missed him after he was gone."

Brody absently twisted a strand of her hair. "He liked to look at my drawings. Told me I had talent."

"He sounds like he was a very good man."

"Reckon there ain't many men keen on having a son who

draws in his spare time instead of doing something more productive. But not Pa."

Her heart warmed just thinking about Brody's father. Now she knew why each McQuaid man was good and kind. "I can see why you loved him. I love him, and I never even knew him."

Brody's lips twitched with the hint of a smile.

"Is that why you want to save the wild mustangs? For his sake? Because he loved them?"

"Maybe. Partly." Brody stared sightlessly at her blanket as though he'd disappeared to another time and place. After a moment he visibly shuddered. "Saw a lot of horses suffer in the war. Told myself if I ever made it out alive, I'd never let a horse suffer again."

It was her turn to shudder. "I can't imagine what you saw and experienced. It must have been horrible."

He nodded and started to rise, as though he intended to leave.

She rapidly changed the subject to a safer topic. "Tell me more about your father and your family. What was it like living on your farm in Pennsylvania?"

Brody settled himself back on the edge of the bed. And while she finished eating the biscuit, he shared about his father, the kind way he always treated their ma, the quality time he spent with all his children, the sacrifices he made for their family, and some of the most difficult horses he gentled.

As she ate the last crumb, contentment settled over her. Even if her stomach wasn't full, her soul was. She relaxed into the mattress but couldn't keep chills from racking her body.

His brow furrowed. "You're still cold?"

She tried not to shiver, but her limbs shook regardless of her efforts.

He peeled back the covers enough to see her lacy chemise. It still hadn't dried completely and was cold against her skin.

Concern flashed across his face. "You gotta get out of your . . ." He gave a pointed look at her chemise but then muttered and glanced away.

Feeling bare, she tugged the blankets back to her chin.

He stood and stuffed his hands into his pockets. His gaze darted to the window and door, as though he was seeking an escape. Then he stared down at his boots. "Can you take 'em off yourself? Or am I gonna have to do it?"

"Brody McQuaid, you'll do no such thing." She was sure her cheeks had turned a bright red.

"There's ways for me to do it without looking."

"I'll manage just fine without assistance."

"Then go on and get to it."

She wasn't about to bare herself around him, even under the covers. "You'll need to hand me my other garments. Please."

He stepped toward the clothing he'd draped across the benches and table to dry. As he picked up her bodice, he shook his head. "Still damp."

"What about something else from my bag?" Her haversack sat by the door next to his.

He dug through it and pulled out a couple of items. But even in the low light, it was clear everything was wet. Crossing his arms over his chest, he narrowed his eyes. "No way around it. You gotta take 'em off."

She glared back.

"Heaven help me, Savannah. I'm not gonna take advantage of you."

"I know that."

He huffed out a breath. "Then what?"

She honestly didn't know why she was embarrassed.

"If you're worried about saving your reputation, I reckon saving your life is more important." Standing with feet braced, his muscular form showed beneath his damp clothing. He was a mighty handsome man. Every part of him.

And that was the problem. She was too attracted to him. Being here in the cabin alone was just asking for trouble. But being alone *and* taking off her clothes?

She tried to release her grip on the blanket. She was making too much of the situation. After all, she had no energy for staying awake much less starting anything with Brody.

"Promise. You got nothin' to worry about with me."

Surely everything would be fine. She pushed aside her trepidation. "Alright. Turn around."

He did as she asked. And when his back was toward her, she wiggled and maneuvered under the covers until she divested herself of her drawers and chemise.

When she finished, she dropped the cold items to the floor and drew the covers around her tighter.

Somehow—likely from her stillness—he knew she was done and turned. He glanced from her discarded undergarments to the outline of her body under the blankets then back to the garments on the floor.

He palmed the back of his neck, blew out a breath, and crossed to the offending items. Gingerly, as if they were hot coals, he picked up first her chemise and draped it near the stove. Then he did the same with her underdrawers.

When he finished, he didn't look at her. Instead, he shrugged into his coat and yanked on his gloves. As he pressed on his hat, he stopped, one hand on the door. "Be back soon."

"Where are you going?" She hated that her voice was breathless and tinged with longing.

"Out." He tossed open the door and stepped through.

As the door closed heavily behind him, she held herself rigidly until a deep shudder racked her body.

He was right. They had to focus on surviving. That was the most important thing. And just because they were alone together didn't change the future and the obstacles standing between them.

CHAPTER
20

On the stool, Brody leaned against the log wall, trying to get comfortable. He'd tried every single which way and hadn't found any that would allow him some shut-eye.

His muscles burned from shoveling snow, and his legs were wobbly and weak from hiking and searching for animal tracks and any early root vegetables or even dandelions. But he hadn't found a thing.

Savannah thrashed and murmured in her sleep, and he sat forward, his body rigid and his shoulders tight. He didn't dare look in the direction of the bed. Hadn't dared since he'd returned from cooling off.

Thankfully she'd been asleep when he'd come back. Even so, he'd kept his gaze averted from her. It was already too easy to visualize how beautiful she was without lingering over her frame.

He bent forward, propped his elbows on his knees, and rested his head in his hands. He should've been more careful earlier, shouldn't have tugged her blanket down. But he hadn't realized how much he'd see of her chemise or how it would affect him.

And now he couldn't think of much else.

He pressed his palms into his eyes and rubbed. But he couldn't erase the image any more now than when he'd stormed from the cabin all ablaze.

Heaven help him. She was the prettiest woman he'd ever laid eyes on. He pulled in a deep breath and forced himself to visualize the areas he'd explored, the places he'd set traps, and the creek he'd staked for fish.

But his mind could only stay away from thoughts of Savannah for so long before it wandered right back. To the plain fact that she was lying an arm's length away and wasn't wearing a stitch of clothing.

Heat pumped into his veins again, and he hopped up so he wouldn't get scorched. But just as soon as he was standing, he was afraid of his feet carrying him to the bed, and he plopped himself down just as quickly.

He was mighty glad she wasn't watching him. No doubt he looked like a bear dancing 'round a beehive trying not to get stung, especially since he wore nothing but his under-drawers.

His damp clothing hadn't bothered him when he'd kept moving and busy. But inside the cabin after darkness had fallen, the temperature had dropped, and he started shivering. He'd been vigilant about adding fuel to the stove, and it was pumping heat into the little shack. Even so, he finally had to strip down and dry out the same way as Savannah.

His stomach rumbled with pangs of hunger, pangs that took him swiftly to the brink of his past, a past he loathed revisiting. Jumping up, he stalked to the stove and dipped the tin mug into the steaming pot. He forced himself to sip on the liquid, knowing it would provide some sustenance and buy him time.

He had to keep fighting. Couldn't give in to man's greatest enemy—despair. He'd watched too many of his companions fall prey to the killer of hope. And in almost every case, once that happened, it was only a short time later that death caught up with them.

Savannah shifted in her sleep. She was shaking again, and this time her teeth were chattering.

He frowned and dipped the mug back into the pot of melted snow. He filled it and took it to her. As he pressed a hand to her cheek to awaken her, he was surprised at how icy her skin still felt.

He checked her forehead, then neck. Even without her damp underclothes, she wasn't heating up. And her pulse was sluggish.

Frustration pooled inside. She wasn't recovering. If anything, she was getting worse.

He lifted her. "Hey, darlin'. Drink this."

Her head lolled to one side.

He shook her gently. "Wake up, Savannah."

She didn't respond.

His heartbeat kicked into a gallop. Was she unconscious? He lowered her and shook her harder. "Savannah?"

He didn't want to think on December of 1862 and his first battle of the war. But the bodies of the dead and wounded on the slope beneath Marye's Heights at Fredericksburg flashed into his mind. The bitter cold had killed too many.

He had to do more to warm her up. The only thing left

was to give her his body heat. This was no time to worry about propriety. Her life was at stake. And he needed to do whatever he could to save her.

He shoved additional wood into the stove, hoping it would pour out the warmth. Then he climbed in beside her. He hesitated, then peeled away all but one blanket, which he made sure was wrapped securely around her. While he suspected skin-to-skin transfer would be the best, he couldn't make himself do it, especially after how hesitant she'd been to take off her wet undergarments.

He positioned himself between her and the wall. Maybe he could act as a buffer from the air that managed to get in between the cracks. He pulled all the covers over them and wrapped his arms around her, gathering her as close as he possibly could.

She trembled even in her unconsciousness. Frantically, he rubbed her arms and then her legs and back. The blanket caused the friction he wanted. All the while, he pressed against her, desperate to give her his heat. He only stopped to add more fuel to the stove, keeping it blazing.

At some point, his own exhaustion overcame him. He held her, wrapped securely in the crook of his body, alternating between dozing and rubbing her, praying like he never had before that if someone had to die, this time it would be him.

⁂

The sound of a cough brought him out of his slumber—the kind of half-sleeping, half-wakefulness he'd perfected over recent years, where he was safe from having to relive the memories of the war that came too vividly to life in his dreams.

He started massaging Savannah's arms again, his hands moving with the same steady rhythm he'd used for the past hours.

She released another soft cough and then a sigh.

Was she waking up?

His pulse spurted. "Savannah?"

"Hmmm . . ." Her response was sluggish, but it was something.

"You getting warm?"

This time she snuggled in against him, her back pressed to his chest. "Um-hmm."

She was conscious. He fought back a wave of relief.

"Brody." Her voice slurred, almost as if she were drunk. "I like this."

"Like what, darlin'?" He continued to rub her arms.

She lifted a hand through the slit in her blanket and stroked his arm back. "This closeness to you. Can we stay here like this forever?"

He paused. Did she know what she was saying? Or was she mumbling in her sleep? He'd witnessed men whose brains turned sluggish from prolonged exposure to the cold. They often said and did strange things while they were suffering.

"Please, Brody." She curled into him, her body fitting against his like it was made to go there. "Can we live here?"

He wasn't sure how to answer and figured the best way was to go along with her, just like he'd had to do with some of his friends who'd been so far gone they'd hallucinated.

He pressed a kiss into her long silky hair. "Reckon we can, darlin', if that's what you want."

She released what seemed like a contented sigh. "You're

very good to me, Brody. No one else loves me like you do, you know that?"

Yep. He was well aware of how much he loved her. But how had she recognized his love? He hadn't spelled it out for her yet. Hadn't wanted to pressure her or scare her away. Figured she was skittish like a wild filly needing a little more gentlin' before being ready to fully trust him.

"And you know what else?" Her voice was definitely slurred. She wasn't back to normal. But at least she was conscious.

"What?"

She hugged her arms over his and tilted her head toward him. "The truth is that I love you too."

He froze. Oh, heaven help him. Was she telling the truth? Or was it the blamed delirium doing the talking?

Part of him wanted to twist her around so he could kiss her and leave no doubt to either of them that this was real.

But this wasn't the time or place to kiss. Not with her still suffering. Not with her still half-asleep. He'd told her she had nothing to worry about from him. Vowed he'd do the right thing. And he aimed to make sure that happened, no matter how enticing this situation was.

He shifted her face gently down, hiding the temptation to kiss her, and settled her into a comfortable position.

She relaxed into him, her breathing growing even. Her skin was warmer and her pulse stronger. He could sense she'd fallen asleep, and that her body was making it through the worst of the ailment.

Closing his eyes, he kissed the back of her head again, long and hard. Yep. He loved her. Trouble was, it was scary just how much.

CHAPTER

21

The heaviness in Savannah's chest and the burning in her throat prodded her awake. Her body ached, and her stomach gurgled uncomfortably. But blissful warmth coursed through her. The cold in her bones was gone.

She wiggled her toes to find they were warm again, along with the rest of her body. Somehow, she'd finally been able to thaw. Thank the Almighty. She'd been afraid she'd never feel normal again.

She released a relieved sigh.

Immediately, arms tightened around her. Steady breathing filled the crook of her neck. And she was aware of a cheek almost flush against hers.

Brody.

Her eyes flew open. The darkness of the shuttered cabin was broken by the light of flames in the stove as well as cracks in the boards covering the window. Even though shadows shrouded them, she didn't need light to know they were wedged together in the bed big enough for only one person.

A new heat shimmied through her. She was lying in bed with Brody, his chest pressed against her back. What if someone—like the cabin's owner—arrived, threw open the door, and discovered them together?

She shifted, needing to put some distance between herself and this man who was entirely too attractive in ways she couldn't even begin to describe.

At her movement, his hands against her stomach drew her toward him more securely. The long length of his fingers splayed across her ribs almost possessively. He wasn't touching her directly. A coarse woolen blanket covered her skin. Her bare skin.

Mentally she took in her state of undress beneath the blanket, and a flush worked through her. Her predicament was more indecent than she'd realized.

His fingers skimmed up her arms, sending tingles along her nerve endings. He rubbed her lightly, absently, clearly not fully awake.

She rolled to her back, and this time, she realized he was bare, too, except for underdrawers.

Mortification swept through her. She started to push away, but at his weary sigh in her ear, she stopped. She knew without his explanation that the only reason he'd climbed in next to her was because she hadn't been warming up on her own. By drawing her close and transferring his body heat, he'd helped her.

That's all it was. Help.

But now that she was warm, she had to get up, move away.

Carefully, she attempted to extricate herself. But then, half facing him, she stopped.

Yes, all he'd done was help her. If she told him she was fine, he'd scramble out of bed and put proper distance between them. But from the even rise and fall of his breathing, she was reluctant to wake him. She didn't know how much time had passed since he'd fallen asleep, but he likely hadn't slept often or long.

Her gaze fell to his chest, to the puckered ridge of a scar near his collarbone. Before she could stop herself, she traced the jagged flesh. A painful ache formed in her throat along with the need to bring him comfort. As she came to the end, her fingers brushed a second raised welt, this one more terrible than the first. She pressed her hand against it only to feel another one a short distance away.

Was his entire body riddled with scars? From the war?

His breathing quickened, and even without his moving, she could sense he was awake. Did he dislike her touching his scars? Would he protest?

She let her fingers glide to the next uneven ridge.

His muscles stiffened against her, but he didn't pull away.

"How did you get this one?" she whispered.

He was silent so long she wasn't sure he would answer. Finally, he whispered one word. "Fredericksburg."

She skimmed it again. She'd been so far removed from the war that she hadn't paid too much attention to the specific encounters. They'd gotten the news long after each battle was over. Even so, she'd heard enough to know Fredericksburg had been a horrible loss for the Union.

Did she dare press him to talk about it more? Was he ready to confront additional demons of the past? Lightly, almost reverently, she let her fingers linger over the old wound. "Were you shot?"

Again, he didn't respond right away. She didn't move and didn't say anything, just waited patiently.

"It was from a bayonet." His voice dropped to a ragged whisper. "We pierced the right wing. Got closer to the grey-backs than other regiments . . ."

She tried to picture what a battle would have been like from his perspective and the horrors he'd witnessed.

"Killed a man there for the first time." The raw anguish in his tone told her exactly how he'd felt about having to take a life. "Didn't want to do it. But when he stuck his bayonet into me, reckoned I had to defend myself."

She closed her eyes to block out the image of Brody killing someone. If it was hard for her to envision him taking a life, she could only guess how difficult it was for him to think back on what he'd had to do in the name of war.

He shuddered.

Surely, he had to know he wasn't at fault for his participation in the war and the killing. "You aren't defined by your past, Brody."

He held himself rigidly.

She had the urge to bend down and kiss this wound, along with all the others, and show him they weren't ugly to her. "You no longer have to be condemned by your scars. God can redeem anything. Whenever you look at or feel your battle wounds, instead of seeing all the ways you failed, you can see the strength you've gained through the hardships and realize wounds might shape us, but they can't determine who we are."

After a moment, he seemed to relax again. The silence inside the cabin was broken by a crackle of a log in the stove.

"You warmed up?" The question rumbled near her ear and sent a delicious shiver through her, one very different from the others that had racked her body recently. This one was filled with awareness of him, of his scruffy jaw brushing her cheek, of his warm exhalations against her neck.

"I'm much better."

As he situated himself, his legs and chest brushed up against her. His very masculine physique. Too close. Too tempting.

Now that she was stabilized, they needed to extricate themselves from the impropriety of their situation. She gingerly lifted her hands from his chest but didn't know where to put them.

Maybe she should get out of the bed first. As she moved, the blanket surrounding her body loosened, and she quickly grasped it to keep it closed.

He hesitated, but only an instant, before he pushed himself up, letting the covers fall away. "Need to go clear more grass for the horses." He crawled off and stood in the open space between the bed and stove.

The moment he was no longer beside her, the bed felt empty and too big.

He swiped up his shirt and kept his back to her, giving her full view of the patchwork of battle scars, just as battered as the front. As he tugged on his shirt, she could only think of Hades, how the scars made the stallion even more magnificent.

Brody didn't bother buttoning his shirt before he reached for his trousers. As he stuffed the first leg in, he cast her a glance over his shoulder. Something in his eyes smoldered and lit a spark of heat inside her belly.

He didn't look at her long and dropped his attention to his dressing. "Recollect anything you said to me?"

She thought back to the restless sleeping and waking, but the hours were blurry, filled only with images of shivering and trying to get warm.

He stabbed his other leg inside his trousers.

"Did I say something memorable?"

"Yep. It was memorable alright."

She cringed. Had she inadvertently told him how much she liked kissing him? "What was it?"

He pulled up his trousers and began to strap his suspenders over his shoulders. Watching him dress like this wasn't appropriate for a young woman. Not in the least. And yet, she couldn't tear her gaze away.

"You were talking about us. . . ."

"Oh no." She rose to her elbow. "I said something embarrassing, didn't I?"

"You don't remember?"

Once more, she tried to recall everything that had happened, but she'd been so cold she was sure it had affected her ability to think. "You'll just have to forget whatever it was. I'm sure it wasn't true."

He sat down on the bench and pulled on his socks and then stuffed his feet into his boots. As he rose and put on his coat, he looked at her sideways but then rapidly turned his back toward her. "I won't be forgetting it anytime soon."

She sighed. She wanted to pester him to tell her, but at the same time she was afraid of what he might reveal.

He swiped up his gloves and didn't bother to put them on or fasten his coat before he opened the door, almost as though he couldn't leave her fast enough. Halfway out, he paused. "I ain't no saint. Reckon you best get your clothing on soon as you can manage."

The words barely left his mouth before he closed the door, leaving only a cold draft of air in his wake.

What had just happened? She stared at the door for a moment, then glanced at herself only to find that her blanket had slipped down. One of her shoulders and part of her upper arm were exposed. Not an indecent amount, but certainly more than she should be revealing to Brody.

No wonder he'd raced to get out of the cabin.

A mixture of embarrassment and strange longing swirled inside, the longing to have him back in bed beside her where they could lie together and talk and hold each other. It was a wanton thought.

His words, *"I ain't no saint,"* rumbled through her. The truth was, she wasn't a saint either. And now that she was feeling better, she had to act like a lady.

As she pushed up, dragging the blanket around her, a wave of dizziness and weakness washed over her, nearly capsizing her and sending her back down. She fought against it and forced her legs over the edge of the bed. She had to get stronger because they couldn't stay in this secluded gulch for much longer, not without food.

She stood, feeling lightheaded. She grasped the table to keep from buckling. The ache in her chest pressed uncomfortably. But she managed to shuffle to her garments, which were stiff and dry.

By the time she finished putting everything back on, her

breathing was labored, and a low burning had flamed in her chest. A cough pushed up into her throat, but she stifled it. It was nothing.

Somehow, she made it back to bed, covered herself, and pretended she was fine.

CHAPTER

22

Savannah's deep, hacking cough penetrated the log walls and rattled Brody's bones. He paused in feeding Molasses in the lean-to and balled his fists. Every time he listened to Savannah, his frustration and anxiety mounted, making him mad enough to tear a bite out of an ax.

He'd hoped she'd passed through the worst of the troubles. But after four days of being stranded in the cabin by snow and cold temperatures, her condition was getting real bad. Though she muffled her cough whenever he was inside, she released the pent-up coughing every time he stepped out. And tonight was the worst yet.

In the falling darkness, he offered a last handful of hay to Molasses, from what was left of the mattress. Savannah had been the one to suggest using the hay after she'd questioned him whether the horses were getting enough. He hadn't admitted how hard shoveling the snow was, especially in his weakening condition, but she must have guessed.

Molasses snorted her thanks, releasing a cloudy white puff into the coldness of the oncoming night.

"You're welcome." He brushed a gloved hand over the mare's fine black coat. Then he gave his horse a last handful before twisting closed the muslin mattress cover. There wasn't much hay left, but he had to stretch it out for as long as possible so that when the snow started to melt, the horses would have enough strength to make it off the mountain.

After checking the perimeter of the cabin, he made his way toward the door. The darkening sky overhead was clear and studded with thousands of stars. The beauty of it was stunning. If only their situation wasn't so blamed dire, he might have been able to stop and appreciate it.

As it was, he dreaded having to go in and tell Savannah the traps had been empty, and they still had no food. She never once complained. Never once hinted she was hungry. But with his own stomach and body wrestling like two bobcats in a gunnysack, he knew well enough that the hunger pangs were hard on her. He just prayed Ivy and Dylan weren't going through this same suffering somewhere else.

He'd hoped by now the temperatures would rise, at least during the daytime, to begin melting the snow. From what he calculated, at least three feet had fallen. With how wet it was, along with the layer of ice underneath, the horses wouldn't be able to travel in such deep drifts. They would sink down and get stuck. Some of the accumulation had to go down before they could leave—at least by horse.

More than once, he'd considered hiking out by foot. But with just one pair of snowshoes, the going would be tough, if not impossible. Their only hope was that they'd get a warm spell, and that the snow would melt off real quick. It could happen. Happened all the time in the lower elevation around the ranch. They'd get snow one day, and the next it'd be gone. But here . . .

He glanced at the shadows caused by the rocky ledges of the ravine on both sides, the dark pine trees still wearing their crystal ice covering, their boughs weighed down, some having broken off completely. This was the wilderness, and there was no predicting what might happen in a place of such untamed beauty.

He kicked the wet snow from his boots against the doorjamb and tried to expel his frustration. The last thing he wanted was to worry Savannah. As it was, she'd been as sweet as a maple-sugar cake, doing her best to help him pass the time and taking his mind off their difficulties.

She'd asked him to find her supplies and had rigged up a checkerboard, using black and white stones he collected from the creek bottom. She'd introduced him to the art of telling tall tales and had convinced him to spin his own yarns. At other times, she watched him sketch and once tried a picture of her own under his guidance.

Through it all, somehow she managed to get him to share more about his childhood, about his pa and ma, those years when everything had been perfect and life had been good. When he asked her about her past, she easily opened up and told him about growing up on her family's Georgia plantation, how one of her uncles had fostered her love of animals, and how excited she'd been when they'd moved to Colorado Territory and her father had taken up ranching. She'd spent the past seven years learning everything she could about animals, not only from the cowhands but from the veterinarian her father had hired on.

Even if Brody figured he had the talent of saying a whole lot in mighty few words, he still found himself enjoying their conversations. And whenever his hankerings turned his thoughts toward pulling her into his arms and holding her again, he put on his coat and went outside to cool off.

Though he bedded down on the floor next to the stove, keeping as much distance from her as he could, he'd still had to step out of the cabin twice last night to get his mind on other things. He'd told her right—he wasn't a saint by any long shot. Couldn't take many more nights of wrangling himself back. Another reason he needed the sun to melt away the snow. He was afraid of losing control.

As he swung open the door, she stopped coughing. From her spot in the center of the box bed, now empty except for the blankets, her face was flushed, her hair tousled, and her eyes welcoming. Too welcoming. All he wanted to do was stalk across to the bed, bend down, and kiss her.

He pivoted and took his time closing the door, lowering the bolt, and shedding his coat. She started to say something but then couldn't hold in her coughing. She buried the sound in the crook of her arm, but it was harsh and heavy and uncontainable.

The anxiety he'd been holding at a standstill advanced through his chest like an army on the attack. He crossed to the pot of melted snow he kept on the stovetop. "Your cough sounds worse."

She managed a nod through the hacking.

He dipped the tin cup into the hot water and approached her. As he sat down on the edge of the bed frame, he waited for her to bring it under control. But she couldn't stop and was running short on air.

With a growl of frustration, he scooped her up and carried her to the pot on the stove, white clouds rising into the air. Vesta had used steam one time when Flora had been suffering from a cough, and the hot air had helped his little niece breathe. He could only pray it would help Savannah now.

He held her as close as he could.

Her expression was taut with pain. And panic.

"Breathe in the steam, darlin'."

Leaning into the rising mist, she let the hot air hit her face. After several long minutes, her coughing subsided. As it did, she laid her head against his shoulder. Wisps of hair stuck to her forehead, and red stained her cheeks.

"I'm not doing so well, Brody." Her whisper was raspy.

"Shh. You're doin' fine now." He didn't budge from the pot. Figured he'd hold her there all night if he had to.

She didn't move either. Just lay listlessly. "I've got pneumonia."

The mention of the word caused the army of anxiety inside him to re-form their lines for another charge. "You don't know. Could be better now."

"I know, Brody. I've been on enough house calls to treat cattle for it. I have all the symptoms of pulmonary edema, a fluid buildup between the layers of my lungs and chest cavity."

Half her words made no sense. But he did know pneumonia was deadly. At least it had been in the army camp. "What can I do to help you get better?"

"I have to keep breathing."

He nodded. He'd do everything he could to help her breathe, even if he had to give her his own air.

The night dragged on. He fed the fire, boiling melted snow

nonstop. Every time she had one of her coughing spells, he held her above the steam until her breathing steadied again.

Even so, she was deteriorating. Not only had her cough worsened, but she'd developed a fever. Whenever he wasn't helping her breathe, he was bathing her face with cold compresses.

By the time first light crept through the cracks in the window and door, he'd made up his mind. He needed to get her back to civilization and a doctor. If they stayed another night, he suspected she wouldn't make it. No matter how difficult the trek would be, they had to leave.

⁂

He fashioned a litter of two long branches, the way he'd witnessed the Utes construct theirs, attaching the canvas to the poles and making a projection at one end to keep her from sliding off. With the snow, he intended to drag the canvas like a sled. Once he reached the lower elevations and the snow melted, he'd have more difficulty and would have to figure out something else.

He tended to the horses one last time, then untied and set them free. He hoped they'd find enough to eat and eventually make their way down into lower elevations, but there were no guarantees.

Savannah wouldn't want to leave Molasses behind, but she'd grown lethargic, hardly paying attention to what he was doing. Even if she'd known, she was too weak to protest.

As he carried her out into the sunshine, she didn't stir. Bundled in all the blankets and situated on the litter, she opened her eyes. They were glassy with fever, but she smiled at him anyway. "It's a beautiful day, isn't it?"

He wanted to shout at her that no, it wasn't. That it was awful. That he was angry and frustrated and nearing the end of himself. But he managed a nod.

Using a blank page from his sketch pad, he penciled a note to the owner, promising reimbursement for all the supplies he'd used, including the snowshoes, then he closed up.

As he strapped on his snowshoes, she roused again. "Thank you for taking such good care of me, Brody."

"Hush now. Save your strength."

As he straightened and hefted the litter poles, he had the sudden need to tell her he loved her. Was afraid he might not get another chance. But just as soon as the fear wafted through him, he angrily started forward.

He wasn't losing Savannah today.

He was aiming to get her out of the mountains and close enough to civilization that he could send someone for a doctor.

Besides, she hadn't remembered declaring her love to him. For all he knew, she hadn't meant it. The delirium she'd experienced from the coldness might have confused her.

Whatever the case, he started down the ravine, following the creek and going as fast as the conditions would allow. Even though the snow made the pulling easy, he was weak from lack of food and was soon winded and tired. But he pushed onward. He wasn't sure where the stream ended, but like most creeks and rivers, it formed a natural road that would probably take him into the foothills.

He stopped frequently to check on Savannah. But she slept most of the way, waking occasionally with a coughing spell. He was grateful for the mostly easy terrain, likely cut back by the miner who owned the cabin. Only a time or two did Brody have to heft a fallen branch or log out of the way.

Regardless, he feared he wouldn't make it out of the higher elevation by nightfall. He wanted to be low enough that they wouldn't have to worry about freezing temperatures when they made camp and low enough that he could hunt for wild game.

By midafternoon, he had no choice but to stop when one of Savannah's coughing fits got the better of her. After scrounging for dry wood, he started a fire and soon had water boiling in the pot he'd taken from the cabin. He lifted her onto his lap, placed the pot near her head, and formed a tent from a blanket to trap the steaming air.

After she was breathing evenly, she tossed aside the blanket, wrapped an arm around his neck, and rested her head in the crook of his chin and chest.

The worry that had been warring within pummeled him again. He wanted to get going, hated wasting time, but he didn't want to push her.

As the smoke from the fire rose through the haze of sunshine, he found himself back on the battlefield. His inhalations quickened as the gun smoke began to choke him. His shoulder wound radiated pain down his arm.

Gunshots and cannon blasts boomed in the distance. Faint. Far away. But the cries of the wounded rose around him. Closing his eyes tight, he gritted his teeth, the urgency of all those lying on the battlefield prodding him. Somehow, he had to pick himself up and drag them to safety.

Didn't they know he was injured too? Couldn't they see he was as trapped as they were in the carnage?

"Brody?" Gentle fingers stroked his cheek.

His heart thudded so hard it hurt his chest.

The fingers continued caressing his face. "Are you thinking of the war again?"

He blinked, trying to see through the haze.

Savannah was watching him, concern radiating in her glassy eyes. "I think you were back on the battlefield for a minute."

His mouth was dry with fear and his body stiff, but he managed a nod.

"Which battle this time?"

"Gettysburg."

She removed his hat and combed her fingers through his hair, as if she had every right to do so. As far as he was concerned, she *did* have every right. She could do whatever she wanted, whenever she wanted.

"The smoke and the sunshine." He glanced the opposite direction down the creek away from the rising steam. "Guess it triggered something inside."

"What did you see?" The tenderness in her voice beckoned him to unburden himself. After the pieces he'd already shared with her, the idea of telling her a little more didn't seem quite so daunting or impossible.

"The smoke was thick as fog." Her fingers in his hair felt so good. He let it drive the worry from his shoulders and loosen his tongue. "I reckoned I could use the smoke as a cover to crawl off the hillside and get to safety."

"Did it work?" Her innocent question was filled with such kindness, emotion swelled to clog his throat.

He choked it down. "Zach and Jesse were alive but torn up so bad they couldn't move. Figured I could somehow sneak 'em both out of there."

She kept combing his hair.

"I tried." He'd spent hours but could barely move them a few feet behind a boulder. He wanted to blame his failure on the hot sun, dehydration, the loss of blood, the pain coursing through him from his wound. But the fact was, he'd been scared. "Stayed with 'em all day."

She stroked his cheek and chin, her gaze full of compassion.

"When darkness fell, I left." He loathed himself all over again for his failure to move them and for his cowardice in leaving them behind. "Told 'em I'd be back with help. But when I reached the closest regiment, I passed out. By the time I woke up in the hospital, it was too late."

He'd been frantic and had crawled out of bed, intent on returning to rescue Zach and Jesse. He only made it two steps before he collapsed. His best friend, Newt, had been at his bedside and promised to do what he could. But when they found the fellas where Brody had indicated, they were both dead.

"They're gone because of me."

"No, Brody. You can't blame yourself."

"If I'd tried harder . . ."

"You did what you could. And sometimes that has to be enough."

He wished he could believe her, but the guilt was too heavy to shake off.

She pressed a kiss to his cheek.

He relished the sweetness of it, knew she meant nothing other than offering him comfort. Even so, it stirred up the longing that had been building all week. The keenness of his desire swirled faster. His muscles tightened.

Heaven help him. He wanted more than anything to kiss her.

He couldn't—wouldn't. Not when she was sick. Even so, as she shifted back, he angled in and grazed her neck.

At the touch, she gasped.

The soft sound fueled him, and he dropped another kiss, this one lower, a kiss that contained his gratefulness for her compassion and understanding and kindness. Whether she realized it or not, she was helping him find solid ground after so many years of floundering. She was bringing him life, giving him purpose, and making him want to be a better man.

"Brody . . ." Her voice contained a question. Both of her hands moved into his hair, digging in and weaving through the strands, locking him in place.

He needed no other permission to kiss her neck once more, gently brushing the soft skin by her collarbone. He wanted her to know how much he cared about her. Maybe she'd remember telling him she loved him. Maybe she'd say it again.

"Savannah?" A man's voice broke through Brody's haze.

Her eyes flew open, filled with confusion.

Brody sat up. Riding toward them was a gentleman on a powerful roan gelding at least seventeen hands tall. The fellow's face was lined with worry. But as he took in Savannah's position on Brody's lap, her hands in his hair, and his splayed around her, something flared in his eyes.

Savannah dropped her hold as quickly as if she'd been caught stealing. "Chandler? What are you doing here?"

CHAPTER

23

Savannah blinked, expecting her vision of Chandler to disappear. Surely she was hallucinating. But he was still there, guiding his mount through the snow alongside the creek toward Brody and her. He was riding his favorite horse and had on his tan-colored hat with the braided leather hatband. His trimmed auburn beard showed above his neckerchief. And his serious hazel eyes were fixed on her.

Chandler really was here. She wasn't seeing things.

Brody stood, lifting her and cradling her against his chest. She needed to insist on him putting her down, needed to gain some distance between them, needed to pretend she hadn't just been relishing his soft kisses on her neck.

But from the frown marring Chandler's features and the dark slant of his brows, she guessed pretending wouldn't do any good. Chandler had witnessed the exchange and hadn't liked it.

He didn't say anything, but each jolt of his horse practically shouted his anger. Brody didn't speak either. Just waited, drawing her in more closely, almost possessively.

"Savannah, are you alright?" Chandler took in her appearance. No doubt she was bedraggled from a week without grooming. In addition, her face felt flushed and overheated. From Brody's kisses or her fever?

"I'm alright." She tried to keep her voice from cracking, but it did anyway. "What are you doing here?"

"We have search parties out looking for you and have been combing up and down this range. Saw the smoke of a campfire and came to investigate." He nodded toward the fire Brody had used for boiling water.

Chandler's appearance meant only one thing. He'd come to South Park to get her, had likely arrived sometime after she'd left with Brody.

"Your daddy's been worried sick about you." Chandler reined in beside them, his gaze pinned upon Brody, radiating with coldness.

She'd never witnessed him being anything other than kind, and she wasn't sure what to make of his demeanor. "I didn't mean to worry you or Daddy. Did he ride along up here?"

"Yes, he's searching farther north. He's hardly rested since he heard you were kidnapped."

"Kidnapped?" At the same time she spoke the word, Brody tensed and his expression hardened. "You're mistaken, Chandler—"

"Brody McQuaid?" Chandler jumped down from his horse, his focus on Brody.

Brody braced his feet. "Yep."

Chandler jerked his revolver out of his holster and jammed it against Brody's head.

"Chandler! No!" Her cry tore from her raw throat.

But Chandler was leaning in, the muscles in his jaw flexing at the same time he fingered the trigger.

"Brody didn't kidnap me. He saved my life."

Chandler and Brody had locked gazes, and she doubted Chandler heard a word of what she'd just said. Down the gulch, she caught a glimpse of more horses and riders making their way up the creek. She hoped one of them was Daddy, who could talk some reason into Chandler. At the very least, she hoped they'd hurry before Chandler hurt Brody.

"You have my woman, McQuaid." Chandler's tone was deadly. "Give her back."

"Chandler, please." She could feel the tingle of a cough working its way up her throat.

Brody's grip only tightened around her. His expression was unreadable, but his dark eyes filled with mocking as he stared at Chandler. "Reckon if she was yours, she wouldn't have felt the need to run into my arms."

Chandler rammed the barrel against Brody again and clicked the hammer.

She tried to scream, but her coughing spilled out instead and racked her body.

Immediately, Chandler lowered the gun and focused on her, his brow furrowing. "What's wrong?"

"She's got pneumonia." Brody answered for her. "Needs a doctor in a bad way."

Chandler's frown deepened. "How sick is she?"

"Getting worse by the day."

Even though Brody had done all he could, she could tell her condition was deteriorating. He'd been wise to construct the makeshift sled and drag her down from the cabin.

The past hours of hiking and hauling hadn't been easy on him. His face had grown strained. His steps had wavered a time or two. And his pace had slowed. But he'd clearly seen the urgency of getting her help before it was too late.

She ought to be glad Chandler had shown up. Now Brody didn't have to work so hard to save her, and soon they'd be warm and well fed.

But Chandler's appearance wasn't assuring her. Instead, it was filling her with apprehension.

"Looks like I found you just in time." Chandler's gaze turned tender upon her, filled with the same care and love she'd seen so often over the past several years. He truly was a good man, and she couldn't forget that.

Chandler lifted a hand as though he might caress her cheek, but he tipped up the brim of his hat instead. He was too much of a gentleman to touch her, not without her permission. Brody, on the other hand, didn't need anybody's permission but his own, not even to leave a trail of kisses down her neck.

Chandler's jaw flexed as though he was thinking about those kisses too. Then with strong, confident steps, he crossed to his horse and mounted. "Hand Savannah up to me." His order to Brody held the hint of a challenge.

Brody didn't move.

"You've done enough damage." Chandler's gelding shied sideways, sensing the tension. "It's time to give her over to the people who can take care of her the way she needs."

"Brody's been kind," she managed between coughs. "He saved my life."

Brody still didn't budge.

Chandler grabbed up his reins and jerked on them, bringing

the gelding into submission. "Come on now, McQuaid. You need to let me take her directly to the closest doctor."

Her coughing abated, but her breathing was shallow. A part of her wanted to ask Chandler to give his horse over to Brody and she'd ride with him. But she couldn't be so cruel to Chandler, not after his efforts at searching for them and coming to their rescue. Besides, she was suddenly too dizzy and weak to protest anything. She just wanted to close her eyes and sleep.

When Brody started toward Chandler, she clung to him a little tighter. Even if the conditions had been difficult over the past days, she couldn't deny the bond she'd developed with Brody. It was a beautiful bond born out of desperation and survival. And a part of her was sad to see their time together end.

As Brody stopped beside Chandler, he hesitated. She guessed he was feeling that same tug of sadness. She had the urge to comb her fingers through his hair one last time, but with Chandler staring down at them, she tried for a smile instead. "I'll see you again soon."

"Just get better, y'hear?"

"I will."

His dark gaze took her in with the kind of look he used when he was memorizing something and storing it away for sketching later.

Brody lifted her up, and Chandler took her gently, then settled her into the saddle sideways in front of him and tucked her blankets around her. "There. Are you comfortable, my dear?"

She nodded and shifted, wanting a final good-bye with Brody. But before she could say anything more, Chandler spurred his horse forward, pushing it through the snow. Within a dozen paces, he pivoted, pulled out his revolver, and pointed it in Brody's direction.

She released a cry and batted at his arm. He raised the gun up out of reach. "Chandler, you can't hurt Brody!" Her voice was raspy but loud and anguished enough that he halted.

"Please. He's a good man."

"He kidnapped and molested you." Chandler's eyes sparked with wrath. "He deserves to die."

"No! You have no idea what you're talking about!"

"I saw him molesting you with my own two eyes."

"He was doing no such thing." *Oh my.* Of course Brody hadn't been molesting her. She'd been a willing participant. Before she could figure out an explanation, three other men on horseback reined in a few paces away. She scanned them. Daddy wasn't there. The newcomers were cowhands from the Double L, Chandler's closest friends. They'd do whatever he asked them to.

Chandler tilted his head in Brody's direction. "Don't let him get away."

Chandler didn't wait for his men to respond. Instead, he pivoted to face Brody. "I will see you brought to justice. One way or another I intend to make you pay for your crimes."

"Stop, Chandler. Brody's innocent. I vow it." Her reprimand was lost in the flurry of his spurring his horse onward and a fresh fit of coughing. At the jarring of the ride, she clung to Chandler as best she could. But she was too weak and tired and within moments fell into the blackness of oblivion.

CHAPTER
24

Brody's muscles ached with the need to punch something. He'd held back from hauling off into Chandler's face. But inside he was blistering Chandler's hide with words hot enough to melt the snow off peaks for miles around.

The fella was so arrogant he'd probably gotten his calluses from patting his own back. It was too bad Savannah couldn't see it for herself. Yep, Brody understood—and even liked—that she always looked for the good in people. But in this case, she needed to start seeing the truth about the Double L's manager.

At least Savannah would get to the doctor faster. Brody was grateful for that even if he'd had to hand her over to the last person on earth he'd wanted to.

The three men in Chandler's search party drew nearer. The way they were eyeing him and clutching their six-shooters set him on edge. His own revolver was holstered at his belt. But the day he'd walked away from the war was the day he'd vowed never to end another man's life.

Hadn't stopped him from taking out his wrath with his fists. But he'd never once used his gun. Didn't plan to now, even when Chandler had threatened him with his.

Instead, Brody spread his feet and fisted his hands.

The man in the lead halted and pointed his revolver at Brody. "Best come along nice and easy so no one gets hurt."

In their long waterproof slickers and felt hats, they had the weatherworn look of typical cowhands. They weren't overly menacing, and Brody figured in a fistfight he'd be able to knock 'em right down. But he didn't have the strength today, not after near to a week without any food. He was spent. All he wanted was a way off the mountain and some grub to fill his belly.

He stood unmoving as the first fella dismounted and inched his way forward. The other two did the same thing. When they reached him and grabbed his arms, he didn't resist.

They bound his hands in front of him, keeping a line long enough that they could guide him as they remounted. But as they started back down, dragging him along behind, they realized soon enough how weak he was. Even though he did his best to keep hold of his pride and hike behind them, he stumbled and fell too many times. Eventually the leader of the three gave him the mount and walked alongside.

Exhausted, Brody dozed the rest of the way. When darkness started to fall, they reached a campsite with a few tents and a blazing fire. The snow had already melted in the lower elevation. All that remained were soggy splotches in areas the sun didn't reach. The scent of roasting game filled the air and set his stomach to rumbling worse than a skinny hound growling after a bone.

He scanned the faces for Savannah. But there was no sight

of her or Chandler. After listening to the conversation, he learned Chandler, Sawyer Marshall, and several others had hurried on with Savannah, intending to make it to Fairplay by the night's end. They'd sent a rider ahead to fetch the doctor so he'd be waiting when they arrived.

Those left behind had apparently been tasked with bringing him in. For kidnapping Savannah.

He'd decided to let them think what they would. Chandler could trump up all the charges he wanted, but the fact was, Brody hadn't kidnapped Savannah, and she'd make sure everyone knew it. In the meantime, all that mattered was getting her to the doc.

They didn't give him much grub, but he'd learned after Andersonville that a starving man had to go slow, that a stomach deprived of food for too long was finicky. He asked after Ivy and Dylan, hoping to get news of their whereabouts and whether they'd made it out of the storm, but the cowhands only shrugged, not knowing or caring.

At dawn as they broke camp, he was rested and eager to go. This time when they made him walk, he had more strength. The lower they hiked, the warmer it got, until finally the snow was completely gone, making the way easy.

Still, it took most of the day to reach Fairplay. By the time they arrived at the outskirts of town, he was tired and weak again. More than anything, his anxiety had a stranglehold around his neck. He could hardly breathe with his need to find out how Savannah was doing and prayed the doctor had been able to help her.

"Brody!" A shout from Main Street drew his attention.

Ivy hopped off a hitching post and ran toward him, her hat flapping against her back.

His chest constricted. Thank the Almighty she was safe. He scanned the area for Dylan, but the kid was nowhere around. Wyatt and Flynn, along with a number of Healing Springs ranch hands, were congregated together with townspeople Brody recognized: Mr. Steele and his son, Logan; Father Zieber, the Methodist minister; Mr. Fehling, the proprietor of Hotel Windsor; and other family friends.

Ivy sped toward him, her feet pounding the road, her arms outstretched. When she met him, she threw herself at him. "Oh, Brody! We thought for sure you and Savannah got buried in snow and died."

He would've hugged her back if his hands hadn't been bound. As it was, the fella who'd been towing him along had enough decency to stop and let him talk to Ivy. As she pulled away, she swiped at the tears streaking her cheeks.

He dragged in a breath of relief that as far as he could tell, she was fine. "Was hoping you and Dylan made it out in time."

"The minute we saw the snow clouds rolling in, we high-tailed it down the mountain. Figured you'd seen the storm a-comin', too, and were right on our trail."

He'd already beaten himself up enough for not paying better attention. And even though he took all the blame for getting trapped in the snowstorm, a part of him knew that even if they'd left at the first sign of snowflakes, they still wouldn't have made it down. They'd been too far up, and the storm had come on too fast.

Ivy brushed at more dampness on her cheeks. "By the second day of waiting, we knew you'd gotten stuck. And that's when Wyatt and Flynn organized the search parties."

Brody's gaze shifted to his brothers. From where they'd

been loitering, they'd straightened and were now walking toward him. Wyatt and Flynn had been out looking for them? He wasn't sure why that surprised him. But it did. For too long he'd kept them at spitting distance. Anytime they'd tried to talk or get close, he'd been as thorny as a cactus. He wasn't proud of the fact.

Truth was, he hadn't given them much reason to put their work on hold and go searching in the mountains for him. Why had they done it? Why did they keep on loving him when he didn't deserve it?

"Been searching all week 'til this morning when we got word you were found and Savannah was rushed down to the doctor."

"She with the doc now?" He scanned Main Street, hoping for a glimpse of Chandler, her father, or the doctor. Anyone who could tell him how she was doing.

"Fairplay Hotel." Ivy gave a nod in the direction of the two-story establishment with a white balcony across the second floor. "Doctor's been with her since she arrived."

"How is she?"

Ivy's expression turned solemn. "Last we heard, she's having real trouble breathing. It ain't looking good."

He fought back the despair and found himself swaying. Ivy reached out to steady him at the same time the fella holding him captive jerked on his binding. He was too weak to stay standing and dropped to his knees, even as Ivy tried to catch him.

Wyatt and Flynn ran toward him, shouting at Chandler's cowhands who had him roped up like a criminal. At a gunshot in the air, everyone halted and turned their attention to the cowboy on the horse beside Brody. His six-shooter was pointed at the sky.

"I got word to lock this fella up and put lead in anyone who tries to interfere." The man's voice filled the silence that had rapidly fallen over the busy thoroughfare.

Brody couldn't stand. Couldn't get his muscles to listen to his mind. Even though Ivy was trying to help, he'd run out of fuel.

"What's he done?" Flynn's challenge was hard.

"He kidnapped Miss Marshall."

"He doesn't need to resort to kidnapping to get a woman." Flynn edged closer, his gun drawn. "Savannah was sweet on him before they left to drive the horses west."

Wyatt, too, had his revolver aimed at the posse. Both his brothers were dusty and haggard, no doubt from the past days of living in the wilderness while searching for him.

They'd done so much for him, and this was just one more thing. As much as he'd respected his pa, these two men embodied everything he'd loved in his pa and more, everything good and decent and loving. He'd just been too blinded by his own pain and selfishness to see it.

Wyatt had labored harder than any fella he knew in order to build a home for them here in the West. And Flynn had too. Not only had Flynn put his life on hold to ride east after the war, but he'd sacrificed work and sleep for the past couple of years to watch over him.

Brody swallowed the emotion that swelled into his throat. Why hadn't he ever thanked either of his brothers? Was it because he'd resented them for saving his life? For having hope for his future when he'd had none? For forgiving him when he'd been bent on punishing himself for all he'd done during the war?

What had happened to change his perspective?

He couldn't single out a specific incident. Couldn't remember when he'd given himself permission to get on with living. But somehow, somewhere, he'd stopped hating himself. And he knew Flynn and Wyatt and their unconditional love for him had played no small part in that.

Brody lifted his head. Even now Flynn was looking at him like he'd rush in and switch places in a heartbeat if he could.

Flynn took several more steps closer, but at the cocking of a hammer, he froze. "Whoa, now."

Chandler's cowhand had shifted the gun to Flynn, and his finger was close to squeezing the trigger. "Saxton gave us orders. And we're aiming to follow them."

"Don't shoot him." Brody pushed up, letting Ivy assist him even as he placed himself between her and his captor. He wasn't gonna give the fella any more targets, especially not his little sis.

The cowhand swung his revolver in an arc. "Tell these folk to stay out of the way, and if they do, then ain't no one gonna get hurt."

"Stay on out of the way, Flynn." Brody met his brother's gaze head-on.

Flynn's brows dipped into a fierce scowl, one that could frighten the spine off a lizard. Brody had seen that look too often in recent months. The one that worried over him doing something stupid, something that might put his life in jeopardy.

Yep, he could admit he hadn't had much respect for his

own life. Because of that, he'd been all too willing to plunge headlong into dangerous situations. But this was different. This time, he was putting himself into danger to keep the ones he loved safe.

"I ain't done what they're accusing me of," Brody said, "but I ain't willing to let anyone get hurt right here and now on account of it."

Flynn's frown only deepened. "And I ain't willing to let you throw your life away—"

"Flynn, you've been there for me all along. Picked me up every time I've fallen down. And I'm mighty grateful." Brody hoped his brother could feel his sincerity. He hadn't made things easy on everyone, but he was thankful Flynn hadn't stopped trying to help him. "Reckon it's time for me to pick myself up."

Flynn's mouth closed, and his brows rose, revealing his serious green-blue eyes.

"Let me go with these fellas peacefully. And I'll get things straightened out soon enough."

Flynn didn't budge. The man was a rock. Strong and unmovable. Brody had a lot to learn from his brother, and when he got out of this mess, he intended to let Flynn know it.

But for now, this was his battle to fight.

He squared his shoulders and gave a nod toward Chandler's men. "Go on and lock me up. I'm aiming to keep the peace. And these folk will too."

As Chandler's cowhand gave the rope another tug, Brody plodded forward. He met Flynn's gaze again. This time his brother stood back and watched Brody, not with the usual disappointment but with respect.

Respect. Brody's chest squeezed with a strange sense of satisfaction.

"Wounds might shape us, but they can't determine who we are." Savannah's words from their time together in the cabin pushed to the front of his mind. His scars might never go away, but it was past time to stop letting his wounds define him and to find out who he really was.

CHAPTER
25

Brody leaned his head back against the shed wall. The past two days of being locked away had been a form of torture because he hadn't been able to see Savannah and check for himself how she was doing.

He'd gotten reports from Ivy. She'd been the only one allowed to visit him, bringing both food and news. While he was grateful for both, with each passing hour he was growing more desperate to be with Savannah.

Trouble was, Chandler was doing his best to keep them apart. That was becoming mighty clear the longer he was locked up. He reckoned Chandler wasn't gonna let him go until Savannah was well on her way home.

The door rattled, and Brody sat forward, the chains on his legs clinking together. From the low voices outside, he knew his visitor wasn't Ivy. Every time she came around, she was loud and heated, giving the guards a tongue-lashing with enough sting to make a bucking bronc go wild.

Maybe this was the mayor coming to question him— someone finally willing to listen to his side of the story. Ivy'd already reported that Wyatt, Flynn, Mr. Steele, and several other prominent men of the community were negotiating with Chandler and Mr. Marshall for Brody's release.

But apparently, Chandler had a whole bunch of witnesses from the area willing to testify just how violent and volatile Brody was, how he was always fighting with one man or another and stirring up trouble. Chandler had discovered how he'd broken Gill's arm and threatened to do worse to the cowhands at the Elkhorn Ranch barn dance. Apparently Lonnie Quick had come forward saying Brody had threatened violence after the recent confrontation in town with Sitting Bear.

'Course, Brody couldn't claim innocence in any of the cases. But everyone had to see that the accusations were exaggerated.

"It ain't looking good, Brody," Ivy had said earlier that morning when she'd brought him a cup of coffee and a plate of grub. "Chandler's been talking with all the ranchers 'round these parts, telling them you're nothin' but a criminal. And he doesn't have to jaw long to convince them, since they're already plenty mad at you for giving them trouble over Hades and the other wild mustangs."

Chandler had persisted in charging him for kidnapping Savannah. The story going around was that he got wind of Chandler and Mr. Marshall's arrival in town and had convinced Savannah to go along on the horse drive. He'd sent Ivy and Dylan home because he intended to run off with Savannah. When the snow had trapped them and she got sick, he'd been left with no choice but to bring her back.

Chandler's accusations had enough hot air to keep a windmill going. All Brody needed was for Savannah to tell everyone the truth. One word from her would put an end to Chandler's attempt to ruin him. But Savannah was still too sick to leave her hotel room or have visitors—according to the doctor. Only Chandler and Mr. Marshall had access to her, and Brody knew blamed well Chandler wasn't gonna let Savannah in on the tall tale he was spinning.

The shack door swung open, and bright sunlight poured in, blinding Brody. He stuck up a hand to shield his eyes but was jerked to his feet.

His sight adjusted in time to see Chandler's fist flying toward his nose. The wallop slammed his head into the wall, and blood gushed over his upper lip. Chandler sent another blow into his midsection.

Brody wanted to lash out, but before he was given half the chance, his arms were wrenched behind him and twisted so painfully that he had to grind his teeth together to keep from crying out. Only then did Brody realize two cowhands were holding him in place as Chandler's punching bag.

Tall and slender and attired like a gentleman in a fine suit and spiffy hat, Chandler took a step back and combed away a strand of hair that had fallen over his forehead. "That's for touching what doesn't belong to you."

Brody figured Chandler had seen him kissing Savannah when he'd ridden up into the gulch. He hoped more than ever that Chandler had seen Savannah's reaction to those kisses. That's all the proof they needed to determine who she belonged to. Didn't matter how much Chandler denied it. The truth was plain as day. Savannah was his.

As if sensing the defiance, Chandler looked him over, then

spit at his feet, the spittle landing on his boot. "Men like you ought to remember your place in the order of things." Chandler slid his fingers into his leather gloves. "You're a poor man with nothing to your name but a long list of offenses."

The saltiness of blood tinged Brody's tongue, and he had half a mind to spit on Chandler's boot. But he forced down the anger and the desire to fight. He was trying to do better, be better. Couldn't let this fella goad him into losing his temper.

"It's too bad you didn't figure out your place sooner." Chandler finished adjusting his glove and then straightened his shirt. "As it is, you've left me in an unfortunate position of having to set an example of what happens to hotheaded cowboys who think they deserve better than they have."

For a second, Brody could imagine Chandler talking to his slaves in the same tone and manner, likely had interacted with them with such superiority during his days of living in the South. It was clear that even though the war was over, plenty of people still had a heap to learn about treating all people with dignity.

Chandler tilted his hat back into place. "Do you have any final words to say on the matter, McQuaid?"

Brody guessed that hobbling his lip was for the best. But at the smugness in Chandler's eyes, he couldn't keep his jaw in a sling any longer. "Stand by what I told you already. If she was yours, then she wouldn't have come running into my arms."

He was exaggerating a mite. But he couldn't keep from riling up the ornery cuss.

Chandler's face blanched.

A sharp sliver pricked Brody. He didn't want to ruin Savannah's reputation with his tales. But at the same time, he wanted to rub Chandler's face into dung. At least long enough to make him squirm.

Chandler had grabbed hold of the handle of his revolver. A killer glint flashed in his eyes.

Brody tensed.

"I was thinking this little lesson I was giving you might be enough to set you on the right path." Chandler's voice was calm and cold. "But I can see you're beyond reforming and that only one thing will put an end to your interference with Savannah."

Brody had faced death enough to know he was facing it again. But for the first time in a long time, he wasn't ready to die.

He shoved against the fellas holding him, but they twisted his arms hard. Any movement he made felt as though his tendons were tearing from the socket.

"That's right." Chandler lifted his chin. "I sure do like the way justice is served up here in the Rockies. Criminals like you are punished swiftly."

"You know I ain't a criminal." Brody ground out the words through the pain rippling through him.

"I've got a dozen men out there—" Chandler nodded toward the street outside the shack door—"a part of the vigilante committee who agree you should be hanged for kidnapping and molesting Savannah."

"I didn't kidnap or molest her, and we both know it."

Chandler had already moved to the door.

How had things gotten so twisted up? "Listen, Saxton. Savannah and me . . . we didn't do nothin'—"

"Shut it, McQuaid." Chandler halted but didn't turn. "She told me you forced her to undress and then got in bed with her."

Why had Savannah told Chandler that? Didn't she know how incriminating it sounded? "She was freezing. Did it to keep her from dying."

"It's pretty obvious to everyone in this community you're smitten with her. You were just waiting for an opportunity to get her alone and use her."

"That's hog feed." This wasn't going the way he'd hoped.

"In my mind, bringing ruination to a woman like Savannah is a hanging crime. And fortunately, the men on the vigilante committee agree with me."

Maybe he shouldn't have had Savannah undress after all. And maybe he shouldn't have climbed into bed with her. Guess he could see how the whole thing might look to someone else. Regardless, he hadn't taken advantage of her, and he had to make sure everyone knew it. "She's innocent—"

Chandler spun with a furious glare. "Savannah is the sweetest woman I know. And you sullied her."

Brody swallowed his retort. He hadn't meant to sully her, but he supposed being alone with her in that cabin for a few days was enough to get men thinking all the wrong things.

"Lucky for her," Chandler continued, "I love her enough that I'm willing to overlook this unfortunate situation. I'm intending to take her home and marry her and put all this behind us."

Brody shook his head. "This is ridiculous."

Chandler stepped through the door.

"She ain't gonna marry you, Saxton."

"You won't be around to stop her." The reply wafted back

as Chandler moved out of the shack. Chandler was attempting to get rid of him, knew nothing was forced, was jealous. Plain and simple.

Brody strained against his captors, wished he could rush after Chandler and bury his fist into the man's face. But somehow he sensed that he'd lost even before he'd had the chance to get started.

"Tie him up good," Chandler called from outside. "It's time for a hanging."

∽ৎৢৣৎ∽

Savannah pushed up from the bed. After two days of vapors, rest, and nourishment, she'd survived the worst of the pneumonia and was finally improving.

She was more than ready to see Brody. But Daddy, Chandler, and the doctor had insisted she refrain from having visitors. In fact, Chandler had posted two men outside her hotel room door to make sure no one disturbed her unnecessarily.

While it was kind of them to be so concerned for her well-being, she was worried about Brody, even though Chandler insisted his men had brought Brody back to town and that he was fine.

She stood, smoothed her damp hair away from her face, and took a deep breath of the humid air filling the room from the big pots boiling on the corner stove. The private room was the best one Fairplay Hotel had to offer. The large bed with its mahogany headboard and footboard took up a prominent place at the center of the room, with a matching bedside table and the chair Daddy had sat in frequently over the past two days.

She'd been too sick the first day to speak. But on the

second morning, she'd squeezed his hand and managed a smile, relieved when he smiled tenderly in return.

His distinguished, handsome face had been lined with worry. And the dark hair at his temples and sideburns contained extra gray hair she suspected she'd put there.

"I'm sorry for worrying you, Daddy," she'd croaked.

He hugged her tight, his bony frame reminding her of his grieving over Hartley and the weeks of not having an appetite and picking at his food. "You don't have anything to apologize for, sweetheart. I'm just glad my little girl is safe."

"I've made a mess of things, haven't I?"

He kissed her forehead. "You don't worry about a single thing except getting better. Understand?"

The doctor had stepped in then to begin breathing treatments. And she hadn't had the opportunity to talk to Daddy too much about all that had happened. She could only imagine his worry, not only while she'd been gone from the ranch, but then in learning she was stranded in the mountains, not knowing what had become of her, whether she'd lived or died in the snow.

He hadn't needed the trauma of thinking he'd lost another child. And now she was plagued with the guilt of having put him through such an ordeal.

She wrapped a blanket around her nightgown. She had Ivy to thank for retrieving her belongings. At the thought of the young woman, Savannah wished she could see her, thank her in person, and hear more about her adventure in returning to Fairplay after the snow had started. As it was, Chandler had been the one to deliver her haversack, unwilling to let Ivy visit her, even after assurances that the girl's presence would be a welcome relief.

With a sigh, Savannah started across the room, the wood floor cold against her bare feet. She walked directly to the window and pulled back the curtains. The back of the hotel faced the west, and the snow-covered mountains greeted her, a vivid reminder of the danger she and Brody had faced.

She offered a prayer for their horses, hoping the two beautiful creatures would find grass and be able to make their way down the mountain.

The morning sunshine glistened off the bright-white peaks. The memory of her picnic with Brody on one of those distant summits came rushing back. It had been one of the most amazing moments in her life. She'd never felt so free as she had up there watching Hades and his band grazing.

The freedom had come with danger. She'd nearly lost her life for that moment of independence. But it had been worth it, hadn't it?

She reached up and touched her lips, reliving the softness of Brody's kiss, tasting him, feeling his heat on that mountaintop with the wind and clouds and the sky whispering that she was free.

The distant heights seemed to beckon to her to break away again and to truly live. Even with the danger.

Blocking out the calling, she let the curtain fall into place. She didn't want to face the room, but it closed in around her, the humid air confining and stifling her.

It was the same feeling she'd had those last few weeks before her weddin'. Confined. Stifled.

Was it because Daddy and Chandler always took charge of her life, made decisions for her, and expected her to follow along? She usually agreed with their plans, didn't question their decisions because they meant well.

Even though they thought they knew what she needed and wanted to take care of her, they treated her like a piece of delicate porcelain needing to be displayed rather than utilized for its purpose.

She'd didn't doubt both of them cherished her and wanted to protect and take care of her. But she longed for more than being a showpiece. She wanted to fulfill the purpose God had created her for, whether that was helping animals or people.

She released a frustrated breath that ended in a hacking cough, one that weakened her limbs. Weariness weighed upon her shoulders, and she slid down until she was sitting with her back against the wall and her legs stretched out in front.

She'd hoped the time away from home would give her clarity, at the very least would help her accept the future that Daddy and Chandler wanted for her. But she'd only grown more certain she couldn't move forward with the plans. She couldn't deny her identity and sacrifice her dreams.

Yet, she didn't want to deny her parents their dreams either. . . .

Sitting in the hot room with the four walls closing in around her, she only wanted to run away again.

"Oh, Lord." Savannah buried her face in her hands.

There had to be a way to assist her parents without marrying Chandler. When he'd charged up the gulch, she was grateful for the rescue. But she despised the way he treated Brody, jumping to conclusions and treating him like a criminal.

Maybe Chandler had always been a little arrogant and unfair. And maybe she'd simply overlooked those qualities, telling herself no one was perfect. But she couldn't ignore his faults any longer. She didn't want to be with someone who thought he was better than others. He was the opposite of Brody, who didn't control her but instead worked at earning her trust and respect. Brody challenged her when she needed it, but he also valued her for who she was.

At a knock outside the window, she sat up with a start. A face peered through the glass past the curtains. Ivy. The young woman was searching around the room frantically. "Savannah?" Her muffled voice radiated with distress.

Savannah struggled to her feet.

Ivy was standing precariously on the windowsill. Two stories above the ground. With a steep drop below her. She was too daring for her own good.

"Ivy, what are you doing?" Savannah tugged on the window-pane and inched it up.

Holding on to the narrow frame, Ivy tottered.

Savannah shoved the window open more quickly, until it was high enough for Ivy to slide her legs through. At least in her boy's trousers, Ivy didn't have to worry about a skirt getting tangled.

"How did you get to the window?" Savannah pulled the young woman all the way into the room.

Straightening, Ivy glanced toward the door and spoke in a whisper. "Crawled from the balcony on the other side up onto the roof and down this side."

"Why didn't you use the door?" Even as Savannah asked the question, she already knew the answer. If Ivy had made it inside the hotel, the guards outside the room would have stopped her.

Ivy gripped Savannah's arms, and only then did Savannah

see the tears streaking the girl's cheeks. "Brody needs you in a bad way."

Savannah's heartbeat plummeted. "What's wrong?"

"Chandler's vigilante committee is taking him down to the hanging tree."

CHAPTER

26

"You gotta stop them." Ivy's whisper was ragged with desperation. "Please. Please. Please."

"A hanging?" Savannah peered out the window but couldn't see anything but the dry, grassy outskirts of town. Ivy wasn't making any sense. Why did Chandler have a vigilante committee, and why were they hanging Brody?

"Chandler's riled everyone up, telling them Brody kidnapped you." Ivy's words ended on a sob.

Savannah's backbone turned rigid. Chandler had accused Brody of that when he'd first come upon them. She assured Chandler that Brody had acted with honor, that even when she had to get undressed because of her wet garments, Brody had done everything he could to save her life and hadn't taken advantage of the situation in the least.

Why was Chandler persisting in his accusation? And attempting to hang Brody?

"You have to hurry."

Savannah finally understood the urgency in Ivy's voice, and she hastened toward the door.

"They might already be stringing Brody up."

"Where are Wyatt and Flynn? Why aren't they putting a stop to this?"

"They're not in town yet this morning. And I don't have time to ride on back to the ranch to get 'em."

Savannah flung the door wide, revealing the two cowhands in the hallway, playing cards on a barrel between them. At the sight of her, they dropped the cards and jumped up.

"Miss Marshall, can we help you?" one of them asked. As Ivy appeared behind her, their eyes widened, no doubt wondering where the young woman had come from.

Savannah pulled her blanket around her nightgown more fully. This wasn't the time to worry about indecency, not when Brody's life was in danger. And this wasn't the time to worry about explaining herself to these men.

"I'm stepping outside for a few minutes." Her stomach knotting, she started down the hallway past them with Ivy close on her heels. She had to make it outside before the men thought to detain her.

She made it to the top of the stairway before footsteps thudded after them.

"Mr. Saxton said you ain't supposed to leave your room" came the call behind her.

She hurried down the steps, her bare feet slapping hard in her haste. "I'm sure he won't mind my going out for a breath of fresh air."

"No, ma'am. He made it real clear he didn't want you goin' nowhere."

"I assure you," she said over her shoulder, "Chandler won't care in the least."

Would he, though? Brody had expressed his worry about Chandler during one of their first conversations. Brody had been hesitant to reveal the negative things he knew about Chandler. Obviously, he hadn't felt the need to disparage Chandler to make himself appear better or to sway her opinion.

Yet, what if Brody had been right in telling her she should to take a closer look at Chandler? Maybe, if she examined him more thoroughly, she'd find additional qualities besides his arrogance she didn't like.

She shook off the thought. Right now, she had to think about Brody. All that mattered was finding him and making sure he didn't suffer today on account of her.

When she reached the bottom of the stairs, she noticed the dining room was eerily silent. The long tables and benches were deserted. Not a patron in sight.

Was everyone outside watching the goings-on?

"Miss Marshall, wait," the cowhand behind her called more urgently.

She picked up her pace and escaped through the establishment's front door. Even though her lungs were already burning from the exertion, she ran outside.

Where was the hanging tree?

She glanced both ways, the morning sunlight warm and bright. A crowd of men on the north edge of town milled together. Ivy latched on to Savannah's arm and dragged her toward the gathering surrounding a lone bare-branched pine tree. Its thick black branches twisted up to the sun like gnarled fingers, and a rope dangled from one of the limbs.

Bile swirled in her stomach. "No! Brody's innocent!"

Her voice was drowned out by the commotion. But Ivy began shouting with her. As they elbowed through the throng, the men stepped aside, growing quiet as they recognized Ivy and her. When she stumbled to the front of the crowd, Savannah took in the scene at the foot of the hanging tree.

Chandler stood with a dozen cowhands surrounding Brody—most of them from the Double L, but a few she recognized as locals. Blood trickled from Brody's nose, and a bruise was forming under one of his eyes. Had someone been beating him up?

He was unshaven and still wearing the same clothing from when they'd been trapped in the cabin. His hands were tied, and chains encased his ankles. Did all of this mean he'd been detained—possibly jailed—for the past few days?

Who had done all this? And why?

In the process of tying a noose in the end of the rope suspended from the tree, Chandler paused. He took in the quiet of the crowd and followed their attention to her.

Brody's gaze had landed upon her as well. He held himself rigidly but calmly. As their gazes connected, she could see the relief there and knew he hadn't gone willingly, that he wasn't ready to die, that he wanted to live.

"Chandler." She shifted and pinned her gaze on the man her daddy wanted her to marry. "Let Brody go. I already told you he didn't kidnap me."

At her declaration, several men in the vigilante committee took steps back, their brows rising, their eyes registering surprise. What exactly had Chandler been telling everyone about Brody and her?

Chandler dropped the rope and started toward her. "Savannah, my dear, you shouldn't be out here. Not with how sick you are. And not like this." He nodded to her nightgown and the blanket now dragging by her bare feet.

"I'm here. And I'm staying." She hefted the blanket to her shoulders. "Someone's got to tell the truth about Brody, because it doesn't look like you're planning on it."

"I've done nothing but unearth the truth the past couple of days." Chandler drew closer.

She held out her hands, suddenly afraid of him getting close enough to pick her up and haul her back into the hotel.

"Where's Daddy?" She scanned the crowd for his familiar face. She'd told him briefly about Brody and the help he'd been during the days stranded in the mountains. He believed her, didn't he? Surely he'd sort out this mess.

"Mr. Steele offered to give your father a tour of his mine this morning."

Something in Chandler's eyes told her more than words could that he'd plotted everything. "You're doing this"—she waved toward the tree and the rope—"while they're gone because you know they'd stop you."

"The mayor is friends with the McQuaids. Of course he's been attempting to obstruct justice."

"The only justice here is to let Brody go free."

Chandler had stopped an arm's length away. His men from the hotel room now stood behind her. Was she trapped? "Everyone agrees Brody McQuaid's nothing but trouble. And after kidnapping and molesting you—"

"He did neither of those things."

"From the indecencies you described, that's exactly what he did."

"Indecencies?" She hadn't described anything to Chandler. What was he talking about?

Chandler darted a glance at the men standing around, then lowered his voice. "I'd rather not mention the details publicly and bring any more ruination to your reputation."

"Brody didn't ruin my reputation." But even as the words slipped out, she tugged the blanket closed more firmly. Was he referencing Brody's saving her from freezing to death? When Chandler had asked her pointed questions about how Brody had warmed her up, she'd thought honesty was for the best. But it appeared he'd taken everything she said the wrong way.

"Brody could have brought you right home with his brother and sister." Though Chandler spoke gently, his features had hardened. "Instead, he kept you out there intending to hole up in that secluded cabin and seduce you."

She fought back a shudder. The way Chandler described her time with Brody sounded downright vulgar. "We had a picnic, and that detained us."

"Brody figured he'd get you alone and take advantage of the situation and you."

"Brody's not like that."

"A dozen men will testify differently." Chandler nodded to the vigilante committee. She spotted Lonnie Quick, the foreman of Stirrup Ranch. Gill was there, his broken arm in a sling. The man Brody had threatened at the barn dance stood with others she didn't recognize.

Just because Chandler had rounded up all the fellows Brody had offended didn't mean he deserved to hang, especially not on account of her.

The way Chandler pressed his lips together told her he

wouldn't be swayed. "I'm doing this to preserve your honor. You may not realize that now in your sick and weakened condition, since you're not thinking soundly. But someday, you'll conclude this is for the best."

Chandler truly believed Brody was guilty of enticing her and leading her astray. And he'd convinced a majority of people in the area that Brody had done so too. How could she persuade everyone otherwise, when they believed she was too sick to process everything rationally?

She met Brody's intense brown gaze. He wasn't silently pleading with her or defending himself. Instead, his expression was steady, as if he had faith she'd speak the truth and that justice would prevail. He was a man of integrity. And in spite of Chandler's attempt to undermine Brody's reputation, he hadn't done anything wrong.

But how could she prove it when her word wasn't enough?

The morning sunshine beat upon her bare head, the heat and light suddenly making her dizzy.

"I can't in good faith let Brody go free." Chandler crossed his arms. "What's to stop him from coming after you when you leave, kidnapping you again?"

"He's not like that—" As she spoke the words, shouting and the pounding of hooves drew near.

As the men parted, Flynn galloped up, his revolver out and his eyes frantic. Ivy, who'd been standing beside Savannah during the entire exchange with Chandler, expelled a breath but stopped abruptly at the sight of Jericho riding in on Flynn's heels. His horse was foaming at the mouth, the same as Flynn's.

"Jericho was in town this morning," Ivy said softly. "He must've rode out to the ranch and got Flynn."

Jericho reined in beside Flynn and glanced around the crowd, his attention coming to rest on Ivy. Only for the briefest of instances. But it was long enough for Savannah to see his concern for Ivy and to know he'd gone after Flynn for her sake.

"Let Brody go!" Flynn jumped down from his horse and aimed his revolver at Chandler.

Chandler's hand fell to his Colt. He'd become a proficient gunman in recent years and had gained a reputation for his shooting skills among the Double L cowhands. Savannah had no doubt Chandler would be able to put a bullet in Flynn or Brody before either of them could duck out of the way.

A fresh sense of urgency coursed through her. She had to stop Chandler before anyone died.

The truth was, she'd never expected Chandler to act so irrationally or be so jealous. Maybe he was afraid she'd want to stay in South Park with Brody instead of going home. Maybe he felt Brody stood in the way of their future together.

Whatever the case, she needed to convince him Brody wasn't a threat. And maybe the best way to do that was to underplay her feelings. Yes, she could admit she'd grown to care about Brody deeply, especially during the past week together. But nothing could come of it, could it? Even if she didn't marry Chandler, she had to go home and find a way to help her parents. But what other way would she find?

A part of her feared there was no other way, that maybe Chandler was the only answer to their problems.

Flynn planted his feet apart and fixed a glare on Chandler. "You got no right coming to Fairplay and riling everyone up against Brody."

"I didn't need to do any riling." Chandler lifted his chin.

"From what I can tell, Brody's already done a good enough job of that for himself."

"People 'round here know he's a good man even if he's still hurting from the war."

"You can make excuses for him, but the war's been over for two years."

Flynn glanced at Brody. "Healing takes time."

Flynn's statement was just what she needed, hopefully one that could sway Chandler. She pushed past her trepidation and found her voice. "That's why Flynn hired me on. He saw my healing touch and decided it might be worth a try with Brody."

Brody's attention snapped to her, but she didn't dare meet his gaze for fear he'd see right past her attempts to defuse the situation.

Chandler's brows rose.

"It's the truth. My focus was on helping Brody heal." Now that she'd started down this path, she couldn't stop. "Ask Flynn."

Flynn stilled.

She held back her regret that she was having to reveal Flynn's intentions. He probably hadn't wanted Brody to know his true motivation for hiring her. But she had to remember that even if her declaration might hurt Brody and Flynn in the short term, it would save Brody's life and be worth the heartache.

More people had gathered around and were watching the exchange with interest. No doubt she was giving them plenty of gossip for the days and weeks to come.

"She telling the truth?" Brody stared at Flynn, and his tone was cold enough to freeze prairie grass.

Flynn's shoulders slumped.

"You hired Savannah with the hope of her fixin' me?"

"Reckoned it couldn't hurt."

Brody said something under his breath.

Chandler was watching the exchange, and with each passing moment, the tension eased from the lines in his face.

"I was nothin' but a critter to doctor? That's all?" Brody's question seemed to be directed at Flynn. But a moment later, he shifted to look at her. The hurt within the depths of his beautiful brown eyes stabbed her heart.

While she may have started out wanting to help him, somewhere along the way he'd become much more than just another creature to heal. Therein was the problem. She'd grown to care about him too much. And staying up in the high country with Brody wouldn't solve her parents' problems the way a match with Chandler would.

She couldn't tell Brody the truth. But neither could she lie. So she didn't speak at all.

At her silence, Brody just shook his head.

"I'm sorry," Flynn said.

"I don't want your apology." Brody's growl echoed in the silence.

Flynn's warning rushed back. He'd told her to be careful, that he didn't want Brody to end up worse because of her. Was that what she was doing? Hurting Brody more?

She loathed the thought of wounding him. After how much he'd already suffered, she didn't want to cause him this pain. But what other choice did she have at the moment?

Flynn holstered his gun. "Let Brody go."

Chandler hesitated, again glancing from Brody to her and back. Was he thinking about the moment of intimacy he'd witnessed when he'd come upon them in the gulch? How could she explain it?

"Please, Chandler." She tried to keep the desperation from her tone. "I was trying to help Brody. But he doesn't need me any longer. He's doing well enough on his own." She meant it. She just hoped Brody could believe it for himself and would continue the progress he'd made.

She tried to catch Brody's eye, but he stared down at his boots, his jaw flexing.

"Let him go." Chandler's pronouncement rang out, making Savannah's knees weak. She reached out to hang on to Ivy, but the girl had bounded forward toward Brody. Flynn, too, quickly crossed the distance, reaching Brody and using a knife to saw through the binding around his arms.

Savannah wanted to go to him with the others, but she refrained, knowing to do so would only put more suspicion upon him. And she didn't want to chance Chandler changing his mind, not until Brody was safely away from town.

She pressed a hand to her head, overwhelmed with exhaustion. In the next instant Chandler was at her side, sweeping her off her feet and carrying her toward the hotel.

She closed her eyes and pretended everything would be fine. But with each step away from Brody, her heart tore until it felt like it was ripping from her chest.

CHAPTER

27

Brody kicked the hay in the mow, sending pieces into the air so that the slants of sunshine revealed particles of dust hovering in the barn. He slammed his palm into the stall rail and then kicked again.

He wanted to cry out, shout, yell, and even sob. But he couldn't find a way to release his anguish except through punching and kicking. After Flynn had freed him of his manacles, Ivy offered her horse for the ride to the ranch. He'd pushed hard, his chest burning the entire trip. He'd needed to put as much distance as he could between himself and Savannah, as if that could somehow take away the ache.

But once he galloped into the ranch yard and handed the horse over to Elmer, the ache only pulsed harder. With Flynn hot on his tail, Brody had been tempted to stalk over to his brother, yank him down from his mount, and pummel him hard. He needed a release for all his frustration.

Instead, he'd forced himself to enter the barn and had taken out his anger on the haymow. In spite of the turmoil, he maintained a measure of self-control he hadn't thought possible.

"He's doing well enough on his own." Savannah's words reverberated through him. He hated what she'd said but couldn't deny the truth. He was doing better.

Even so, he took another swipe at the pile, scattering strands and making a mess of the place. He paused to look at the dust flying around and let his shoulders slump. He could kick the hay all the way back to Pennsylvania, but it wouldn't change what had happened. Nothing could.

He'd lost Savannah.

He leaned into a post, letting his head rest against the rough plank.

Had he ever really had her to begin with?

Probably not. Truth was, she'd reached out to him because he'd been hurting and broken. Couldn't blame her. That's the way she was. She was drawn to the wounded. That trait made her an excellent veterinarian.

And of course in hiring her, Flynn had jumped in to try to rescue him again.

Brody glanced sideways at the barn door to find Flynn leaning against the frame, mostly outside, but still hovering nearby, keeping an eye on him as always, worried he'd do something stupid.

Even though Brody was angry at his brother, he couldn't blame Flynn either. Brody had been the one to push Flynn into hiring Savannah. Had pushed him real hard that day. And Flynn hadn't wanted to say no—rarely said no to him—probably out of fear of what he might do next.

Brody sighed and gripped the post, resisting the urge to slam a palm against it.

Maybe Flynn shouldn't have cooked up the arrangement with Savannah. Should've left the two of them alone to figure things out on their own. Maybe Flynn needed to back off on all the hovering.

But what if he needed to give his brother more reassurance? Maybe he needed to prove he could handle the stress and pain of life better than he had in the past—including this pain of having Savannah leave him. In fact, maybe he oughta start showing Flynn he wasn't gonna fall apart every time something bad happened.

He could do that, couldn't he?

The image of Savannah standing in the middle of Main Street rushed back into his mind. She'd been beautiful with her long blond hair blowing in the breeze, swirling around the blanket she'd donned. Her eyes had been bright and rested, her cheeks flushed, her expression etched with fear and worry.

Ivy had been with Savannah, likely had been the one to alert her to what was happening. Even if Chandler had staged the hanging when no one would be around to stop him, the fella hadn't counted on Ivy's ingenuity and determination. Thank the Almighty for his sister. Ivy'd realized the same thing he had—that Savannah would come to his defense and save him.

He just hadn't figured Savannah would cut him loose in the process.

No matter what she'd said, he knew blamed well there'd been a whole lot more between them than just her helping him heal. He hadn't imagined the attraction between them or her reaction to his touches and kisses. She'd felt everything too. And she'd said she loved him, even if she'd been delirious.

The stab in his chest radiated throughout his whole body. He tried to suck in a deep breath, but the agony turned into anger. Made him want to lash out again.

He loved her, deeply and truly. And the prospect of losing her forever was almost more than he could bear. It sent his thoughts spiraling down into a dark place, the same dark place he'd found himself too often when he faced loss in the past. Loss of his pa, then ma. Loss of Wyatt when he'd moved. Loss of so many companions during the war. Loss of Newt. Loss of his own humanity.

He balled his fists. He'd let his inner demons have the upper hand for too long, and it was past time for him to get on with fighting them and waging an all-out assault so they were no longer controlling him.

Lord Almighty, help me. He lifted the silent plea heavenward. He was still too weak to fight any battles on his own. He was gonna need reinforcements from outside himself and had to start by turning back to the Almighty for strength.

And maybe it was time to let Flynn in on the reinforcing, too, leaning on his brother instead of pushing him away.

"I know you're there, Flynn."

Flynn straightened and moved as though to leave.

"Reckon you lost a lot of time this week searching for me and Savannah."

Flynn paused.

Brody wasn't exactly sure how to let Flynn in on his pain, but he was determined to figure out a way. "No sense standing around. Might as well come in, and we can get to work."

Flynn shuffled inside several steps.

Brody tried to draw in another breath and this time managed it. He pushed away from the post, grabbed a fork leaning against the wall, and began to pitch the hay back into a neat pile.

A second later, Flynn was shoveling beside him. No questions. No condemnation. No need to talk. Just silent acceptance.

Tears stung the backs of Brody's eyes. He wanted to tell Flynn how much he loved him, that he'd never stopped. But emotion tightened his throat.

The battle ahead was far from over, especially in combatting his grief over losing Savannah. But this time, he wouldn't push away those who cared about him and were ready to fight by his side.

CHAPTER
28

Savannah peered over her shoulder at the outline of Fairplay. The haze of the sun in the dust blurred the small town with its smattering of weathered buildings in the barren prairie. Her attention snagged upon the twisted, blackened hanging tree.

A shiver shimmied up her spine. Brody had come so close to dying there.

On the horse beside her, Daddy watched her with concern in blue eyes so much like hers. His face had aged since she'd left home. More crinkles at the sides of his eyes and mouth. More worry lines in his forehead. More weight loss.

"Are you sure you're ready for the long ride?" he asked gently.

"I'm sure." After Brody's near-hanging two days ago, the urgency to leave had been building. No matter how much Daddy and Chandler had pleaded with her to wait until the end of the week, she'd needed to go.

The confining hotel room had closed in on her again. The

wide-open spaces of the mountains had beckoned. But most of all, she'd wanted to protect Brody.

If, for some reason, he decided to see her and talk to her, he'd only put himself in danger with Chandler, especially because if she spent any length of time with Brody, Chandler would be sure to see just how attracted they were to each other.

Now that she was leaving, she understood just how attracted. So much that the ache in her chest hammered painfully. Even though a part of her had known all along she would eventually need to leave, she'd never imagined it would be so difficult.

"Even if the doctor said you're doing better," her daddy said, "you're still weak."

After four days abed, her fever was gone, her cough was subsiding, and she was breathing easier. She was still tired. But more than anything, she was heartsore. "I'm doing the right thing." She tried to give her daddy a smile, but it felt forced and stiff.

When Daddy had returned from visiting Mr. Steele's mine two days ago, he'd been surprised to hear the news of the near-hanging. Apparently, he hadn't expected Chandler to pursue such drastic measures against Brody, and he'd told Chandler as much. Of course, Chandler had been as smooth talking with Daddy as he'd been with her, making himself seem noble for attempting to bring about justice for the wrongs Brody had perpetrated.

Daddy tipped up his brimmed hat and glanced in Chandler's direction, his expression just as troubled now as it had been then. "Yes, you're probably right. Heading home is for the best."

Did Daddy want to avoid any further confrontations too?

Chandler rode at the head of their group with some of his closest cowhands. His shoulders were straight and proud. He was a born leader, and he'd done much to make the Double L Ranch successful over the years. She was grateful for his hard work and all he'd done. And she was grateful he cared enough for her parents that he wanted to provide a way for Daddy to get out of his financial woes.

But she hadn't liked how he handled the situation with Brody, especially his jealousy, quick judgment, and spitefulness. He'd been slow to show mercy and hadn't displayed any remorse. Would she ever be able to relate to Chandler again without thinking of how he tried to hang Brody and likely would have if she hadn't intervened?

She didn't want to lose her ability to see the best in others, but had she been too naïve, too trusting? Especially of Chandler? Even Daddy?

In his finely tailored riding suit, her daddy stood apart from the cowhands. Even after all the years in the West, he was still a gentleman. He'd never truly fit in here, had only come to save Hartley from the war. Now that her daddy no longer had a reason for staying, she wanted him to be able to leave.

Yes, she truly wanted the best for him. But she also needed him to understand her perspective, and so far, she hadn't figured out a way to share it. "I hope you know Brody Mc-Quaid didn't do any of the things Chandler accused him of doing."

"You're a very caring young woman, Savannah." Daddy's soft comment contained a note of caution. "And I know you meant well. I'm just afraid you put a blemish on your reputation. Thankfully, Chandler's a decent fellow and will still have you . . . in spite of everything."

A part of her wanted to apologize again for bringing Daddy more heartache with her blemished reputation. But another part of her pushed to be heard, to persist in saying what she needed to. "Brody is a decent fellow too. He never once took advantage of the situation or of me. You have to believe me."

Her daddy stared ahead at the grasslands spreading out for miles before them. Gopher hills dotted the landscape, which was green and filled with wildflowers. "From everything I've heard about Brody McQuaid, he's a broken and troubled man. Even so, I believe you, Savannah. I know you wouldn't lie to me about something like this."

"Thank you, Daddy." If Chandler truly loved her, why wouldn't he trust her too? In fact, she couldn't understand why he'd spoken so publicly about the things she'd shared with him in private. Had he put her reputation on the line so he could retaliate against Brody?

Now that she was returning home, both Daddy and Chandler had naturally assumed the weddin' would continue as previously arranged. She wanted to set them straight, tell them she wasn't going through with it. But the words stuck in her throat.

It would be easier to break the news once she had a solid plan in place, one that would make everyone happy.

But what? If she had all the time in the world, would she ever be able to think of such a solution? Wasn't that what she'd hoped to do by running away from home in the first place? It hadn't done much good. She was still in the same predicament with the same pressing problems.

She sighed. "I know you're eager to leave for Atlanta. But could you give me one more week before we talk about the weddin'?"

"Of course, of course. I hope you realize I just want what's best for you."

"Thank you, Daddy."

"And if you start feeling the need to put it off longer, promise you won't sneak away again? That you'll talk to me first?"

She hesitated. Could she talk to him honestly without him trying to persuade her into doing what he wanted? Maybe she would have to keep on learning how to state her opinion and stand up for herself.

"Please, Savannah."

"I promise." She just prayed that in one week she'd know what to do.

CHAPTER
29

Brody awoke with a start. The blast of gunfire and cannons was only a distant sound. The wafting smoke and heat encircled him, but the cries of the wounded and suffering were strangely silent.

His body trembled and his heart pounded. The nightmare wasn't as intense as it used to be, but even so, he glanced across the hallway to Savannah.

The moonlight revealed her neatly made bed. She was gone.

A different kind of pain shot through him, right through his chest. He sat up so suddenly, he slipped off his bed and landed on the floor with a thud.

On the stairs, the soft squeak of a floorboard told him Flynn was there, waiting, making sure he was alright.

Was Flynn always gonna jump out of bed at the least sound of thrashing? Was his brother worried he'd try to take his own life again?

Brody buried his face in his hands. He'd endured the terrors of the war, the nightmares, the heartache for Newt's sake, to make sure he stayed alive. His friend's life had been his one redemption. He'd told himself that if he could keep Newt alive, then he'd be able to bear up under the weight of all the atrocities he'd committed in the name of war.

After Newt was gone, Brody had no more reason to live. His sins overwhelmed him with guilt. He hated that he survived when others hadn't. That first night in New York City, he wrapped a belt around his neck and attempted to strangle himself.

In the next room, Flynn heard him and came to investigate. Flynn's face had filled with horror as he frantically worked to cut him loose. . . .

Brody pressed his palms into his eyes to block out the memory. But couldn't. Heaviness settled in his stomach at the heartache and frustration and fear he'd caused Flynn.

"Flynn?" he whispered.

For several heartbeats Flynn didn't respond, almost as if he was embarrassed at being caught in the stairwell. "Just checking on Flora," he whispered.

"I'm real sorry for what I put you through these past years."

Flynn was silent again.

"I regret it all." And he truly did regret it. Even though he'd fallen into a darkness so deep and hadn't known how to get out of it, he shouldn't have looked for the easy way to end his pain.

Fact was, the heartaches in life weren't ever gonna go away. If it wasn't one trouble, it was another. Like losing the woman he loved. Even now, after a week of nursing his broken heart over Savannah's leaving, the pain had only gotten worse. Made him downright cranky and miserable.

Although he relished the source of comfort she'd been, he couldn't love her sacrificially if he was using her for the peace and healing she could give him. He wouldn't be able to love her the way she deserved until he first found peace and healing in the One who was waiting patiently for him.

He'd been angry at everyone, including God, for too long. But the anger had been aimed mostly at himself. He could see that now.

Savannah had told him to be on the lookout for ways to fight those inner battles. First thing he needed to do was clear enough.

He scrubbed a hand over his jaw and spoke before he could find an excuse not to. "Can you forgive me, Flynn?"

Flynn didn't respond for so long, Brody started to think his brother had left. Finally, Flynn cleared his throat from outside the doorway. "Yep. I forgive you." His voice was clogged with emotion, and when he stepped into the doorway, he swiped at his cheeks.

Brody pushed up until he was standing. Tears pricked his eyes. "You're a good man. Just like Pa."

Flynn brushed at his cheek again. "You're a good man too, Brody."

"Got a long way to go." Brody spoke past a tightening in his chest. "But reckon I'll be happy if I end up half the man you are."

Flynn's throat worked up and down.

"Pa?" Flora's sleepy voice broke through the silence.

Flynn nodded at Brody, a nod that contained the same

respect from earlier in the week. A respect Brody could get used to.

As soon as Flynn stepped out, Brody sank to his knees beside his bed. Time to ask forgiveness from the Almighty. If a hardheaded man like Flynn could forgive and love him, Brody reckoned God could too.

God, I'm sorry. He was done pushing the Almighty away. Wanted Him there helping to fight the battles from now on.

I'm sorry. It was about as much as he could say, even silently. But he meant it from deep in his soul. Reckoned God knew exactly all the things he was sorry for without him spelling it out.

Forgive me, please. I don't deserve it but I'm asking anyway. His chest hurt with the pain he'd locked away there for so many years.

He expelled a breath, and somehow his chest loosened. The pain eased out, almost as if the lock had been opened.

Savannah's words from the mountain cabin came back to him almost as if God was saying them to him this time: *You no longer have to be condemned by your scars. God can redeem anything.*

He was still gonna have scars that would never go away and hurts that might always bother him—just like his shoulder wound did from time to time. But the burden inside him was gone. He was free.

CHAPTER

30

Savannah sat on the edge of her bed, the low glow of her bedside lantern chasing away the shadows of her room. The cool night breeze fluttered the lacy curtains and brushed against her, sending chills across her skin.

Tomorrow was one week. She'd asked Daddy to give her one week before talking about the weddin', and he allowed it. Even though everyone—including Chandler—had respected her wish, tomorrow they expected her to set a new date.

No one questioned *if* she'd marry Chandler, only *when*.

"Oh, Lord." She closed her eyes in prayer. "What should I do?"

She'd offered up dozens of prayers all week, hoping to find a solution that didn't involve marrying Chandler. But every time she tried to quiet her mind, her thoughts flooded with images of Brody, of their time together, of the way he looked at her and made her insides burn. She couldn't extinguish the flame. It only spread until it was like a forest fire, sweeping through her, consuming her, and ravaging her all at once.

Being with Brody, even when neither of them was talking, brought her pleasure. Simply riding alongside him was more satisfying than anything else. Not to mention how much she appreciated his support and encouragement and help with her veterinary calls. He didn't merely tolerate her being a vet. He genuinely cared about what she did and took an interest in each animal she doctored.

But it wasn't fair to consider a life of happiness with Brody at her parents' expense, was it?

She hugged her arms to her chest. "I can't think on him anymore. I can't." She needed to squelch the desire for him.

Even if she never saw him again, she couldn't walk down into the dining room tomorrow morning to the special breakfast Momma was planning and set a new weddin' date. At the same time, she couldn't bear seeing the disappointment on both of her parents' faces when she told them the truth. They were counting on her. They needed her. Their future happiness depended upon her.

The panic that had been stirring inside all week suddenly bubbled up. She stood abruptly and glanced around her room. She had to leave, had to get away from everything. If she stayed, she didn't know if she'd have the strength to say no to everyone.

Her frantic gaze landed upon her haversack still sitting beside her dresser. The servants had asked about cleaning it out, and every time she'd shaken her head, not ready to see her clothing and all the items that would only remind her of the weeks she'd spent at Healing Springs Ranch with Brody.

But now she crossed to the bag. She untied the drawstring, turned the sack over, and dumped out the contents. She had to pack quickly and head out before anyone awoke.

She didn't have the option of waiting until morning and riding along with Mr. Pritchard this time. All week during their calls, he'd made sure she was by his side at every moment. He probably had strict instructions from Chandler or Daddy not to let her out of his sight.

With each visit, she'd experienced the same restlessness she'd felt in the hotel room last week. She'd tried to analyze the discontentment and could only surmise that after having the freedom to practice by herself, she'd slowly gained the respect of the people in South Park. They'd begun to accept her, not just as a tagalong assistant but as a veterinarian in her own right.

At the Double L, she'd never had the kind of respect she'd had in the high country. She'd always been seen as the Cattle King's daughter. Mr. Pritchard's assistant. And with Chandler, she would have been seen as his wife and nothing more.

She didn't want her identity and dreams to continue to be defined by the men in her life.

With a final shake, the last item fell from the haversack. A book.

She gasped and sank to her knees. It wasn't just any book. It was Brody's sketch pad, the one he'd drawn in during their picnic and while stranded in the miner's cabin.

How had it gotten into her bag? Had he packed it there when they'd left the cabin? Perhaps he'd wanted her to have it as a gift, a reminder of their time together?

Sitting back on her heels, she brushed a hand across it reverently. She imagined Brody's strong, callused fingers holding it while his other hand danced across the page with a pencil, bringing to life whatever his eyes touched upon.

For a man who'd experienced so much death, he was able

to breathe life into anything he saw. Whether he realized it or not, he'd even breathed life into her with his confidence and acceptance.

Slowly, she opened to the first page, to a drawing of the mustang he'd rescued the day she met him. She traced the strong lines. As she turned from one page to the next, she halted at the sketch of her he'd drawn on the mountain peak the day of the snowstorm.

"Ain't never gonna get tired of drawing you, darlin'."

Cocking her head, she analyzed Brody's likeness of her. Her expression was flirtatious. And the look in her eyes? Love. Was that really what he'd seen?

Had she fallen in love with Brody?

She snapped the sketchbook closed and pressed a hand to her cheek. She couldn't have fallen in love with Brody in so short a time of knowing him, could she?

Even as denial rose swiftly, Brody's strange question from the night she'd been delirious came back to her, when he'd asked her if she remembered anything she'd spoken to him. He told her she said something memorable, something about them.

At the time, she'd been too tired and cold and sick to guess what it was she'd said. But here, now, she didn't have to think on it. She'd told him she loved him.

"Oh my." How had she been so bold?

She supposed her sickness had given her the ability to speak her mind. She'd lost her inhibitions, and the truth had come out easily without worry of repercussions, without worry of the future, without worry of what anyone else would think.

What *had* Brody thought? Of course, he said he wouldn't forget what she told him. But that didn't mean he reciprocated the love, did it? He liked her, was attracted to her, cared about her. But love?

She opened the notebook again, and this time turned to the pictures he'd sketched during their time stranded together. Several were of the cabin and horses and landscape with the snow covering everything like a thick feather coverlet.

But he'd drawn some of her too. Several of her sleeping. One of her resting and watching him, her eyes bright and her face flushed, but satisfaction and happiness in her expression. Each picture was carefully crafted, so much so that she couldn't believe he didn't feel the same about her as she did about him.

She had to go to him and find out. All the more reason to leave tonight. The need prodded her with such force that she pushed to her feet.

But even as she started toward her wardrobe, her footsteps slowed. Brody wouldn't want her to run away again. He'd want her to stand up and be strong and tell the truth. The truth was, as much as she wanted to help Daddy and Momma, she couldn't help everyone. That's what Brody had told her when he claimed she wasn't responsible for bailing Daddy out of trouble.

He was right. A part of her knew it. But the other part was having a hard time letting go of having to fix everything that was broken.

Clutching Brody's notebook against her chest, she shook her head. In fixing everyone else, she was only hurting herself.

Her parents would have to do the hard work of healing on their own, the same way Brody was working on his healing. She couldn't fight her parents' battles any more than she could fight Brody's. All she could do was be there for them and love them through the pain.

With shaking legs, she returned to the bed and sat down. She wasn't running away tonight. This time she needed to do what she hadn't done the first time. Tomorrow morning, she had to go down to Momma's special breakfast and inform Chandler and her parents there wouldn't be a weddin'. Not now and not ever. At least not to Chandler.

The truth was, Daddy would need to find another investor. Or search harder to locate a buyer for the ranch who could give him what it was worth. Or perhaps there was a stream of income he hadn't yet tapped, one that wouldn't bankrupt the ranch and yet would allow him to take Momma east and make her happy.

Savannah pulled her legs up under her and situated Brody's sketchbook in her lap. She opened it again and fingered one of the drawings of the wild stallion he'd corralled and trained. Somehow through seeing the work of his hands, she felt connected to him. It eased the ache in her heart just a little to have a part of him with her.

The work of his hands.

Her heart gave an extra thump. She flipped to the next page in Brody's sketchbook. Then to the next and the next, her pulse surging faster with each drawing of the wild mustangs. This might not mean anything, might not be a big enough answer to the problem. But it was a solution worth exploring.

At the squeak of floorboards in the hallway, she stilled. The heavy-slippered shuffle belonged to Daddy. Ever since Hartley's death, he'd had a hard time falling asleep, and she occasionally heard him making his way downstairs, where he'd head to his office and work on business for a while.

Her refusal tomorrow was only going to make things worse for him.

Indecision crept back through her. "No." She quietly chastised herself. "Even if it does make things worse, I can't let that stop me." It was time to let go of having to please everyone else. Instead she had to lead her own life the way God had intended. And maybe she needed to tell Daddy tonight. Right now.

She scooted to the edge of the bed. But how? How could she gather the courage to finally speak her heart?

She pressed Brody's notebook closer. Maybe she needed to fight her demons every bit as much as Brody did.

Pulling her robe closed around her, she left her room and started down the hallway and stairs. The faint glow of light from Daddy's study guided her steps past the parlor and dining room. When she reached his open door, she paused and lifted her eyes heavenward. *Help me do what I need to and not back down.*

She stepped into the room lit by a lantern he'd placed on his large desk. "Daddy?"

At the curio cabinet where he stored his liquor and glasses, he took a quick step back and fumbled at a decanter before he composed himself. "Savannah. You startled me."

"I'm sorry, Daddy." She ventured farther into his office.

Attired in a deep-burgundy bathrobe and a nightcap, he reached for a tumbler. "I hope I didn't wake you."

"No, I was still up."

"So, you're having trouble sleeping now too?" He approached his desk, set his cup down, and unstopped the decanter.

"Yes, tonight." She hesitated. She had to tell him and couldn't stop now.

As though sensing something amiss, he paused his pour and looked up. Even with the additional worry lines creasing his forehead, his features were still handsome, retaining a refined air. "What's troubling you, my dear?"

How could she do this to him? She just couldn't. She couldn't hurt him. But at the same time, she had to let go of her old patterns of interacting.

"Savannah?" He placed the glass and decanter on his desk and turned his full attention upon her.

She swallowed the appeasement that rose so naturally and easily. "Daddy, I'm not going to marry Chandler."

He stared at her and didn't speak. But the disappointment that flashed across his face spoke clearly enough.

"I know you wanted the union. And I feel terrible to let you down. But I can't do it."

He was quiet, and the ticking pendulum inside the large standing clock filled the silence.

Her insides twisted, and she fought back the sting of tears. Even if he was angry with her, she was doing the right thing. At least she hoped she was.

"I'm sorry, Daddy." Her lips trembled through the whisper.

He expelled a sigh. "No, I'm the one who should be sorry, Savannah."

She shook her head, still fighting the tears.

"When you ran away, I should have figured out I was putting too much pressure on you. But I guess I wanted to pretend everything was okay."

"And I wanted to pretend that too . . . because I love you

and Momma, wanted to help you. And I thought I could do it. But now I know I can't. I can't marry a man I don't love."

"Oh, Savannah." Chagrin creased his face. He was quiet for long moments before he lowered himself into a chair near his desk.

"You alright, Daddy?" She wanted to cross to him, hug him, and promise him everything would be okay. But, as difficult as it was, she refrained.

"This isn't a surprise. But it's hard to accept."

Had she done the right thing? Maybe she'd been too hasty. Selfish. Unloving. As soon as the thoughts came, she pushed them aside. No, sometimes loving people meant letting them go through their difficulties instead of providing a way for them to escape.

Her daddy bowed his head.

An ache settled in her heart. But Brody's chastisement nudged her once more. She silently chanted the truth: She wasn't responsible for her parents' happiness, and she couldn't take their burden back on herself.

"I don't want you to marry Chandler if it won't make you happy."

Her pulse stuttered. "You don't?"

Daddy lifted his head, his expression haggard, his gaze filled with sadness. "I've tried to ignore the misery in your eyes this past week, but I admit I've seen it."

He'd seen her misery? Even though she'd tried to pretend everything was okay?

"I've been selfish, Savannah. I've been pushing you into something regardless of how it affects you."

"It's not your fault entirely, Daddy. I went along with it.

Thought I could do it. But when the weddin' day crept up on me, I was scared."

He stared unseeingly ahead.

With each passing moment, her body tensed. And she lifted up a silent prayer. *Courage, God. I need courage to stay strong.*

Finally, he focused on her again. "We'll just have to figure out another way to make things work."

"Are you sure?"

"If we don't, we'll learn to adjust."

"But I know how much you and Momma want to move to Atlanta." She clasped her hands together over the sketchbook to keep them from shaking.

He was silent for several heartbeats. "When you were gone, all I could think about was that I was losing you." His voice dropped to an anguished whisper. "I've already lost one child. And I can't bear the thought that I might drive you away and lose you too."

She crossed to him, knelt, and threw her arms around him, hugging him tight. He wrapped his arms around her in return and placed a kiss on her head.

"You're a sweet and helpful woman, Savannah. I took advantage of that, and I'm sorry."

"It's okay, Daddy."

"How can I blame you for running away when that's what I've been trying to do too?"

She pinched her eyes closed, but tears slipped past.

He squeezed her harder. "Running from this place and the memories of Hartley might give us a fresh start, but no matter where we go, we'll never outrun the pain."

Tears trickled down her cheeks, tears of sorrow for what

they'd lost, but also tears of realization that they were growing stronger through the pain.

He pressed another kiss against her head. "I'm guessing you were thinking of running away tonight?"

She hesitated but then nodded. "It crossed my mind."

"I'm glad you came and talked to me instead." He released her and wiped the tears from her cheeks.

"I'm glad I did too." She was relieved she hadn't run off and broken his heart again, that she'd had the courage to stay and be honest.

He stood, reached for his decanter, and poured the dark liquid into the glass.

She waited until he finished putting the stopper back on before speaking. "I won't leave *tonight*, but I am leaving soon."

In the process of lifting his glass, he halted. "Leaving soon?"

Her stomach quivered, and for a moment her voice got lost somewhere inside.

"You don't need to go anywhere, Savannah—"

"I want to go." The words came out on the edge of a plea.

"But I understand about Chandler. I admit, I didn't like the way he behaved up in Fairplay."

"This is about more than marrying Chandler." She forced herself to keep going. "It's about me. About needing to be me."

He'd been understanding so far about her decision not to marry Chandler. Could he also accept that she wanted more from life than the usual course set out for a woman? "South Park needs a veterinarian, and if you'll give me your blessing, I'd like to take the job until they're able to find a full-time vet. Probably through the end of summer."

He appraised her before he lifted his glass and took a sip. "Does this have anything to do with Brody McQuaid?"

"He's a good man, Daddy. And I believe once you get to know him, you'll think so too."

Since she'd been the one to leave Brody, she doubted he'd seek her out. And after the way she'd hurt him, he might not want to see her again. But she had to at least try to tell him how she felt and let him know about her decision not to marry Chandler.

Daddy took another drink, this one longer.

She pushed down her trepidation and opened Brody's sketchbook. "In fact, I think you'll like Brody a great deal once I propose to you how he might be the investor you've been looking for."

CHAPTER
31

Brody slowed his horse's gait as Flynn's place came into view. The two horses trotting behind him snorted, both weak and hungry and ready for a rest.

"Hang in there. We're almost home." After he'd been gone near to a week, the house and barn and outbuildings were a welcome sight. With the mountains rising in the distance and the vibrant green of new leaves, the view was awe-inspiring enough to clear the air straight from his lungs.

Home. Never thought he'd feel that way about a ranch or the people waiting for him there. But he was mighty happy to be back, eager to wrap Flora in a hug, to hear her prattle on about the kitties, and to have her boss him around. His stomach rumbled with a hankering for one of Vesta's home-cooked meals. And he was looking forward to listening to Ivy's yammering on about local news from while he'd been gone.

When Brody had brought up the idea of going to search

for Savannah's and his horses up in the Mosquito Range, he'd been surprised when Flynn hadn't opposed him. He'd been even more surprised when Flynn hadn't suggested he take someone along. Even if a thin line had creased Flynn's brow, his brother had cut him loose.

Since that night over a week ago when he'd asked Flynn to forgive him, Brody had sensed a shift, that Flynn was trying harder to trust him to stay safe. And he'd sensed God's redemption at work inside, little by little, taking his scars and hurts and making him stronger through them.

Brody could admit he still had a long way to go. He'd had nightmares a couple of recent nights and hadn't been able to sleep well. Partly, he'd been thinking on Savannah and missing her something fierce. The ache of her not being around had been worse than his most painful battle wounds. He'd had to open a sketchbook and draw her so he wouldn't go mad with the wanting.

He'd hoped to be able to move on. But in the two weeks she'd been gone, he couldn't get her out of his blood. She'd become a part of him, a part he'd never be able to lose, not without losing himself.

Now that he had Molasses, he had the perfect excuse to ride down to the Double L Ranch.

Urgency had been nudging him harder with every passing day. He didn't think Savannah would go through with marrying Chandler. But what if Chandler came up with a way to force her into a union? What if the ornery cuss had already done it?

Brody glanced at Molasses. The beautiful Morgan was in need of a good grooming, plenty of hay, and some rest. As anxious as he was to ride on until he reached the Front

Range, he couldn't force the horse to keep going, not without time to recuperate from the ordeal in the mountains.

Thankfully, he'd found the two horses quickly. The snow had melted enough that they'd made it to the lower part of the gulch. But even there, the grass had been sparse and covered in patches of snow, leaving them malnourished.

He'd put out inquiries about the miner's cabin and learned it belonged to a fella from Buckskin Joe. At some point soon, Brody intended to ride out and repay the man for the damage he'd caused and supplies he'd taken.

First, he needed to see Savannah. Had to tell her he loved her and ask her to come back. Not to be his healer. But because he wanted the chance to love her unselfishly, the way she deserved.

Even though the thought of her rejecting him again scared the gizzard right out of him, he couldn't let her go without at least trying to get his loop on her. He wasn't a prize or a parlor ornament like Chandler, but she couldn't deny something special had developed between them.

He gave a gentle tug of the lead lines guiding the two horses. "Ready?"

Molasses responded with a soft, excited snort, her big eyes trained on the barn as though she hoped Savannah would come walking out.

"Sorry, girl." Brody started forward. "Know how you're feeling. But it's gonna be a few more days 'til we get to see her."

He lifted his hat and wiped the sweat from his forehead, then resettled it. The June afternoon on the grassland was downright hot after the cooler mountain temperatures. Summer was finally making its way into the high country, and hopefully they'd seen the last of the snowfall.

As he rode up into the ranch yard, Flynn exited the front door of the house.

At the sight of his brother, Brody's heart clattered like a pot taking a tumble. What was Flynn doing home? Why wasn't he out on the range with the cattle?

Hopefully nothing bad had happened.

Brody reined in his mount and tried to glimpse Flynn's expression beneath the brim of his hat as he walked down the steps and started across the yard. His limping amble was unhurried and his shoulders at ease.

"Looks like you found 'em easy enough." Flynn's tone contained a note Brody didn't recognize. Was it anticipation?

"Yep." Brody glanced around, taking stock of the out-buildings, corrals, barn, laundry swinging from the lines, and garden with plenty of new growth. Nothing seemed unusual or out of the ordinary. "Everything go okay here?"

"Everything's fine."

"Flora?"

"Napping."

Brody scratched the back of his neck. "Linnea?"

"Drying all the new grass specimens she's been busy collecting."

"Ivy?"

"Been and gone today." Flynn's lips twitched with the start of a smile. "Far as I can tell, Dylan and Wyatt and Greta and Tyler and Ellie are doin' just fine too."

If everything was so fine and dandy, why on God's green earth was Flynn standing around jawing with him in the middle of a busy workday?

"Brought in several steers with foot rot." Flynn cocked his head toward the barn.

Brody released a tense breath. Why didn't Flynn say so to begin with instead of letting him get worked up for nothing?

Flynn stuffed his hands in his pockets. "Could use your help with 'em."

Help the steers with foot rot? Usually, Elmer took care of stuff like that. Brody peered through the open barn door. Hoped to see the old cowhand. But maybe he was in town, and Flynn had decided the steers couldn't wait.

Brody swung his leg over and dismounted. "Need to see to the horses first. Reckon I can lend a hand when I'm done."

"I'll take care of the horses." Flynn had a hold of the lead lines before Brody could protest.

Brody stood motionless for a moment, that strange feeling hitting him again. Something wasn't quite right.

"Go on now." Flynn gave him a small but forceful shove toward the barn door. "They're in the stalls in the back."

Brody slogged forward like he was knee-deep in mud. He had half a mind to grab Flynn's collar and tell him to shoot straight, that he wasn't so fragile anymore and could handle whatever news he had for him.

When Brody reached the open doors, he paused.

"I'll be there in a minute." Flynn's tone was firm, giving Brody little choice but to continue. As Brody entered the barn, the familiar scent of old hay and horseflesh greeted him.

He wound through the haymow and down the set of stalls near the back. The rear door leading out into the corral was open, and sunlight cascaded inside, giving some light but leaving plenty still shadowed. He almost stopped to grab a lantern, but at a soft murmuring voice from the nearby stall, his pulse picked up its pace.

Someone was already here.

"That's right." The voice was more distinct. "You'll feel better in no time."

Savannah. His heart jumped into his throat, and he stumbled to a halt. What was she doing here? When had she arrived?

His mind scrambled to make sense of the fact that she was just a few paces away. Flynn had known she was in the barn. And that's why he'd been so adamant. He was giving Brody time and space to make things right with the woman he loved.

Brody'd been waiting and praying and hoping to have this chance. And now that it was here, his mouth was as dry as a watering trough at high noon, and he was as nervous as a tenderfoot riding a rough string for the first time.

He breathed in and squared his shoulders. Time to claim this woman for his own and make sure she never got away again. Only one surefire way to do it. He was gonna have to kiss her and kiss her good.

❧

Savannah rubbed a hand over the steer's nose, between his eyes. He gave a soft, contented moo.

At the thud of the stall door closing, she glanced up. Her heartbeat skittered to a halt, and her fingers stilled.

Brody was half a dozen feet away, leaning against the stall door that he'd obviously just shut. He hooked one bootheel into the lowest rung. The brim of his hat was tipped down, shadowing his eyes.

Even so, she could feel his gaze raking over her, and she wiped her hands on her skirt before she tucked back a strand of hair that had come loose.

When had he arrived home?

She'd been waiting impatiently for him for the past three days since she'd ridden out to the ranch with Daddy. When Flynn had told her Brody had gone up into the mountains to try to find their horses, she felt a twinge of hope that if he was searching for Molasses, maybe he wasn't too angry with her. But the moment she allowed the hope, she reminded herself that she shouldn't read too much into his efforts. Brody didn't like seeing animals suffer any more than she did.

She hadn't told Flynn about her desire to reconcile with Brody. That was too personal. But she had informed him she wanted to stay on as the veterinarian for the summer if he'd still have her. The words hadn't even fully left her mouth before he nodded and said the job was hers as long as she wanted it. That even if they got a permanent vet up in South Park, Healing Springs Ranch would always have need of her help.

When she'd mentioned she was staying at the hotel in Fairplay, he insisted that she live at the ranch like she had before. As much as she wanted to be close to Brody, she refrained. She couldn't agree yet, not if he didn't want her.

As it was, Flynn had sent word to her every day of one livestock ailment or another. And each time she'd ridden to the ranch, she'd hoped to see Brody. Not only because Daddy was there, too, and eager to talk to him about the business deal, but because she was becoming almost desperate to tell him how she felt.

Now here he was. And she was speechless.

If only he wasn't so incredibly good-looking. With the way he was leaning back, the hard, rounded muscles in his legs and arms were visible against the strain of his clothes. Even though his stance was casual, he radiated a rugged intensity and masculinity that were magnetic.

He crossed his arms as though he had all the time in the world to stand there and let her admire him.

A flush moved to her cheeks, and she tore her attention away, focusing on the steer. "You're probably wondering why I'm here."

He didn't respond.

Was he mad? Of course he was mad. After she humiliated him in front of Chandler and then left without apologizing, he ought to hate her. She hadn't meant what she said that day about only being concerned about healing him and had done so to protect him. But she should have been stronger and spoken the truth even then.

She tossed aside everything she'd rehearsed and instead said the only thing left. "Daddy wants to go into partnership with you in selling your tamed horses to eastern buyers."

Brody tipped up the brim of his hat a fraction, but it still wasn't enough to see his eyes. She could see his mouth, and his lips were pressed tightly. In displeasure?

She had to finish telling him the plans before he walked away and never spoke to her again. "He's telegrammed a friend, a breeder, who wants to use your drawings of the mustangs to auction off the horses to the highest bidders. He thinks he can generate quite a bit of interest among his wealthy eastern buyers."

Brody suddenly pushed away from the railing and straightened. Was he leaving already?

"You stand to make a hefty profit." She spoke hurriedly about the plan she'd developed at length with Daddy during the past week. "You'll do the capturing and taming. And then when the mustangs are ready, the Double L will take care of getting them to their buyers."

Instead of opening the stall door and stalking away, he started toward her.

She took a step back. "If you agree to the arrangement, Daddy will build a horse barn for the mustangs, which means you can train here in South Park and down at the Double L—"

He approached so swiftly, she had no place to go except into the wall. As she flattened herself, one of his hands landed on her hip. The contact sent a heated jolt through her that went all the way to her toes.

"You'll be able to go back and forth between the two places, wherever you're most comfortable." The words tumbled out. "It's a good solution for the mustangs, Brody. We'll be able to save them and give them wonderful homes in the East."

He was so close she could hardly think, hardly breathe. Before she could figure out what to say or do next, his hand at her hip pulled her toward him at the same moment he bent in and covered her mouth with his. The touch was explosive and all-encompassing. He pressed in hard with a passion that demanded her response. Except he didn't have to demand. She gave herself to him willingly and eagerly and with all the need that had been building during the time away from him.

Somehow in the process of kissing him, her hands found their way around his neck. And his arms wound around her, drawing her as close as he could so that she could feel the thud of his heart against her chest. She was right where she wanted to be—a place she never wanted to leave again. She could only pray this kiss meant he felt the same way.

Even so, she had to be sure.

She broke the kiss and leaned back. "Does this mean you forgive me?"

"It means I love you."

The world around her stopped spinning. For a moment, she let his declaration sink in and soothe the heartache and stir her longings. He loved her. How was it possible?

"Besides, ain't nothin' to forgive."

"But I hurt you—"

"Don't matter how things started out between us. What matters is how we move forward."

"You never were just another creature to heal. But I had to let Chandler believe it so that he'd let you go."

Brody released a taut breath and then drew her against him, tucking her head under his chin and holding her tight.

"I finally did it. I told everyone the truth. That I couldn't marry Chandler."

"Good. Guess all my convincing worked." His voice hinted at a smile.

She clung to him, tears stinging her eyes—tears of joy. "You are rather convincing when you need to be."

"Think I can convince you to give us another chance?" His muscles tensed as though he was preparing himself for another rejection.

She pulled back enough so she could see his face. Then she tipped up his hat and lost herself in his dark, soulful eyes. "I remember what I said that night I was delirious in the miner's cabin."

"You do?"

"Um-hmm."

"Then tell me." He settled his hands at the small of her back.

She lifted on her toes and brushed her lips against his, the warmth and firmness a heady mixture that beckoned her deeper. "I told you I love you."

He brushed her lips in return, softly, sweetly. "You weren't just letting the sickness do the talking?"

"No. I was doing the talking then, and I'm doing it now. I love you, Brody McQuaid."

His lips curved up into a smile right before they captured hers in a kiss that left no doubt she was exactly where she needed to be, with the man she was destined to love.

"You were right, Pa." A little girl's voice chirped behind them. "Uncle Brody's smoochin' with Vannah."

Brody released Savannah and stumbled back a step. Savannah smoothed her skirt, trying to compose herself but unable to keep her hands from shaking, flustered Flynn had caught her doing anything other than what he'd hired her to do.

Flora was climbing through the stall rungs, her little body sliding through effortlessly. Flynn stood on the other side, a sheepish look on his face.

"Thought Flora was napping." Brody growled out the words.

Flynn shrugged. "Must've heard you ride up. She couldn't wait to see you."

Flora skipped through the straw toward them. Brody reached for her and caught her up in a big hug. The girl wrapped her arms around his neck. "Missed you, Uncle Brody."

"Missed you too, darlin'." As he spoke the words, his gaze connected with Savannah's as though the words were meant for her.

Flora laid a hand against Brody's cheek. "The kitties missed you too."

"I'll bet they did."

Savannah's heart squeezed with all the love she felt for this tenderhearted man.

Flynn lifted his brows at Brody. "Reckon you'll be wanting to build a house of your own this summer."

Brody focused on Flora, who had pressed both hands to his cheeks. "Reckon so."

"Why's that, Uncle Brody? Don't you like living in the room next to me?"

"Sure I do, darlin'. . . ."

"Brody's ready to have a place of his own." Flynn spoke with such assurance that Savannah suspected it had to do with Flynn letting Brody go.

"Best make it a big house," Flynn continued, his tone laced with teasing. "Have a feeling you'll be filling it soon enough."

Brody's lips twitched with the beginning of a grin. And when he looked at Savannah, the love in his eyes left no doubt he intended her to be by his side every step of the way, no matter what the future held.

CHAPTER

32

Brody patted his pocket before bringing his steed to a halt on the overlook.

On the trail behind him, Savannah clucked to Sugar, her Appaloosa, and the silvery white-and-spotted horse stopped next to him.

"Reckon this is a good place for a rest." He took in the view of the Front Range that spread out endlessly. It was the perfect setting he'd been looking for during the past hour of traveling.

The red sandstone formations jutted into the sky below them in an artistic display, reflecting the late-afternoon sunshine. With summer coming to a close and autumn on its way, the days weren't as long. But he had time to do what he'd been planning and would still make it the rest of the distance to the Double L before darkness fell.

Ahead, down the trail, the cowhands kept on going, leading the newest band of tamed mustangs, the second herd Brody had trained over the past few months with help from

Sitting Bear and Tall Arrow. They liked the steady work and wages. Even though Brody had offered to hire them on for good, he wasn't sure how long they'd stay. He had the feeling they'd move to the proposed reservation in the western part of the state at some point.

When he'd taken the first mustangs down to the Double L and learned from Sawyer Marshall exactly how much money buyers from the East were willing to pay for the beautiful horses, he'd been so staggered he had to sit down in the chair across the desk from the Cattle King. After seeing his drawings, wealthy easterners had bid on the horses higher than anyone had expected. And now that word had spread about his gentled mustangs, the demand was only growing.

The profits had allowed Mr. Marshall to finally move his wife to Atlanta. They'd left at the beginning of August, taking Brody's drawings of the latest herd he'd been working with. Not only were the horses popular, but the drawings had gained interest as well.

Savannah sidled next to him. Recently another veterinarian had moved up to South Park, allowing Savannah to focus entirely on the mustangs. She was still using her veterinary skills with the horses but was also helping him with the training.

"Should we tell the others to stop?" she asked.

"Naw, we'll catch up."

She nodded and peered out over the majestic expanse, delight filling her face.

He dismounted and offered a hand to her. Once she was down, he pulled a blanket from his saddle.

Under the brim of her hat, her brows rose in a silent question.

"Figured this is a good spot for a picnic."

"A picnic?"

"Yep." He flipped open the leather strap on his saddlebag and dug inside for the small bundle of food he'd set aside for the occasion.

When he turned to her, she was smiling. The sunshine glinted off the flyaway strands that had come loose from her hair tied back with the usual leather strip. "Are you hoping we'll get stranded again?"

"Wouldn't mind."

She laughed lightly, ending on a breathy note of delight.

The sound sent heat through him, heat he was having a harder time banking. All summer he'd doused his desires, mainly by working himself to the point of exhaustion. He'd kept extra busy between building his house and taming mustangs. But he was getting mighty tired of squelching everything he was feeling for this beautiful woman.

"Don't you know I've been praying for a snowstorm all day?" he teased as he laid out the blanket. "Reckon I might have to invent another excuse to stay out here with you."

"Brody McQuaid." She laughed again, her eyes sparkling. "The manager's expecting us tonight." Mr. Marshall had hired a new fella shortly after Chandler left and took his promises of investments with him. The new manager had a real fondness for horses, something Mr. Marshall had made sure of before hiring him on.

Brody held out a hand to Savannah.

As she took hold, his heart swelled to overflowing. He'd never imagined he'd be in a position like this with the woman he loved and his future ahead of him so full of possibility. To think he'd almost thrown it all away. He'd been a fool and was all the more thankful for the grace of God reaching down to keep him safe through the trials.

He lowered himself onto one knee in front of her and at the same time pulled the telegram out of his pocket. "Got this from your father yesterday."

She studied his face.

"Asked him for his blessing."

"His blessing?"

"Yep. And he approves."

"Of what?"

"Of us getting married."

Savannah's eyes widened with what he hoped was anticipation.

He swallowed his nervousness and pushed on, taking hold of her hand. "I've loved you from the first day I met you. But I wanted to take the summer to make sure we didn't rush into things, especially since I needed time to grow."

She nodded, her fingers tightening within his.

With every passing day, he felt himself becoming the kind of man she deserved. "Reckon I've waited long enough."

"Reckon so." Her whisper was followed by a flush to her cheeks.

He took courage from her response. "Then you'll be my wife? You'll make me the happiest man in the world if you say yes."

"Yes." Her answer was eager and breathless and full of longing.

Relief rushed through him along with gratefulness to God for this beautiful woman who was willing to spend her life with him.

He stood and reached for her other hand. "You're sure?"

She nodded and bit her lower lip, as though hesitating.

"What?" He brushed his thumb over her knuckles, never getting tired of holding her hands, about all he'd allowed himself over the summer, knowing if he kissed her he'd have a hard time stopping.

"When did you want to plan for the weddin'?"

How about now? The words pushed for release, but he bit them back. "Anytime you want, darlin'."

She dipped her head.

He didn't want to push her. He loved her too much to let his own desires stand in the way of what she needed. She might want to wait until her folks could come back and she could have all the fancy trimmings with a big party and lots of guests.

She stared down at their intertwined fingers. "I was hoping we could get married soon."

His mouth went dry, and he cleared his throat so he didn't squeak. "Soon sounds good to me."

"Does it?" She glanced up. "I know you don't want to rush. . . ."

"I'd marry you tonight if I could." The words slipped out just as fast as if his tongue was greased and his lips oiled.

The flush in her cheeks deepened.

He wanted to take the whip to his own backside for letting his eagerness get the best of him. "Listen. I know weddings take time—"

"Okay."

The wind stuck in his lungs.

She peeked up at him shyly. "We might as well."

"Might as well what?" This time his voice did squeak.

"Get married tonight. It will make the logistics of traveling together much easier. We won't have to worry about chaperones and finding separate housing and neighbors gossiping and—"

He pressed his finger to her lips, cutting her off. "I ain't worried about none of that." Her mouth was warm beneath his touch, and his thoughts went straight to kissing her. He couldn't. Not yet. "If we're getting married, it's 'cause we want to. Plain and simple."

"Oh, Brody." She spoke his name like a prayer. "I love you."

As he studied her face, trying to figure out what she really wanted, she lifted her arms around his shoulders. She removed his hat and then flipped hers back. Gently, she guided him down until her lips touched his. She pressed in, offering herself to him.

The exquisite meshing stirred his soul, and he moaned. He let himself linger in a way he hadn't before, needing the kiss as much as he needed to breathe.

She was the first to break away, resting her head against his chest. "Tonight, then?"

At the hint of her eagerness, he smiled and wrapped her close. "Tonight."

She released a happy sigh, one that couldn't compare to his own happiness. As he pressed a kiss to her head, he gazed again at the majestic landscape that opened up before them. Here with Savannah and her agreement to marry him, he was about as close to heaven on earth as he could possibly get.

There would still be dark days ahead. Of that he had no doubt. But with this woman walking by his side, he'd always come out the other side better and stronger.

CHAPTER
33

IVY McQUAID
HEALING SPRINGS RANCH
SEPTEMBER 1867

Ivy sat up in bed, the heat of the September night too much to bear a moment longer. The month had started out unusually warm, without a lick of rain. After several days of high temperatures, the dormer room she shared with Astrid was as hot as a Kansas prairie at midday in the blazing summer sun.

Well, maybe not quite as bad as that. But still . . .

Ivy kicked off the sheet covering her nightgown and climbed out of bed. She tiptoed to the open window and felt for a breeze. But only the stillness of the night greeted her.

A quick dip in the creek would cool her. Yep. That's what she needed.

She reached for Astrid's foot and squeezed it.

The girl shifted. "Hmmm?"

"Let's go swimming."

"No."

"C'mon."

"No." Astrid's sleepy voice was full of censure. "I'm not going out."

"Please, please, please." Ivy wiggled the girl's foot.

Astrid tucked her feet out of reach, turned over, and snuggled against her pillow. "You turned seventeen, Ivy. You're too old to sneak out."

Ivy harrumphed. They'd had plenty of adventures in years past with midnight swimming, calf tipping, rope practicing, and other stunts. "I'll never be too old to have fun."

"W-e-l-l, I'm aiming to be a fine lady. And ladies don't sneak out of their bedrooms in the middle of the night." At fourteen, Astrid was petite and delicate in stature, but she was very pretty. So much so that Ivy had begun to feel gangly and awkward around the girl. It didn't help that Astrid had decided she was gonna get all mannerly and proper, making Ivy look like a backwoods ruffian in comparison. Astrid had even taken to wearing a corset. Something Ivy was never gonna do.

And now Astrid was apparently deciding she was too ladylike to have any more of their adventures. "Too bad you're turning into a boring and stuffy adult."

"Too bad you're still acting like a child." Even though whispered, Astrid's words contained a brittleness that stung.

Ivy hoisted her backside onto the window ledge. Astrid had become like a sister to her, and there wasn't anything she wouldn't do for the girl. But lately Astrid was about as much fun as tar in the bottom of a bucket. "Ain't nothin' wrong with letting loose and living a little."

"There *isn't anything* wrong with it"—Astrid had taken to correcting her grammar, too, and it irked Ivy to no end—"if you want to end up a spinster."

"Got plenty of fellas taking a shine to me."

"Only because they know they can get fresh with you—"

"That ain't true." Ivy's voice rose, then she glanced across the hallway to where her little nephew, Ty, slept, and she banked her anger.

Astrid finally pushed up to her elbows, her light brown hair flowing all silky and soft around her, making Ivy's dark hair feel stiff and coarse in the long braid down her back. "No good man wants an easy woman or one who acts like a boy."

"Then it's a good thing I don't care about having a man."

"A very good thing."

"I'm going out." Ivy swung her legs around until her bare toes touched the slanted roof. As she crawled down, she waited for Astrid to appear in the window behind her and whisper at her to stop, that she was sorry, that she hadn't meant what she'd said.

But as Ivy reached the roof that jutted out over the porch, the bedroom window remained dark and empty. A familiar frustration pushed up inside Ivy. She hated arguing with Astrid, felt like she was losing a friend, but she didn't know how to stop the change in their relationship.

'Cause she sure as heaven above wasn't planning on changing the fact that she was taking a midnight swim in the creek to cool off. Didn't matter if it was childish.

She shimmied down the porch rail and hopped the last of the distance. The two cow dogs sleeping by the front door lifted their heads to watch her and sniff the air before settling down. Thankfully, they'd gotten used to her nighttime comings and goings and didn't cause a ruckus. Last thing she wanted to do was wake Greta and the new babe.

The moon and stars were hidden behind clouds, but she didn't need the light to know where she was going. She'd crept down the path behind the house to the creek so many times that she was there in no time. She dropped her nightgown, let it pool on the ground, and wearing her undergarments, she waded in until she was knee-deep. The cold rushing water always took her breath away at first. But once she adjusted to the temperature, she lowered herself until her body was submerged and only her head was above the water.

For several minutes she reveled in the swiftly moving creek, letting it soothe away the heat as well as loosen the knot inside that often teased her with the feeling that somehow she wasn't good enough, that she never had been and never would be.

At a movement along the bank, she stilled her thoughts and listened. In all the years she'd been sneaking down to the creek at night, she'd never once run into problems with wild animals. But with how hot it had been lately, maybe some critter was out cooling off just like she was.

The rushing water made identifying any sounds difficult, and the darkness was thick and impenetrable. Even so, she sensed she was no longer alone and that whatever lingered nearby was waiting for her.

Her muscles tensed, and she closed her fingers around two large stones in the creek bed beneath her. Maybe she should have brought a pistol.

She started to rise from the creek when a hand closed over

her mouth. A scream pushed up into her throat, but the hand pressing against her was large and hard. A man's hand.

With a burst of panic, she wiggled and fought, swinging her hands back, hoping to hit her attacker. One of the rocks connected, but in the next instant, the attacker grabbed her arms, pinning both wrists. "Stop your fighting, Ivy."

At the familiar voice, she grew motionless. Jericho? With his hand still pressed firmly against her mouth, she couldn't let out the slew of cussing he deserved for scaring her half out of her wits. Instead she bit his finger.

He didn't budge. "Settle down." His voice was irritatingly calm.

She tried to elbow him, but with both her wrists locked securely in his grip, she was at his mercy.

"Blast it all, Ivy. What if I'd been some other man?"

She wanted to answer him that there weren't any men brave enough to sneak around Wyatt's place at this time of night. But his hand only pressed against her mouth harder, as if he didn't want to hear what she had to say.

"Not too many men would walk away from a woman in her unmentionables bathing in a river."

She pinched her eyes closed and held herself still. She was in her undergarments. And Jericho was right there behind her. No amount of pretending was gonna get her out of the mortifying situation.

How much of her indecent state had he seen? Without any light, hopefully he hadn't seen anything.

"If I take my hand away, promise you'll be quiet?" His voice rumbled near her ear, and his breath was warm against her neck. His callused hands were strangely gentle. And suddenly she was attuned to just how near he was, almost engulfing her from behind.

Oh, holy Saint Peter. He felt good.

She'd had a secret—or maybe not-so-secret—infatuation with Jericho since the day she'd met him in Missouri when he and his brother had joined their wagon train to help drive Wyatt's herd of Shorthorns west. Ever since, she hadn't been able to stop liking Jericho—no matter how hard she tried.

Now here he was, with her in an entirely scandalous predicament. Under the circumstances, how could he not finally see her as a desirable woman?

"Promise?" His question was low and did strange things to her middle.

She couldn't remember what she was supposed to promise, but she nodded anyway.

Slowly, he dropped his hand from her mouth. But he kept his grip around her wrists, and for a long second, he didn't move or say anything. His solid chest wasn't touching her back, but she could feel the heat radiating from him.

What was he thinking? How he wanted to sweep her up into his arms, carry her away, and marry her? In the West, she'd heard of other women, some at sixteen and seventeen, getting married. Now that she was seventeen, she was plenty old as far as she was concerned. And he was twenty, surely ready to take a wife.

"You shouldn't be out here by yourself." He leaned in, his voice strangely breathy.

Delicious shivers skittered over her skin, prickling her and stirring her desire. Couldn't he sense the wanting too? Surely, she wasn't the only one feeling it.

His grip around her wrists tightened, and a second later he

thrust her from him, almost as if he was disgusted with her. "I oughta take you across my knee and give you a walloping."

She sank into the creek, the water spilling into her mouth, choking her. Wallop her? What? Did he still think she was a child? She spluttered and coughed, indignation rising hotly inside.

Through the darkness, she could see him slosh to the shore, his back rigid. When he reached the bank, he stood facing the opposite direction, tension and frustration rolling from his shoulders like steam from a hot spring. "Get out and get dressed. Before I really do wallop you."

She stared at him a moment longer, the ache inside welling up into her chest and throat. Was he rejecting her like he always did? "You're a toad."

"Blast it all, Ivy," he growled without looking at her, "get something on."

She made her way to the riverbank. "I can do whatever I want."

"No, you cannot. Clearly you need someone watching over you."

"I already have more than one pa and don't need another."

"Let me tell you something." He gave a mirthless laugh. "The last thing I plan to be is your pa."

She shivered. Even in the warm night, the water on her skin sent chills through her. She bent and picked up her nightgown.

"Do you know how dangerous it is for you to be out here alone like this? Someone oughta lock you in your room and throw away the key."

"Some men happen to like me." She lifted her nightgown and began to jerk it down over her wet skin.

"So that's what you're doing out here just now?" His tone was low, almost deadly. "Meeting up with a fellow secretly?"

Did he really think the worst of her? That she was loose enough to give herself away so freely? *"No good man wants an easy woman."* Astrid's words from earlier came back to her. As angry and hurt as she was, Ivy didn't want Jericho thinking she was easy.

"I came out here because I was hot. That's all." She finished tugging the nightgown down. "Question is why you're here spying on me. Reckon you were hoping to see me taking a bath."

Jericho gave a soft snort. "Wish I was here for something so simple."

Simple? Her taking a bath? "You're impossible." She couldn't get away from him fast enough. She headed toward the path, her hurt driving her.

"Dylan's got a death warrant out on his head." His statement chased after her, making her stumble to a halt.

"Death warrant?" She spun and stared at Jericho. Though she couldn't see him fully, his strong, lean outline was visible, along with the determined set of his shoulders.

"He's landed himself in big trouble this time, Ivy." Something in Jericho's voice sent fear spiraling through her. "He's racked up a big gambling debt to Bat and his boys."

No one knew Bat's real name. But he and a handful of his friends had a claim not far from Fairplay in one of the many gulches. Bat had earned his nickname because he wore a black cape that made him look like he had bat wings, and he never went anywhere without it. More than that, he had a reputation for his ruthlessness at the gaming tables among Fairplay's saloons.

"How much does Dylan owe Bat?"

"Hundreds of dollars. Bat gave Dylan until tonight to pay off the debt. But Dylan couldn't produce a single cent. By the time one of the ranch hands brought me word and I got to Bat's place, they'd beat Dylan up pretty good."

Oh, Dylan. Her heart ached for her brother. "Where's he now? Does he need a doctor?"

"No, he's battered and bruised, but he's resting upriver a quarter mile or so. He asked me to come and get his things. I was hoping you'd help."

Of course Dylan would have to leave the area if Bat had a death warrant out for him. Unless they figured out a way to pay off his debt. But hundreds of dollars? How could they? How could anyone?

The hopelessness of Dylan's situation stalked her as she crept into the cabin he shared with Judd. She was quiet and sneaky enough that she was able to get Dylan's things without waking the older man from his slumber.

She filled a sack of food before heading back down to the creek, where Jericho was waiting. Then she followed him upriver until they met up with Dylan. He was half-drunk and half-asleep as she hugged him good-bye.

Her heart filled with desolation, not only at the swollen bruises and cuts on his face, but at the realization he wouldn't remember their parting in the morning. How had he fallen so low from the principled young man he'd been only a few years ago?

Jericho secured Dylan to his horse. Then Jericho stuffed his hands in his pockets. His handsome face was shadowed with a sadness that reflected hers. "Thank you, Ivy."

She crossed her arms over her nightgown. "I should be the one thanking you for looking out for Dylan."

"He'll be fine once I get him out of South Park and someplace Bat can't reach him."

"Where will you go? Denver?"

He was silent for a heartbeat. "We're leaving Colorado Territory."

Her pulse halted. His statement was so final. "You'll come back, won't you?"

Again, he paused and then shook his head. "No. With Nash's death hanging over me here, it's time for me to move on."

A strange desperation took hold of her chest. "You can't just up and leave, can you?"

He kicked a rock, and it landed in the creek with a *plop*. "I resigned from the ranch a few days ago."

The desperation spread throughout her body so that she was tempted to launch herself against him, wrap her arms around him, and tell him he couldn't go.

But a sudden truth punched her low in the stomach. Jericho had been planning to leave, didn't like her enough to want to stay and be with her.

She'd been the one to care about him all along, had clung to the hope that someday he'd care about her in return. But apparently she'd just been shooting at the wind.

She took a step away and lifted her chin. "Guess you better go."

He kicked at another rock. He seemed to want to say something, and a part of her willed him to say he'd come back for her, that he wouldn't be able to live without her, that he'd miss her.

He tipped up his brim and met her gaze. In the moonlight, his eyes were a churning blue storm. Oh, she loved those eyes. Yep. She loved him. Why couldn't he feel the same about her?

Something flashed in his eyes, something that hinted he might have feelings. But he blinked, and it was gone. "You've been like a sister to me, Ivy. And I won't forget you."

Sister? Anger reared up. Which was worse, insinuating she was a child or calling her his sister? "I ain't your sister and never will be."

He didn't respond.

"Go on now. And don't come back." She spun and stalked down the creek bank toward home, needing to get away from him before she started blubbering.

Unable to keep the tears from flowing, she hurried her pace. As she turned the bend, she stopped and swiped her cheeks. If only he'd come racing after her and tell her he was wrong—she wasn't like a sister and he'd find a way to be with her. But as she waited, the horses' hooves moved up the creek bank in the opposite direction. And within moments, the sound was gone.

Jericho was gone.

A sob rose in her chest. She pressed her hand against her mouth and caught the anguish. Even so, the pain was too much to bear. She dropped to her knees in the tall grass, buried her face in her hands, and let the sobs come.

About the Author

Jody Hedlund is the bestselling author of over thirty historicals for both adults and teens and is the winner of numerous awards, including the Christy, Carol, and Christian Book Award. Mother of five, she lives in central Michigan with her husband and busy family. Visit her at jodyhedlund.com.

Sign Up for Jody's Newsletter

Keep up to date with Jody's news on book releases and events by signing up for her email list at jodyhedlund.com.

More from Jody Hedlund

Traveling the Santa Fe Trail on a botanical exploration, Linnea Newberry longs to be taken seriously by the other members of the expedition. When she is rescued from an accident by Flynn McQuaid, her grandfather hires him to act as Linnea's bodyguard, and Flynn soon finds himself in the greatest danger of all—falling for a woman he's determined not to love.

The Heart of a Cowboy • COLORADO COWBOYS #2

More from Jody Hedlund

On a trip west to save her ailing sister, Greta Nilsson is robbed, leaving her homeless and penniless. Wyatt McQuaid is struggling to get his new ranch running, so the mayor offers him a bargain: He will invest in a herd of cattle if Wyatt agrees to help the town become more respectable by marrying . . . and the mayor has the perfect woman in mind.

A Cowboy for Keeps
COLORADO COWBOYS #1

Upon discovering an abandoned baby, Pastor Abe Merivale joins efforts with Zoe Hart, one of the newly arrived bride-ship women, to care for the infant. With mounting pressure to find the baby a home, Abe offers his hand as Zoe's groom. But after a hasty wedding, they soon realize their marriage of convenience is not so convenient after all.

A Bride of Convenience
THE BRIDE SHIPS #3

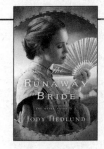

Arabella Lawrence fled on a bride ship wearing the scars of past mistakes. Now in British Columbia, two men vying for her hand disagree on how the native people should be treated during a smallpox outbreak. Intent on helping a girl abandoned by her tribe, will Arabella have the wisdom to make the right decision, or will seeking what's right cost her everything?

The Runaway Bride
THE BRIDE SHIPS #2

◆BETHANYHOUSE

More from Bethany House

Libby has been given a powerful gift: to live one life in 1774 Colonial Williamsburg and the other in 1914 Gilded Age New York City. When she falls asleep in one life, she wakes up in the other without any time passing. On her twenty-first birthday, Libby must choose one path and forfeit the other—but how can she possibly decide when she has so much to lose?

When the Day Comes by Gabrielle Meyer
TIMELESS #1
gabriellemeyer.com

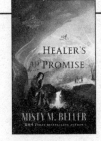

British spy Levi Masters is captured while investigating a discovery that could give America an upper hand in future conflicts. Village healer Audrey Moreau is drawn to the captive's commitment to honesty and is compelled to help him escape. But when he faces a severe injury, they are forced to decide how far they'll go to ensure the other's safety.

A Healer's Promise by Misty M. Beller
BRIDES OF LAURENT #2
mistymbeller.com

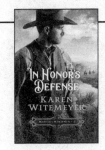

When her brother dies suddenly, Damaris Baxter moves to Texas to take custody of her nephew. Luke Davenport winds up gravely injured when he rescues Damaris's nephew from a group of rustlers. As suspicions grow regarding the death of her brother, more danger appears, threatening the family Luke may be unable to live without.

In Honor's Defense by Karen Witemeyer
HANGER'S HORSEMEN #3
karenwitemeyer.com

⬥ BETHANYHOUSE